THE ROAD BACK

ERICH MARIA REMARQUE

THE ROAD BACK

Translated from the German by
A. W. WHEEN

LONDON

G. P. PUTNAM'S SONS

DER WEG ZURÜCK *first published in Germany April 30th* 1931
THE ROAD BACK *first published in England April 30th* 1931
Reprinted April 1931

PRINTED IN GREAT BRITAIN

LIST OF CHARACTERS

HEEL   Lieutenant, Company Commander

LUDWIG BREYER	2nd Lieutenant	formerly students at the Grammar School and Teachers' Training College
ALBERT TROSSKE	Corporal	
KARL BRÖGER	Cadet	
WILLY HOMEYER	Cadet	
ERNST BIRKHOLZ	Cadet	

ADOLF BETHKE	Lance-Corporal	Shoemaker
JUPP HÜRGENS	Territorial	Clerk
MAX WEIL	Territorial	Clerk
ARTHUR LEDDERHOSE	Territorial	Tobacconist
HEINRICH WESSLING	Reservist	Farmer
VALENTIN LAHER	Reservist	Music-Hall Artist
TJADEN	Rifleman	Peat-digger
GEORG RAHE	Lieutenant and Air Pilot Student at the Grammar School	

THE ROAD BACK

PROLOGUE

WHAT is still left of No. 2 Platoon is quartered in a stretch of battered trench behind the line, and most of them are dozing.

"Funny sort of shell——" says Jupp suddenly.

"What d'you mean?" asks Ferdinand Kosole sitting up.

"Use your ears!" answers Jupp.

Kosole puts a hand to his ear and listens. We also listen into the darkness. But there is nothing audible beyond the dull rumour of gun-fire and the high piping of the shells. From the right sounds the rattle of machine-guns and now and then a cry. But all these we have known some years now; there is nothing in that to make a new song about.

Kosole looks at Jupp suspiciously.

"It's stopped now, of course," says Jupp, by way of defending himself.

Kosole looks him over once more, appraisingly. Jupp remains unperturbed, so he turns away, muttering: "It's the rumble in your own hungry guts; that's all your shells are. Best thing you can do is get an eyeful of sleep." He knocks up a sort of earthen head-rest and stretches out, disposing himself cautiously so that his boots shall not slip down into the water. "God,

and there's the missus and a bed for two at home ! "
he murmurs, his eyes already closed.

" Somebody else is in it by now, I dare say," retorts
Jupp out of his corner.

Kosole opens one eye and gives him a hard look.
For a moment it seems as if he meant to get up again.
" Don't you be too funny, you poor fish ! " And he is
snoring already.

Jupp signs to me to crawl over to him. I step across
Adolf Bethke's legs and sit down beside him. With a
sidelong glance at the snoring figure he says sourly :
" The likes of that don't even know what education is."

Jupp was a clerk in a solicitor's office in Cologne
before the war. And though he has been soldiering
three years now, he still feels himself superior, and in
most curious wise sets great store on education out here
at the Front. What that means exactly, he does not
know himself, of course ; but more than all else that
he ever heard tell of in the days gone by, the word
Education has stayed with him ; and to that he clings,
as it were a plank in the sea, that he shall not go under.
Everybody has something of the sort : this one a wife,
another his business, a third his boots, Valentin Laher
his schnapps and Tjaden the hope of tasting broad
beans and bacon once more.

On the other hand there is nothing so irritates Kosole
as that very word, Education. He always connects it
some way or another with the idea of high collars, and
for him that is enough. Even now it has its effect.
Without interrupting his sleep : " Bloody pen-pusher ! "
says he gruffly.

Jupp shakes his head, resigned and pitying. We sit
on in silence a while, side by side to warm ourselves.
The night is wet and cold, clouds are driving over-

8

head, and it rains off and on. Then we take up the waterproof on which we are sitting and, while the rain lasts hang it over our heads.

Along the skyline are the flashes of gun-fire. One feels that over there must be a region a little less cold, it looks so cosy. Like gaily coloured and silver flowers the flares spring up above the lightning flashes of the artillery. Big and red the moon swims in the wet air over the ruins of a farm.

" Think we're going home ? " whispers Jupp.

I shrug my shoulders. " The rumour is——"

Jupp sighs aloud. " A warm room and a sofa, and going out of nights—can you picture it still ? "

" I tried on my civvies last time I was on leave," I say meditatively, " but they're ever so much too small for me now—I'll have to get new things." How marvellous that all sounds here—civvies, a sofa, the evening —but it brings strange thoughts too—like black coffee, when sometimes it tastes too much of the tin and rust of the dixie, and one coughs it up again, hot and choking.

Jupp is picking his nose absently. " Shop windows— and cafés—and women—oh, boy ! "

" Ach, man, you just be thankful you're back here out of the shit for a bit," I say, and blow into my frozen hands.

" That's true." Jupp draws the waterproof up over his thin, bent shoulders. " What'll you do when you get out of this ? "

I laugh. " I ? I'll have to go back to school again, I suppose. Willy and Albert and I—and even Ludwig over there, too," I say, pointing back to where someone is lying before a dugout entrance, under two great-coats.

" Good Lord ! But you won't do that, surely ? " exclaims Jupp.

" I don't know. Probably have to," I reply, and feel furious, without knowing why.

There is a movement under the greatcoats. A pale, thin face lifts up and groans softly. It is my schoolmate, Lieutenant Ludwig Breyer, our platoon commander. He has had diarrhœa for weeks—it is dysentery, of course, but he does not want to go back into hospital. He would sooner stay here with us, for we are all waiting now in hopes of peace ; then we shall be able to take him back with us at once.—The hospitals are all full to overflowing, no one is properly looked after there, and once a man lies down on it, he is only so much nearer to being dead. Men die all around one. It gets on a fellow's nerves, alone there among it all, and before he knows where he is he has made another himself.—Max Weil, our stretcher bearer, has given Breyer a sort of fluid plaster to eat, so as to cement up his bowels and stay him for a bit. But even so he has his trousers down twenty and thirty times a day.

And now he must go again. I assist him round the corner and he squats down.

Jupp signs to me. " Listen ! There it is again ! "
" What ? "
" The shells I was talking about before."

Kosole stirs and yawns. He gets up, significantly examines his great fist, he looks askance at Jupp and says : " Well, my boy, if you're trying to pull our leg again, you'll soon be sending your bones home in a turnip sack."

We listen. The hiss and whistle of the invisible, arching shells is interrupted by a queer, hoarse, long-drawn sound, so strange and new that my flesh creeps.

" Gas shells ! " shouts Willy, springing up.

We are all awake now and listening intently.

Wessling points into the air. " There they are ! Wild geese ! "

Moving darkly against the drab grey of the clouds is a streak, a wedge, its point steering toward the moon. It cuts across its red disc. The black shadows are plainly visible, an angle of many wings, a column of squalling, strange, wild cries, that loses itself in the distance.

" Off they go," growls Willy. " Damn it all—if only we could pull out like that ! Two wings and away."

Heinrich Wessling follows the geese with his eyes. " Now for winter," says he slowly. Wessling is a farmer and understands these things.

Breyer, weak and wretched, leans against the parados and murmurs : " First time I ever saw that."

But Kosole has brightened up at once. He gets Wessling to explain the matter to him quickly once more, asking particularly whether wild geese are as fat as tame ones.

" More or less," says Wessling.

" My poor belly ! " exclaims Kosole, his jaws working with excitement. " And fifteen, twenty maybe, good roast dinners flying about there in the air ! "

Again the whirr of wings straight above us ; again the hoarse, throaty cry swooping down into our hearts like a hawk ; the lapping pulse of their wings, the urgent cries, gusts of the rising wind all united in one passionate, swift sense of freedom and life.

A shot rings out. Kosole lowers his rifle and peers hungrily into the sky. He has fired into the middle of the flight. Beside him stands Tjaden, ready like a retriever, to dash out should a goose fall. But the flight passes on intact.

"Hard luck," says Bethke. "That might have been the first sensible shot in this whole lousy war."

Kosole throws down his rifle in disgust. "If only a man had some shot-cartridges!" He settles back into gloom, conjuring all the things that might have been. And as he sits, he chews unconsciously.

"Yes," says Jupp, observing him, "with apple sauce and baked potatoes, what?"

Kosole looks at him poisonously. "You shut up, you pen-pusher!"

"You should have joined the Air Force," grins Jupp, "then you might still have gone after them with a butterfly net."

"Arseholes!" answers Kosole finally, and settles down to sleep once more. And that is best. The rain becomes heavier. We sit back to back and drape our waterproof-sheets over us. Like dark mounds of earth we squat there in our little bit of trench. Earth, uniform, and a little life underneath.

A harsh whispering wakes me. "Forward!—Forward!"

"Why, what's the matter?" I ask, drunken with sleep.

"We've to go up the line," growls Kosole assembling his things.

"But we've only just come here!" I say, mystified.

"Such damned rot," I hear Wessling cursing. "The bloody war's over, isn't it?"

"Up! Forward!" It is Heel himself, our company commander, driving us out. He is running impatiently down the trench. Ludwig Breyer is already on his feet. "There's nothing for it, we've got to go," says he resignedly, taking a few hand-grenades.

Adolf Bethke looks at him. "You should stay here, Ludwig. You can't go up with your dysentery——"

Breyer shakes his head.

The scraping sound of belts being tightened, a clatter of rifles, the sickly smell of death suddenly rises up again out of the earth. And we had hoped at last to have escaped it for ever !

The thought of Peace had sprung up before us like a rocket, and though indeed we did not yet believe nor understand it, the bare hope had sufficed to change us more in the few minutes it took for the rumour to circulate, than in twenty months before. Till now the years of war had succeeded each other, year laid upon year, one year of hopelessness treading fast upon another, and when a man reckoned the time, his amazement was almost as great to discover it had been so long, as that it had been only so long. But now that it has become known peace may come any day, every hour has gained in weight a thousandfold, every minute under fire seems harder and longer almost than the whole time before.

The wind miaows round the remains of the breast-works and clouds draw swiftly over the moon—light constantly alternating with shadow. We march close one behind another, a group of shadows, a sorry spectacle, No. 2 Platoon shot to a mere handful of men —the whole company has scarce the strength of a normal platoon—but this remnant is choice, thoroughly sifted. We have even three old timers still from 'fourteen—Bethke, Wessling, and Kosole, who know everything, and often speak of the first months as though

that were away back in the olden days of the gods and
the heroes.

Each man seeks out a corner, a hole for himself in
the new position. There is nothing much doing.
Flares, machine-guns, rats. With a well-aimed kick
Willy tosses one up and slices it in two in mid-air with
one cut from a spade.

A few scattered shots fall. From the left sounds
distantly the explosion of hand-grenades.

" Let's hope it stays quiet here," says Wessling.

" To get it in the neck now! " Willy shakes his head.

" When a man's luck is out, he'll break his finger just
picking his nose," growls Valentin.

Ludwig lies down on his waterproof-sheet. He could,
as a matter of fact, have stayed behind. Weil gives
him a couple of tabloids and Valentin tries to persuade
him to have a nip of schnapps. Ledderhose starts to
tell some smutty yarn, but no one listens. We lie
around and the time creeps on.

I start suddenly and lift my head. Bethke too, I see,
is sitting up. Even Tjaden is on the alert. The year-
old instinct has reported something, none yet knows
what, but certainly something strange is afoot. We
raise our heads gingerly and listen, our eyes narrowed
to slits to penetrate the darkness. Everyone is awake,
every sense is strained to the uttermost, every muscle
ready to receive the unknown, oncoming thing that
can mean only danger. The hand-grenades scrape
over the ground as Willy, our best bomb-thrower,
worms himself forward. We lie close pressed to the
ground, like cats. Beside me I discover Ludwig
Breyer. There is nothing of sickness in his tense
features now. His is the same cold, deathly expression

ive not even realised that the post has been
Flashes continue to burst in the abandoned

quieter.   I am anxious about Ludwig.   But
Then Bethke crawls in.   "Wessling?"——
Wessling doing?"   "Where's Wessling?"
es up suddenly above the dull rumble of
ge guns.   "Wessling—Wessling——"
ears.   "What is it?"
g's missing."

ad been beside him when the word came
fter that he had not seen him again.
asks Kosole.   Tjaden points.   "Damn!"
s at Bethke.   Bethke at Kosole.   Each
this is perhaps our last fight.   They do not
Right for me," growls Bethke.   "Come
Kosole.   They vanish into the darkness.
ut after them.

uts all in readiness to charge immediately
three be attacked.   At first all remains
n suddenly there are flashes of bombs.
ots crack between.   We go forward im-
Ludwig leading—then the sweating faces of
Kosole reappear lugging someone behind
aterproof.

t is Wessling who groans.   And Heel?
m off; it was he that fired.   He is back
t immediately—"Got the whole bunch in
le," he shouts, "and then two with the
He stares down at Wessling.   "Well,
But Wessling does not answer.

lies open like a butcher's stall.   One
how deep the wounds go.   We bandage
ll as we can.   Wessling is groaning for

as everyone's here, the front-line face.   A fierce tension
has frozen it—so extraordinary is the impression that
our subconsciousness has imparted to us, long before
our senses are able to identify the cause of it.

The fog moves and lifts.   And suddenly I know what
it is that has thrown us all into such a state of alarm.
It has merely become still.   Absolutely still.

Not a machine-gun, not a shot, not an explosion; no
shriek of shells, nothing, absolutely nothing, no shot,
no cry.   It is simply still, utterly still.

We look at one another; we cannot understand it.
This is the first time it has been so quiet since we have
been at the Front.   We sniff the air and try to figure
what it can mean.   Is gas creeping over?   But the
wind is not favourable, it would drive it off.   Is an
attack coming?   But the very silence would have
betrayed it already.   What is it, then?   The bomb in
my hand is moist, I am sweating so with excitement.
One feels as if the nerves must snap.   Five minutes.
Ten minutes.   "A quarter of an hour now," calls
Laher.   His voice sounds hollow in the fog as from a
grave.   Still nothing happens, no attack, no sudden,
dark-looming, springing shadows——

Hands relax and clench again tighter.   This is not
to be borne.   We are so accustomed to the noise of the
Front that now, when the weight of it suddenly lifts
from us, we feel as if we must burst, shoot upward like
balloons.

"Why," says Willy suddenly, "it is peace!"   It
falls like a bomb.

Faces relax, movements become aimless and un-
certain.   Peace?   We look at one another incredulous.
Peace?   I let my hand-grenades drop.   Peace?
Ludwig lies down slowly on his waterproof again.

Peace ? In Bethke's eyes is an expression as if his whole face would break in pieces. Peace ? Wessling stands motionless as a tree ; and when he turns his back on it and faces us, he looks as if he meant to keep straight on home.

All at once—in the whirl of our excitement we had hardly observed it—the silence is at an end ; once more, dully menacing, comes the noise of gun-fire, and already from afar like the bill of a woodpecker sounds the knock-knocking of a machine-gun. We grow calm and are almost glad to hear again the familiar, trusty noises of death.

It has been quiet all day. At night we have to retire a little, as so often before. But the fellows over yonder do not simply follow us, they attack. Before we are ready, heavy shelling comes over and behind us the red fountains roar upward into the gloom. For the moment it is still quiet where we are. Willy and Tjaden light on a tin of meat and polish it off on the spot. The rest just lie there and wait. The many months have consumed them ; so long as they cannot defend themselves they are almost indifferent.

Heel, our company commander, crawls up. "Have you everything?" he asks through the din. "Too little ammunition," shouts Bethke. Heel gives a shrug and passes Bethke a cigarette over his shoulder. Without looking round Bethke nods. "Have to make good with what you have," shouts Heel, and springs into the next shell-hole. He knows they will make good right enough. Any of these old hands would make as able a company commander as himself.

It grows dark. The fire catches us. There is practically no cover. With hands and spades we scoop

holes for our hea
pressed close to th
me. A shell lands
beast comes on sc
to save our ear-dr
and our eyes filled
the foul stench of p
Somebody has stop
shell fragment the
head a severed har

Heel bounds into
explosions his face
"Brandt," he gasp

It crashes down
mud and steel ; the
curtain of fire lifts
instant men arise,
bombs in their h
back !" shouts He

The attack lies
for a machine-gun
gun is barking. T
convulsively. Sudd
Immediately the
minutes and it must
He goes over the
nition is tossed up
Bethke, and Heel a
and throw. Heel j
such moments—a p
fellows in the shell-
gun comes again in
together we make
behind us. It has

Tommies
evacuated.
crater.

It grows
he is there.
"What"
—the cry
the long-r

Heel ap
"Wessli

Tjaden
to retire,
"Where?
Kosole lo
knows tha
hesitate.
on," gru
Heel goes

Ludwig
should th
quiet. T
Revolver
mediately
Bethke a
them in

Heel ?
Holding
again al
the shell-
revolver.
how is it

His b
cannot s
them as

water, but he gets none. Stomach-wounds may not drink. Then he begs for blankets. He is freezing, he has lost so much blood.

A runner brings the order to retire still farther. We take Wessling with us in a waterproof-sheet through which is passed a rifle for carrying, until we can find a stretcher. One behind the other we grope our way cautiously. It grows gradually light. Silver mist in the low bushes. We are leaving the fighting zone. Already we imagine it over when a bullet comes swishing up softly and strikes, tock. Ludwig silently rolls up his sleeve. He has stopped one in the arm. Weil bandages him.

We go back. And back.

The air is mild as wine. This is no November, it is March ; and the sky pale blue and clear. In the pools along the road the sun lies mirrored. We pass down an avenue of poplars. The trees stand on either side the road, tall and almost unscathed, except that here and there one is missing. This region lay formerly well behind the lines and has not been so devastated as those miles before it, that day by day, yard by yard, we have yielded. The sun glints on the brown waterproof, and as we go along the yellow avenue, leaves keep floating, sailing down upon it ; a few fall inside it.

At the dressing-station everywhere is full. Many of the wounded are lying outside before the door. For the time being we put Wessling there too.

A number of fellows with arm-wounds and white bandages are lining up to march out. The hospital is to be relieved. A doctor is running about examining the new-comers. He orders one chap, whose leg is hanging loose and bent the wrong way at the knee joint, to be taken in at once. Wessling is merely bandaged and remains outside.

He rouses from his stupor and looks after the doctor. "What is he going away for?"

"He'll be back in a minute," I tell him.

"But I must go in! I must be operated on!" He becomes suddenly terribly excited and feels for the bandage.

"That must be stitched up straight away!"

We try to calm him. He is quite green and sweating with fear: "Adolf, run after him! he must come!"

Bethke hesitates a moment. But under Wessling's eye there is nothing else for it, though he knows it will be to no purpose. I see him speak with the doctor. Wessling follows him as far as he can with his eyes. He looks terrible as he struggles to turn his head.

Returning, Bethke makes a detour so that Wessling shall not be able to get a sight of him; he shakes his head, makes the figure 1 with his finger, and with his mouth shapes inaudibly: "One—hour."

We put on cheerful faces. But who can deceive a dying peasant? While Bethke is yet telling him that he is to be operated on later, but the wounds must heal a little first, Wessling already knows all. He is silent a moment, then he cries aloud: "Yes, you stand there and are whole—and are going home—and I—I—four years and now this—four years—and now this——"

"You're going into the hospital all right, Heinrich," says Bethke comforting him.

But he would not.—"Let be."

Thereafter he does not say much. Nor does he want to be carried in; but to stay outside. The hospital is on a gentle slope, whence one can see far out along the avenue down which we have come. It is all gay and golden. The earth lies there, still and smooth and secure ; even fields are to be seen, little, brown-tilled strips, right close by the hospital. And when the wind blows away the stench of blood and of gangrene one can smell the pungent ploughed earth. The distance is blue and everywhere is most peaceful, for from here the view is away from the Front.

Wessling is still. He is observing everything most narrowly. His eyes are clear and alert. He is a farmer and at home with the country, he understands it better and otherwise than we. He knows that he must leave it now. So he will miss nothing ; nor does he take his eyes from it again. Minute by minute he grows paler. At last he makes a movement and whispers : " Ernst——"

I bend to his mouth. " Take out my things," he says.

" There's plenty of time for that, Heinrich."

" No, no—— Get on ! "

I spread them out before him. The pocket-book of frayed calico, the knife, the watch, the money—one gets to know these things.

Loose in the pocket-book is the picture of his wife.

" Show me," he says.

I take it out and hold it that he can see it. A clear, brownish face. He considers it. After a while he whispers : " So that is finished," and his lips quiver. At last he turns away his head.

" Take it," he says. I do not understand what he means, but I will not ask him more questions, so I thrust it into my pocket. " Take those to her——" he looks at the other things. I nod. " And tell her ——" he looks at me with a strange great gaze, murmurs, shakes his head and groans. I try desperately to understand, but now he only gurgles. He twitches, breathes more heavily, more slowly, with pauses, slackening—then once more, very deep and sighing— and suddenly has eyes as if he had been blinded, and is dead.

Next morning we are in the front trenches for the last time. Hardly a shot is fired. The war is ended. In an hour we must pull out. We need never come back here again ! When we go we go for ever.

What there is to be destroyed we destroy. It is little enough—only a couple of dugouts. Then comes the order to retreat.

It is a strange moment. We stand side by side and look toward the Front. Light trailers of mist lie over the ground. The lines of shell-holes and trenches are clearly visible. They are, indeed, only the last line— they belong really to the reserve position—still they are well within range of the guns. How often we have gone in through those saps ! How often and how few we have come back through them ! Grey stretches the monotonous landscape before us—in the distance what is left of a copse, a few stumps, the ruins of a village, in the midst of it one solitary high wall that has withstood it all.

" Yes," says Bethke meditatively, " it's four years, four years we've been sitting there——"

" Yes, damn it all," nods Kosole. " And now it just fizzles out ! "

" Well—well——" Willy leans back against the parapet. " Funny, eh ? "

We stand and gaze. The farmhouse, the remnants of the wood, the heights, the trenches on the skyline yonder—it had been a terrible world, and life a burden. Now it is over, and will stay behind here ; when we set out, it will drop behind us, step by step, and in an hour be gone as if it had never been. Who can realise it?

There we stand, and should laugh and shout for joy —and yet we have now a sick feeling in the pit of our stomachs, as one who swallows a throat-swab and would vomit.

None knows what to say. Ludwig Breyer leans wearily against the side of the trench and raises his hand, as if there were some man yonder to whom he would wave.

Heel appears. " Can't bear to leave it, eh?— Well, now for the dregs."

Ledderhose looks at him in astonishment. " Now for peace, you mean."

" Yes, that's it, the dregs," says Heel, and goes off, looking as if his mother had just died.

" He hasn't got his ' *Pour le mérite*,' that's what's biting him," explains Ledderhose.

" Ach, shut your mug ! " says Albert.

" Well, let's go," urges Bethke, but still stands on.

" A lot of us lying there," says Ludwig.

" Yes—Brandt, Müller, Kat, Haie, Bäumer, Bertinck——"

" Sandkuhl, Meinders, the two Terbrüggen, Hugo, Bernhard——"

" For Christ's sake, stop, man——"

They are many indeed that lie there, though until now we have not thought of it so. Hitherto we have just all remained there together, they in the graves, we in the trenches, divided only by a few handfuls of earth. They were but a little before us ; daily we became less and they more, and often we have not known whether we already belonged to them or not.

And sometimes too the shells would bring them back among us again—crumbling bones tossed up, scraps of uniforms, wet, decayed hands, already earthy—to the noise of the drum-fire issuing once more from their buried dugouts and returning to the battle. It did not seem to us terrible ; we were too near to them. But now we are going back into life and they must stay there.

Ludwig, whose cousin was killed in this sector, blows his nose through his fingers and turns about. Slowly we follow. But we halt yet a few times and look about us. And again we stand still, and suddenly we know that all that yonder, that hell of terrors, that desolate corner of shell-hole-land, has usurped our hearts ;— yes, damn it, that it should sound such slush !—it seems almost as if it had become endeared to us, a dreadful homeland, full of torment, and we simply belonged in it.

We shake our heads—but whether it be the lost years that remain there, or the comrades who lie there, or all the misery that this earth covers—there is a grief in our bones, enough to make us howl aloud.

And so we march out.

PART I

Roads stretch far through the landscape, the villages lie in a grey light; trees rustle, leaves are falling, falling.

Along the road, step upon step, in their faded, dirty uniforms tramp the grey columns. The unshaved faces beneath the steel helmets are haggard, wasted with hunger and long peril, pinched and dwindled to the lines drawn by terror and courage and death. They trudge along in silence; silently, as they have now marched over so many roads, have sat in so many trucks, squatted in so many dugouts, crouched in so many shell-holes—without many words; so too they now trudge along this road back home into peace. Without many words.

Old men with beards and slim lads scarce twenty years of age, comrades without difference. Beside them their lieutenants, little more than children, yet the leaders of many a night raid. And behind them, the army of slain. Thus they tramp onward, step by step, sick, half-starving, without ammunition, in thin companies, with eyes that still fail to comprehend it : escaped out of that underworld, on the road back into life.

The company is marching slowly, for we are tired and have wounded with us. Little by little our group falls behind. The country is hilly, and when the road climbs we can see from the summit the last of our own troops withdrawing before us, and behind us the dense, endless columns that follow after. They are Americans. They pour on through the avenues of trees like a broad river, and the restless glitter of their weapons plays over them. But around them lie the quiet fields, and the tree-tops in their autumnal colours tower solemn and unconcerned above the oncoming flood.

We stopped the night in a little village. Behind the houses in which we billeted flows a stream lined with willows. A narrow path runs beside it. One behind another in a long file we follow it. Kosole is in front. Behind him runs Wolf, the company mascot, and sniffs at his haversack.

Suddenly at the cross road, where the path opens into the high road, Ferdinand springs back.

" Look out ! "

On the instant our rifles are up and we scatter. Kosole crouches in the ditch by the roadside ready to fire ; Jupp and Trosske duck, and spy out from behind a clump of elders ; Willy Homeyer tugs at his hand-grenade belt ; even our wounded are ready for fight.

Along the road are coming a few Americans. They are laughing and talking together. It is an advance patrol that has overtaken us.

Adolf Bethke alone has remained unperturbed. He advances calmly a few paces clear of the cover. Kosole gets up again. The rest of us recover ourselves also, and embarrassed and sheepish, readjust our belts and our rifle-slings—for, of course, fighting has ceased some days now.

At sight of us the Americans halt suddenly. Their talk stops. Slowly they approach. We retire against a shed to cover our backs, and wait. The wounded men we place in the middle.

After a minute's silence an American, tall as a tree, steps out from the group, stands before us and beckoning, greets us.

" Hullo, Kamerad ! "

Adolf Bethke raises his hand in like manner. " Kamerad ! "

The tension relaxes. The Americans advance. A moment later and we are surrounded by them.— Hitherto we have seen them so closely only when they were either prisoners or dead.

It is a strange moment. We gaze at them in silence. They stand about us in a semicircle, fine, powerful fellows ; clearly they have always had plenty to eat. They are all young ; not one of them is nearly so old as Adolf Bethke or Ferdinand Kosole—and they are not our oldest by a long chalk. On the other hand none is so young as Albert Trosske or Karl Bröger— and they are by no means the youngest of us.

They are wearing new uniforms and greatcoats ; their boots are water-tight and fit well ; their rifles are good and their pouches full of ammunition. They are all fresh and unused.

Compared to these fellows we are a perfect band of robbers. Our uniforms are bleached with the mud of years, with the rains of the Argonnes, the chalk of Champagne, the bog waters of Flanders ; our greatcoats ragged and torn by barbed-wire, shell-splinters and shrapnel, cobbled with crude stitches, stiff with clay and in some instances even with blood ; our boots broken, our rifles worn out, our ammunition almost at

27

an end ; we are all of us dirty, all alike gone to wrack, all weary. The war has passed over us like a steam roller.

Yet more troops gather around us. The square is filled with curious eyes.

We stand in a corner grouped about our wounded men—not because we are afraid, but because we belong together. The Americans nudge one another and point at our old, worn-out gear. One of them offers Breyer a piece of white bread, but though hunger is apparent in his eyes, he does not take it.

With a sudden ejaculation one of them points to the bandages on our wounded. These are of crêpe-paper, made fast with pack-thread. They all have a look, then retire and whisper together. Their friendly faces are full of sympathy as they see that we have not even muslin bandages.

The man who first addressed us now puts a hand on Bethke's shoulder. " Deutsche—gute Soldat," he says, " brave Soldat——"

The others nod emphatically.

We make no answer. We are not yet able to answer. The last weeks have tried us bitterly. We had to return again and again to the battle, losing our men to no purpose, yet we made no protest ; we did as we have always done ; and at the end our company had thirty-two men left of two hundred. So we came out from it thinking no more, feeling no more than that we had faithfully done what had been laid upon us to do.

But now, under the pitying eyes of these Americans, we perceive how much in vain it has all been. The sight of their interminable, well-equipped columns reveals to us against what hopeless odds in man-power and material we made our stand.

We bite our lips and look at each other. Bethke withdraws his shoulder from under the American's hand; Kosole stares ahead into vacancy; Ludwig Breyer draws himself up—we grip our rifles more firmly; we brace our knees, our eyes become harder and our gaze does not falter. We look back once more over the country whence we have come; our faces become tight with suppressed emotion, and once again the searing memory passes through us : all we have done, all we have suffered, and all that we have left behind.

We do not know what is the matter with us ; but if a bitter word were now loosed against us it would sting us to fury, and whether we wanted to or not we would burst forward, wild and breathless, mad and lost, to fight—in spite of everything, to fight again.

A thick-set sergeant with a ruddy face elbows his way toward us. Over Kosole who stands nearest him he pours a flood of German words. Ferdinand winces, it so astonishes him.

" He talks just the same as we do ! " he says to Bethke in amazement, " what do you make of that, now ? "

The fellow speaks German better and more fluently even than Kosole himself. He explains that he was in Dresden before the war, and had many friends there.

" In Dresden ? " asks Kosole even more staggered. " Why I was there once myself for a couple of years——"

The sergeant smiles, as though that identified him once and for all. He names the street where he had lived.

" Not five minutes from me ! " exclaims Ferdinand excitedly. " Fancy not having seen one another ! You will know Widow Pohl, perhaps, at the corner, Johannis Street ? A fat old body with black hair. My landlady."

But the sergeant does not know her, and in exchange submits Zander, a clerk in the Treasury, whom Kosole in his turn cannot recall. Both of them, however, remember the Elbe and the castle, and their eyes light up with pleasure. Ferdinand seizes the sergeant by the arm : " Why, man—you talk German like a native ! So you've been in Dresden, eh ?—— Man, but what have we two been fighting about ? "

The sergeant laughs. He doesn't know either. He takes out a packet of cigarettes and offers it to Kosole, who reaches for it eagerly—there is not a man of us but would willingly give his soul for a good cigarette. Our own are made from beech leaves and dried grass, and even those are only the better sort. Valentin Laher declares that the ordinary ones are made of sea-weed and dried horse-dung, and Valentin is a connoisseur of such things.

Kosole blows out the smoke lingeringly, with relish. We sniff enviously. Laher changes colour. His nostrils quiver. " Give 's a draw," he says imploringly to Ferdinand. But before he can take the cigarette another American has offered him a packet of Virginia tobacco. Valentin looks at him incredulously. He takes it and smells it. His face lights up. Then reluctantly he returns the tobacco. But the other declines it and points energetically at the cockade on Laher's forage cap, which is sticking out from the top of his haversack.

Valentin does not understand him. " He wants to

exchange the tobacco for the cap badge," explains the sergeant from Dresden. But Laher understands that even less. " This spanking tobacco for a tin cockade ? the man must be balmy ! " Valentin would not swop the packet for a commission. He offers the cap, badge and all, to the American, and with trembling hands greedily fills his first pipe.

And now we realise what is expected—the Americans want to exchange. It is apparent that they have not long been in the war ; they are still collecting souvenirs, shoulder-straps, badges, belt buckles, decorations, uniform buttons. In exchange we stock ourselves with soap, cigarettes, chocolate and tinned meat. They even want us to take a handful of money for our dog— but we draw the line there ; let them offer what they will, the dog stays with us. On the other hand our wounded bring us luck. One American, with so much gold in his mouth that his face looks like a brass foundry, is anxious to get some pieces of bandage with blood on them, in order to be able to demonstrate to the folk at home that they actually were made of paper. He is offering first-rate biscuits and, better still, an armful of real bandages in exchange. With the utmost satis-faction he carefully stows the rags away in his pocket-book, especially those belonging to Ludwig Breyer ; for that is lieutenant's blood, you see. Ludwig must write on it in pencil, the place, his name and regiment, so that everyone in America may see the thing is no fake. He is unwilling at first—but Willy persuades him, for we need good bandages sorely. And besides, the biscuits are an absolute godsend to him with his dysentery.

But Arthur Ledderhose makes the best coup. He produces a box of Iron Crosses that he found in an abandoned orderly-room. An American, as wizened as himself, with just such another lemon-yellow face, wants to buy the whole box at one deal. But Ledderhose merely gives him one long, knowing slant from his squinting eyes. The American returns the look just as impassively, just as seemingly harmless. One suddenly saw in them a family likeness, as of two brothers. Something that has survived all the chances of war and death has flashed between them—the spirit of trade.

Ledderhose's antagonist soon sees that there is nothing doing. Arthur is not to be tricked ; his wares will be decidedly more profitable disposed of in retail, so he barters them one by one, till the box is empty. About him there gradually rises up a pile of goods, even butter, and silk, eggs, linen, and money until finally he stands there on his bandy legs looking like a departmental store.

We take our leave. The Americans call and wave after us. The sergeant especially is indefatigable. Even Kosole is moved, so far as an old soldier can be. He too grunts a few words of farewell and waves his hand ; but in him all this has still an air of menace. Then at last he ventures to Bethke : " Quite decent fellows, eh ? "

Adolf nods. We go on in silence. Ferdinand lowers his head. He is thinking. Such is not his habit, but when the fit does take him he is tenacious, and will chew the cud a long time. He cannot get the sergeant from Dresden out of his head.

In the villages the folk stare after us. At a railway-crossing there are flowers in the watchman's window. A woman with ample breasts is suckling a child. She

32

has a blue dress on. Dogs bark after us. Wolf growls in answer. On the roadside a cock is treading a hen. We smoke vacantly.

Marching, marching. We have now reached the zone of field ambulance stations, of supply depots. A spacious park with plane-trees. Stretchers and wounded under the trees. The leaves are falling and covering them in red and gold.

A gas hospital. Bad cases that cannot be moved. Blue faces, waxen green faces, dead eyes, eaten by the acid ; wheezing, choking, dying men. They all want to get away; they are afraid of being taken prisoner.— As if it were not a matter of indifference where they die.

We try to cheer them, telling them they will be better cared for with the Americans. But they do not listen. Again and again they call to us to take them with us.

The cries are terrible. The pallid faces seem so unreal in the light out here in the open. But most awful are the beards. They take on a life of their own, they stand out stiff, fantastical, growing, luxuriating over the sunken jaws, a black fungus that feeds and thrives the more these sag and waste away.

A few of the badly wounded reach out their thin, grey arms like children. "Take me with you, mate," they say, imploring. "Take me with you, mate." In the hollows of their eyes already lurk deep, strange shadows, from which the pupils struggle up with difficulty like drowning things. Others are quiet, following us as far as they can with their eyes.

The cries sound gradually fainter. The road drags on toilsomely. We are carrying a lot of stuff—a man must bring something back home with him. Clouds hang in the sky. During the afternoon the sun breaks through, and birch-trees, now with only a few leaves left, hang mirrored in puddles of rain along the way. Soft blue haze is caught in the branches.

As I march on with pack and lowered head, by the side of the road I see images of the bright, silken trees reflected in the pools of rain. In these occasional mirrors they are displayed clearer than in reality. They get another light and in another way. Embedded there in the brown earth lies a span of sky, trees, depths and clearness. Suddenly I shiver. For the first time in many years I feel again that something is still beautiful, that this in all its simplicity is beautiful and pure, this image in the water pool before me— and in this thrill my heart leaps up. For a moment all that other falls away, and now, for the first time I feel it ; I see it ; I comprehend it fully : Peace. The weight that nothing eased before, now lifts at last. Something strange, something new flies up, a dove, a white dove. Trembling horizon, tremulous expectancy, first glimpse, presentiment, hope, exaltation, imminence : Peace.

Sudden panic, and I look round—there behind me on the stretchers my comrades are now lying and still they call. It is peace, yet they must die. But I, I am trembling with joy and am not ashamed. And that is odd.

Because none can ever wholly feel what another suffers—is that the reason why wars perpetually recur ?

2

In the afternoon we are sitting around in a brewery yard. From the office of the factory comes our company commander, Lieutenant Heel, and calls us together. An order has come through that representatives are to be elected from the ranks. We are astounded. No one has ever heard of such a thing before.

Then Max Weil appears in the courtyard, waving a newspaper and shouting : " There's revolution in Berlin ! "

Heel swings round. " Rubbish ! " he says sharply. " There are disturbances in Berlin."

But Weil has not done yet. " The Kaiser's fled to Holland ! "

That wakes us up. Weil must be mad surely. Heel turns fiery red. " Damned liar ! " he roars.

Weil hands him the paper. Heel screws it up and glares furiously at Weil. He cannot bear Weil, for Weil is a Jew, a quiet fellow, who is always sitting about, reading. But Heel is a fire-eater.

" All talk," he growls and looks at Weil as if he would choke him.

Max unbuttons his tunic and produces yet another Special Edition. Heel glances at it, tears it to bits and goes back into his billet. Weil gathers up the shreds of his newspaper, pieces them together and reads us the news. And we just sit there like a row of sotted hens. This is clean beyond our comprehension.

" It says, he wanted to avoid a civil war," says Weil.

" What rot ! " snaps Kosole. " Supposing we had said that a while back, eh ? Well I'll be damned ! So that's what we've been holding out here for ? "

" Jupp," says Bethke shaking his head, " just give me a dig in the ribs, will you, and see if I'm still here." Jupp establishes the fact. " Then it must be so, no doubt," continues Bethke. " All the same I don't quite catch on to the idea. Why, if one of us had done that, they would have stood him up against the wall!"

"Best not to think of Wessling and Schröder now," mutters Kosole, clenching his fists, "else I'll run amok. Poor little Schröder, a mere kid, and there he lay all bashed to a jelly—and the man he died for just cuts and runs!—Dirty scum!" Suddenly he sends his heels crashing against a beer cask.

Willy Homeyer makes a gesture of dismissal. "Let's talk about something else," he then suggests. "For my part I've done with the fellow, absolutely."

Weil starts to explain how Soldiers' Councils have already been set up in a number of the regiments. The officers are not the leaders any more. Many of them have even had their shoulder-straps ripped off.

He would have us set up a Soldiers' Council too. But he does not get much encouragement. We don't want to set up anything any more. All we want is to get home. And we can do that quite well as we are.

In the end we elect three representatives : Adolf Bethke, Weil and Ludwig Breyer.

Weil wants Ludwig to take down his shoulder-straps.

"Here——" says Ludwig wearily, lightly smoothing his forehead. But Bethke shoves Weil back. "Ludwig belongs to us," he says curtly.

Breyer came to our company as a volunteer and was afterwards given a commission. It is not only with Trosske, Homeyer, Bröger and me that he talks familiarly—that goes without saying, of course, we were former schoolfellows—but, when no other officer is about, he is the same with all his old mates in the ranks. And his credit stands high in consequence.

"Well, Heel then," insists Weil.

That is easier to understand. Weil has often been

ridiculed by Heel—what wonder then if he now means to savour his triumph. That, we feel, is no business of ours. Heel was rather harsh, it is true, but he did go for them ; he was always up and coming where there was trouble. And a soldier gives credit for that.

" Well, you can ask him, of course," says Bethke.

" But take a few bandages along with you," Tjaden calls after him.

The event takes a different turn, however. Heel issues from the office just as Weil is about to enter. He has some message-forms in his hand. He points to them. " You're right," he says to Max.

Weil begins to speak. When he comes to the question of the shoulder-straps, Heel makes a swift movement. For an instant we imagine there is going to be a stand-up fight, but to our astonishment the company commander merely says abruptly : " Quite so ! " Then turning to Ludwig he lays a hand on his shoulder. " You don't understand, perhaps, Breyer ? A private's tunic, that's the idea. The other is finished with now."

No one utters a word. This is not the Heel that we know—the man who would go on patrol at night armed with nothing but a walking-stick, whom everyone regarded as bullet-proof. This man is hard put to it just to stand up and speak.

This evening as I lay already asleep, I was roused by sounds of whispering. " You're pulling my leg," I hear Kosole say. " Fact," persists Willy. " You come and see."

They get up hastily and go out into the yard. I follow them. There is a light in the office, so that it is possible to see inside. Heel is seated at the table.

His blue officer's jacket, the *litefka*, is lying before him.
The shoulder-straps have gone. He is wearing a
private's tunic. His head is in his hands, and—but no,
that cannot be—I go a step nearer—Heel, Heel is
crying.

" Can you beat it ! " whispers Tjaden.

" Hop it," says Bethke and gives Tjaden a kick.
We sneak off embarrassed.

Next morning we hear that a major in one of the
neighbouring regiments shot himself when he learned
of the flight of the Emperor.

Heel is coming. He is grey and worn with sleep-
lessness. Quietly he gives the necessary instructions.
Then he goes again. And we all feel just terrible.
The last thing that was left to us has been taken away
—the very ground cut from under our feet.

" It's betrayed, well and truly betrayed, that's what
we are," says Kosole grumpily.

Very different from yesterday is the column that
lines up to-day and marches dismally off—a lost
company, an abandoned army. The entrenching tool
claps with every step—monotonous melody—in vain
—in vain——

Only Ledderhose is as happy as a lark. He sells us
tinned meat and sugar out of his American plunder.

Next evening we reach Germany. Now that
French is no longer spoken everywhere around us, we
begin at last to believe that the peace is real. Until
now we have been secretly expecting an order to turn
about and go back to the trenches—a soldier is mis-
trustful of good, it is better to expect the contrary
from the outset. But now a bubbling ferment begins
slowly to work in us.

We enter a large village. A few bedraggled garlands hang across the street. So many troops have passed through already that it is not worth while to make any special fuss about us, the last of them. So we must content ourselves with the faded welcome of a few rain-sodden placards loosely looped round with oak leaves cut out of green paper. The people hardly so much as look at us as we march by, so accustomed have they grown to it. But for us it is a new thing to come here and we hunger for a few friendly looks, however much we may pretend we do not give a damn. The girls at least might stop and wave to us. Every now and then Tjaden and Jupp try to attract the attention of one, but without success. We look too grisly, no doubt. So in the end they give it up.

Only the children accompany us. We take them by the hand and they run along beside us. We give them all the chocolate we can spare—we want, of course, to take some small part of it home. Adolf Bethke has taken a little girl up in his arms. She tugs at his beard as if it were a bridle, and laughs with glee to see his grimaces. The little hands pat his face. He catches hold of one of them to show me how tiny it is.

The child begins to cry now that he is pulling no more faces. Adolf tries to pacify her, but she only cries the more loudly and he has to put her down.

" We seem to have turned into first-rate bogymen," growls Kosole.

" Who wouldn't be scared of such a prize front-line phiz," Willy explains to him, " it must just give them the creeps."

" We smell of blood, that's what it is," says Ludwig Breyer wearily.

" Well, we must have a jolly good bath," replies

Jupp, " and perhaps that will make the girls a bit keener too."

" Yes, if bathing were all there is to it," answers Ludwig pensively.

Listlessly we trudge onward. We had pictured our entry into our own country after the long years out there rather differently from this. We imagined that people would be waiting for us, expecting us ; now we see that already everyone is taken up with his own affairs. Life has moved on, is still moving on ; it is leaving us behind, almost as if we were superfluous already. This village, of course, is not Germany ; all the same the disappointment sticks in our gizzard, and a shadow passes over us and a queer foreboding.

Carts rattle past, drivers shout, men look up as they pass, then fall again to their own thoughts and cares. The hour is pealing from the church tower ; the damp wind sniffs us as it goes by. Only an old woman with long bonnet strings is running indefatigably along the column, and in a tremulous voice is asking for a certain Erhard Schmidt.

We are billeted in a large outhouse. Though we have marched a long way no one wants to rest. We go off to the inn.

Here is life in plenty, and a turbid wine of this year's vintage. It tastes wonderful, and works powerfully in the legs, so we are the more content to sit. Clouds of tobacco smoke drift through the low room ; the wine smells of the earth and of summer ; we fetch out our tins of preserved meat, carve off great slices and lay them on thick slabs of buttered bread, stick our knives upright beside us in the big wooden table and eat. The oil lamp beams down upon us all like a mother.

Night makes the world beautiful. Not in front-line trenches, of course, but in peace. This afternoon we marched in here dejected; now we begin to revive. The little band playing in the corner soon gets reinforcement from our fellows. We can supply not merely pianists and virtuosos with the mouth-organ— there is even a Bavarian with a zither. Willy Homeyer will not be out of it. He has rigged himself up a sort of devil's fiddle and with the aid of a couple of enormous pot-lids is treating us to the combined glory and clash of cymbals, kettle-drums and rattles.

But the unusual thing, that goes to our heads even more than the wine, is the girls. They are quite other than they seemed this afternoon, they smile and are complaisant. Or are these different ones perhaps? It is so long now since we have seen any girls.

At first we are both eager and shy at the same time; we are not quite sure of ourselves; we seem to have forgotten how to get along with them. At last Ferdinand Kosole waltzes off with one, a husky wench with massive breastworks that should afford his gun a good lie. Now all the others are following his lead.

The heavy, sweet wine sings pleasantly in the head, the girls are whirling by, and the music plays. We are sitting in a group in one corner gathered about Adolf Bethke. "Well, boys," says he, "to-morrow or next day we'll be home again. Yes—my wife—ten months it is now——"

I lean across the table and speak to Valentin Laher who is looking the girls over coolly, with a superior air. There is a blonde sitting beside him, but he is paying her little attention. As I lean forward something in my tunic pocket presses against the edge of the table. I feel to find out what it is. Wessling's watch.

Jupp has hooked the fattest dame. He is dancing like a question-mark. His paw lies flat upon her ample buttocks and is playing the piano there. With moist lips she is smiling up into his face, and he is growing bolder every minute. Finally he waltzes out through the door into the yard and vanishes.

A few minutes later I go out and make for the nearest corner. But already a perspiring sergeant is standing there with a lass. I trundle off into the garden and am just about to begin when there is a terrific crash immediately behind me. I turn round to see Jupp rolling with Fatty on the ground. A garden table has given way beneath them. The fat lady guffaws when she sees me and puts out her tongue. Jupp hisses. I disappear hastily behind some bushes and tread on someone's hand—a hell of a night! " Can't you walk, you clumsy cow ? " asks a deep voice.

" How was I to know there was a worm there ? " I retort peevishly, moving off to find a quiet corner at last.

A cool wind, very good after the smoke inside there. Dark roofs and gables, boughs overhanging, stillness, and the peaceful plashing as I piddle.

Albert comes and stands beside me. The moon is shining. We piss bright silver.

" Man, but it's good, eh, Ernst ? " says Albert.

I nod. We gaze a while into the moon.

" To think that damned show is over, Albert, eh ? "

" My bloody oath—— "

There is creaking and crackling behind us. Girls laugh out clear among the bushes and are as suddenly hushed. The night is like a thunder storm, heavy with fever of life, erupting, wildly and swiftly flashing from one point to another and kindling.

42

THE ROAD BACK

Someone groans in the garden. An answering giggle. Shadows clamber down from the hay loft. Two are standing on a ladder. The man buries his head like a madman among the girl's skirts and stammers something. She laughs in a coarse, loud voice that scrapes over our nerves like a brush. Shudders purl down my back.—How near they come together, yesterday and to-day, death and life !

Tjaden comes up from the dark garden. He is suffused in sweat and his face is glowing : " Boy ! " says he, buttoning up his tunic. " Now a man knows again what it is to be alive."

We take a turn round the house and discover Willy Homeyer. He has lit a great fire of weeds in a field and thrown on a few handfuls of scrounged potatoes. Now there he sits alone before it peacefully dreaming, waiting till the potatoes are baked. Near-by are laid out a few tins of American cutlets, and the dog is squatting watchfully beside him.

The flickering of the fire throws copper gleams through his red hair. Mists are gathering from the meadows. The stars twinkle. We sit down beside him and fish our potatoes from the fire. The skins are burned black, but the inside is golden yellow and fragrant. We grasp the cutlets in both hands and saw away at them as if they were mouth organs. And we wash them down with schnapps out of our aluminium cups.

Potatoes ! how good they taste !—But where are we exactly ? Has the earth returned on her tracks ? Are we children again sitting in the field near Torloxten ? Haven't we been digging potatoes all day in the strong smelling earth, and behind us with baskets red-cheeked girls in faded blue dresses ? And now

43

the potato-fire ! White mists trailing over the field, the fire crackling and the rest all still. The potatoes, they were the last fruit. Now all is gathered in—now only the earth, the clean air, the loved, bitter, white smoke, the end of the harvest. Bitter smoke, bitter smell of the harvest, potato-fire of our childhood— Wraiths of mist drift up, draw together and withdraw —faces of comrades—we are marching, the war is ended—all is melting, dissolving away—potato-fires have come to their own again, and the harvest and life.

" Ah, Willy ! Willy, my boy ! "

" This is the stuff, eh ? " says he looking up, his hands full of meat and potatoes.

Ach, fathead, I was meaning something far different.

The fire has burned out. Willy wipes his hands on his breeches and shuts his knife with a snap. A few dogs are barking in the village—otherwise all is quiet.— No more shells. No clatter of munition columns. No more the wary scrunching of ambulance cars. A night in which far fewer men will die than ever during the last four years.

We go back into the inn. But there is not much doing now. Valentin has taken off his tunic and stands up on his hands a few times. The girls applaud, but Valentin is dissatisfied. " I was a good artist once, Ferdinand. But that won't do, not even for the village fairs," he says gloomily to Kosole. " Gone stiff in the joints, I have.—Valentini's famous turn on the horizontal bar—that was a sight for sore eyes, I can tell you. And now I've got rheumatics——"

" Ach, you be thankful you've got any bones left at all," says Kosole, and crashes his hand down on the table : " Music ! Willy ! "

Homeyer sets to work with a will on kettle-drum and rattles. Things begin to be lively again. I ask Jupp how he got along with Fatty. But he dismisses her with a most scornful gesture. " Come, come," I say in surprise, " that's pretty sudden, isn't it ? "

He makes a grimace. " Yes, I thought she was gone on me, don't you know ? And the fat bitch, she wanted money from me after ! It was the shock made me bump my knee against that blasted garden-table. I can hardly walk now."

Ludwig Breyer is seated at the table, pale and still. He ought to have been asleep long ago, but he does not want to go. His arm is healing well, and the dysentery has improved slightly. But he remains turned in upon himself and troubled.

" Ludwig," says Tjaden in a thick voice, " you should go out into the garden for a bit, too—that heals all diseases——"

Ludwig shakes his head and turns suddenly very pale. I sit down beside him. " Aren't you glad to be going home ? " I ask him.

He gets up and goes away. I cannot make him out. Later I discover him outside standing alone. I question him no more. We go inside again in silence.

In the doorway we bump into Ledderhose just making off with Fatty. Jupp grins in gleeful malice. " There's a surprise in store for him."

" For her," corrects Willy. " Or do you think Arthur may offer her a ha'penny, perhaps ? "

Wine is running over the table, the lamp is smoking, and the girls' skirts are flying. A warm damp weariness drifts lightly at the back of my brow ; everything has soft, blurred edges, like star shells seen through

fog ; my head sinks slowly down upon the table.—
Then the night roars on, smoothly and wonderful,
like an express train, across the country.—Soon we are
at home.

3

For the last time we stand drawn up on the barracks
square. Part of the company lives here in the neighbourhood and they are being disbanded. The rest of
us must make our own way, for the railway services
are so irregular that we cannot be transported farther
in a body. Now we must separate.

The wide, grey square is much too big for us.
Across it sweeps a bleak November wind smelling of
decay and death. We are lined up between the
canteen and the guard-room, more space we do not
require. The wide, empty square about us wakes
woeful memories. There, rank on rank, invisible,
stand the dead.

Heel passes down the company. And behind him
soundlessly walks the ghostly train of his predecessors.
Nearest to him, still bleeding from the neck, his chin
torn away, with sorrowful eyes, goes Bertinck, company
commander for a year and a half, a teacher, married,
four children ;—beside him with black-green face,
Müller, nineteen years of age, gas-poisoned three days
after he took command of the company ;—and next,
Redecker, forestry-surveyor, two weeks later bashed
into the earth by a direct hit ;—then still paler, more
remote, Büttner, captain, killed in a raid with a
machine-gun bullet through the heart ;—and like
shadows behind them, already almost without name,
so far back, the others—seven company commanders

46

in two years. And more than five hundred men.—
Thirty-two are now standing in the barracks square.

Heel tries to say a few words in farewell. But
nothing will come ; he has to give up. No words in
the world can take the field against this lonely, empty
barracks square, and these sorry ranks of the survivors,
standing there in their greatcoats and their boots,
dumb and freezing, remembering their comrades.

Heel passes from one to another and shakes hands
with each man. When he comes to Max Weil, with
thin lips he says : " Now your time begins, Weil——"

" It will be less bloody," answers Weil quietly.

" And less heroic," Heel retorts.

" That's not the only thing in life," says Weil.

" But the best," Heel replies. " What else is there ? "

Weil pauses a moment. Then he says : " Things
that sound feeble to-day, Herr Lieutenant—kindliness
and love. These also have their heroisms."

" No," answers Heel swiftly, as though he had
already long thought upon it, and his brow is clouded.
" They offer only martyrdom. That is quite another
thing. Heroism begins where reason leaves off : when
life is set at a discount. It has to do with folly, with
exaltation, with risk—and you know it. But little or
nothing with purpose. Purpose, that is your word.
' Why ? wherefore ? to what end ? '—who asks these
questions, knows nothing of it."

He speaks emphatically, as if he would convince
himself. His worn face works. Within these few
days he has become embittered, and he looks years
older. And Weil also, he has altered as rapidly. He
used to be an unobtrusive sort of fellow—but then
nobody could quite make him out.—Now he has come

47

suddenly to the fore and every minute grows more decided, more assured. No one ever thought he could talk like this. And the more agitated Heel becomes, the calmer is Max. Quietly and firmly he says: "The misery of millions is too big a price to pay for the heroics of a few."

Heel shrugs his shoulders. "Price—purpose—pay '—those are your words. We shall see how far they will bring you!"

Weil glances at the private's uniform that Heel is still wearing. "And how far have yours brought you?"

Heel turns crimson. "To a memory," he says harshly. "To a remembrance of things which at any rate are not to be had for money."

Weil is silent a moment. "To a memory," he repeats, then turns and looks out over the empty square, and along our scanty ranks—"Yes,—and to a terrible responsibility."

As for us, we do not make much of all this. We are freezing, and we consider it unnecessary to talk. Talking will not make the world any different.

The ranks break. The farewells begin. Müller, the man next to me, settles the pack on his shoulders, clamps his bundle of rations under his arm; then he stretches his hand to me : "Well, good luck, Ernst——"

"Good luck, Felix——" He passes on to Willy, to Albert, to Kosole.

Now comes Gerhard Pohl, the company singer who on the march used to sing all the top tenor notes, pursuing the melody as occasion offered, up into the clouds. The remainder of the time he would rest on his oars, so as to be able to put his full weight into the

two-part passages. His tanned face with the wart has
a troubled look : he has just parted from Karl Bröger
with whom he has played so many games of skat.
That has been hard for him.

" Good-bye, Ernst——"

" Good-bye, Gerhard." He is gone.

Weddekamp gives me his hand. He used to make
the crosses for the fellows who were killed. " It's a
pity, Ernst," says he, " I suppose I'll never be able to
fit you up now. And you might have had a mahogany
one, too ! I was saving a lovely bit of piano-lid for
you."

" Given time all things must happen," I reply
grinning. " I'll drop you a line when it comes to
that."

He laughs. " That's right, keep smiling, lad ; the
war's not over yet."

Then with drooping shoulders he trots away.

The first group has already vanished through the
barracks gate, Scheffler, Fassbender, young Lucke,
and August Beckman among them. Others follow.
We begin to be troubled. It is difficult at first to get
used to the idea of so many fellows going away for good.
Heretofore it was only death, or wounds, or temporary
transfers that depleted the company. Now peace
must be reckoned with.

We are so accustomed to shell-holes and trenches
that we are suddenly suspicious of this still, green
landscape ; as though its stillness were but a pretence
to lure us into some secretly undermined region.

And now there go our comrades, hastening out into
it, heedless, alone, without rifles, without bombs !
One would like to run after them, fetch them back,
shout to them : " Hey ! where are you off to ? What

are you after out there alone ? You belong here with us. We must stick together. How else can we live ? "

Queer mill-wheel in the brain : too long a soldier——

The November wind pipes over the empty barracks square. Yet more and more comrades go. Not long now and every man will be alone.

The rest of our company all go home by the same route. We are now lounging in the station, waiting for a train. The place is a regular army dump of chests, cardboard boxes, packs and waterproof-sheets.

Only two trains pass through in seven hours. Men hang round the doorways in clusters, in swarms. By the afternoon we have won a place near the track, and before evening are in the best position, right at the front.

The first train arrives soon after midday—a freight train with blind horses. Their skewed eyeballs are blue-white and red-rimmed. They stand stock still, their heads outstretched, and there is life only in the quivering sense of their nostrils.

During the afternoon it is announced that no more trains will leave to-day.

Not a soul moves. A soldier does not believe in announcements. And in point of fact another train does come. One glance suffices. This will do. Half-full at the most.

The station hall reverberates to the assembling of gear and the charge of the columns that stampede from the waiting-rooms and burst in wild confusion upon the men already in the hall.

The train glides up. One window is open. Albert Trosske, lightest and nimblest of us, is heaved up and clambers through like a monkey. Next moment all the doors are blocked with men. Most of the windows are shut. But already some are being shattered with blows from rifle-butts by fellows who mean to get aboard at any price, though it should cost them torn hands and legs. Blankets are flung over the jagged glass points, and here and there the boarding is already in progress.

The train stops. Albert has run through the corridors and now flings open the window in front of us. Tjaden and the dog shoot in first, Bethke and Kosole after them, Willy shoving from behind. The three at once make for the doors opening into the corridor, so as to close the compartment on both flanks. Then follows the baggage along with Ludwig and Ledderhose, then Valentin, Karl Bröger and I, and, after clearing the decks about him once more, last of all, Willy.

"All in?" shouts Kosole from the gangway where the pressure is becoming momently more urgent. "All aboard!" bawls Willy. Then, as if fired from a pistol, Bethke, Kosole and Tjaden shoot into their seats and outsiders pour into the compartment, climb up on the luggage-rack, till every possible inch of space is occupied.

Even the engine has been stormed, and there are fellows sitting on the buffers. The roofs of the carriages are swarming with men. "Come down out of that!" cries the guard. "You'll get your bloody brains knocked out." "You hold your gas! We're all right," it comes back. There are five men sitting in the lavatory. One has his behind sticking out through the window.

The train pulls out. Some, who were not holding on fast enough, fall off. Two are run over and dragged away, but others jump their places immediately. The footboards are full. The crowding gets worse as the train goes on.

One man is hanging on to a door. It swings open and he dangles clear, clutching the window. Willy clambers across, seizes him by the collar and hoists him in.

During the night our carriage has its first casualties. The train passed into a low tunnel and some of the chaps on the roof were crushed and swept clean off. Though the others had seen it, they had no means up there of stopping the train. The man in the lavatory window too dropped asleep and fell out.

Other carriages also suffered similar casualties. So now the roofs are rigged up with wooden grips and ropes, and bayonets rammed into the woodwork. And sentries are posted to give warning of danger.

We sleep and sleep; standing, lying, sitting, squatting in every possible attitude on packs and on bundles, we sleep. The train rattles on. Houses, trees, gardens, people waving. Processions, red flags, guards posted on the railway, shouting, cries, Special Editions, Revolution—but we will sleep first, the rest can wait till later. Now for the first time one begins to feel how tired one has become in all these years.

Evening again. There is one miserable lamp burning. The train moves slowly and stops often because of engine trouble.

Our packs joggle. Pipes are glowing; the dog is asleep on my knees. Adolf Bethke leans across to me and strokes the dog's head. " Well, Ernst," he says after a while, " we're going to separate at last."

I nod. It is strange, but I can hardly picture life now without Adolf—without his watchful eye and his quiet voice. It was he that educated Albert and me when we first came out to the Front as raw recruits; but for him I doubt if I should still be here.

"We must meet sometimes, Adolf," I say. "We must meet often."

The heel of a boot catches me in the face. On the rack over our heads sits Tjaden earnestly counting his money—he means to go straight from the station to a brothel. To bring himself to a proper frame of mind he is now regaling us with the story of his adventures with a couple of land-girls. No one thinks of it as indecent—it has nothing to do with the war, so we listen readily.

A sapper, who has lost two fingers, is boasting that his wife has given birth to a seven months' child and yet in spite of that it weighs eight pounds. Ledderhose jeers at him : "Things don't happen that way ! " The sapper does not follow him, and begins to count on his fingers the months between his last leave and the birth of the child. "Seven," says he, "that's right."

Ledderhose coughs and his lemon-yellow face draws to a wry, mocking smile. "Somebody's been doing a little job for you there."

The sapper looks at him. "What—what do you mean, eh ? " he stutters.

"Why, it's obvious enough surely ! " says Arthur sniffling and scratching himself.

Sweat breaks out on the man's lips. He counts over and over again. His mouth twitches. A fat A.S.C. driver with a beard, sitting by the window, is convulsed with laughter. "You poor fool ! you poor, bloody fool !——"

Bethke stiffens. " Shut your mug, fat guts ! "

" Why ? " asks the fellow with the beard.

" Because you ought to shut your mug ! " says Bethke. " You too, Arthur."

The sapper has turned pale. " What does one do about it ? " he asks helplessly, holding fast to the window-frame.

" One shouldn't get married," says Jupp deliberately, " until one's children are already out earning. Then that sort of thing wouldn't happen."

Outside the evening draws on. Woods lie along the skyline like black cows, fields show faintly in the dim light that shines from the carriage windows. It now wants but two hours for home. Bethke is getting his baggage ready. He lives in a village a few stations this side of the town and so has to get out sooner.

The train stops. Adolf shakes hands with us all. He tumbles out on to the little siding and looks about him with a sweeping glance that drinks in the whole landscape in a second, as a parched field the rain. Then he turns to us again. But he hears nothing any more. Ludwig Breyer is standing at the window, indifferent to his pain. " Trot along, Adolf," he says, " your wife will be waiting."

Bethke looks up at us and shakes his head : " No such hurry as all that, Ludwig." It is evident with what power home is drawing him away ; but Adolf is Adolf—he continues to stand there beside us until the train leaves. Then he turns swiftly about and goes off with long strides.

" We'll be coming to see you soon ! " I call after him hastily.

We watch him go out across the fields. For a long

time he continues to wave. Then smoke from the engine drifts between. In the distance gleam a few red lights.

The train makes a big sweeping curve. Adolf has now become very small, a mere point, a tiny little man, quite alone on the wide, dark plain, above which, vast and electrically bright, ringing the horizon in sulphur yellow, towers the night sky. I do not know why—it has nothing to do with Adolf—but the sight fascinates me.—A solitary man going out over the wide stretch of fields against the mighty sky, in the evening and alone.

Then the trees close up in massive darkness and soon nothing is left but swift motion, and woods and the sky.

It grows noisy in the compartment. Here inside there are corners, edges, odours, warmth, space and boundaries ; here are brown, weathered faces and eyes, bright flecks in them ; there is a smell of earth, sweat, blood, uniforms—but outside the world is rushing obscurely past to the steady stamping of the train ; we are leaving it behind us, ever farther and farther, all that world of trenches and shell-holes, of darkness and terror ; now a mere whirlwind seen through a window—it concerns us no more.

Somebody starts singing. Others join in. Soon everyone is singing, the whole compartment, the next compartment, the entire carriage, the whole train. We sing ever more lustily, with more and more power ; our brows are flushed, the veins swell out ; we sing every soldiers' song that we know. We stand up, glaring at each other. Our eyes shine ; the wheels thunder the rhythm ; we sing and sing——

55

I am wedged between Ludwig and Kosole and feel their warmth penetrating my tunic. I move my hands, turn my head; my muscles brace themselves and a shiver mounts from my knees to my belly; a ferment like sherbet in my bones, it rises, foams up into my lungs, my lips, my eyes; the carriage swims; it sings in me as a telegraph pole in a storm, thousands of wires twanging, thousands of roads opening.—Slowly I put my hand on Ludwig's hand, and feel that it must burn: but when he looks up, worn and pale as ever, all I can drag out of what is surging within me is merely to stammer: " Have you a cigarette, Ludwig ? "

He gives me one. The train whistles, we go on singing. A more ominous rumble than the rattle of the wheels gradually mingles with our songs, and in a pause there comes a mighty crash that travels rolling in long reverberations over the plain. Clouds have gathered; a thunderstorm bursts. The flashes of lightning dazzle like close gun-fire. Kosole stands in the window and shakes his head. " Now for another sort of thunderstorm ! " he mutters and leans far out. " Quick ! see ! there she is ! " he suddenly cries.

We press round. At the limit of the land in the glare of the lightning the tall, slender towers of the city pierce the sky. Then darkness closes over them again in thunder, but with every flash they come nearer.

Our eyes shine with excitement. Expectancy has suddenly shot up amongst us, over us, within us, like a giant beanstalk.

Kosole gropes for his things. " Oh, boys," says he, stretching his arms, " where shall we all be sitting a year hence, I wonder."

" On our backsides," suggests Jupp apprehensively. But no one is laughing now. The city has sprung upon us, gathered us to herself. There she lies panting under the wild light, outstretched, inviting. And we are coming to her—a trainload of soldiers, a trainload of home-coming out of the limbo of nothingness, a trainload of tense expectancy, nearer and nearer. The train tears along ; the walls leap out against us, in a moment we will collide ; flashes of lightning, the thunder roars.—Then the station rises up on both sides of the carriage, seething with noise and cries ; a pelting rain is falling ; the platform gleams with the wet. Heedless, we jump out into it all.

As I spring out of the door the dog follows. He presses close after me and together we run through the rain down the steps.

PART II

I

IN front of the station we scatter like a bucket of water
pitched out on the pavement. Kosole sets off at a
sharp pace with Bröger and Trosske down Heinrich
Street. With Ludwig I turn rapidly into Station
Avenue. Without wasting any time in farewells
Ledderhose and his rag-and-bone shop have already
gone like a shot : and Tjaden gets Willy to describe
briefly the shortest route to the moll-shop. Jupp and
Valentin alone have any leisure. No one is awaiting
their arrival, so they take a preliminary saunter round
the station on the off chance of finding some grub.
They intend later on to go to the barracks.

Water is dripping from the trees along Station
Avenue ; clouds trail low and drive swiftly over.
Some soldiers of the latest class to be called up approach
us. They are wearing red armbands. " Off with
his shoulder-straps ! " yells one, making a grab at
Ludwig.

" Shut your mouth, you war-baby!" I say, as I
shove him off.

Others press in and surround us. Ludwig looks
calmly at the foremost of them and goes on his way.
The fellow steps aside. Then two sailors appear and
rush at him.

" You swine ! can't you see he's wounded ? " I shout,
flinging off my pack to get freer play with my hands.

But Ludwig is down already ; what with the wound in his arm he is as good as defenceless. The sailors trample on him, rip at his uniform. " A lieutenant ! " screeches a woman's voice. " Kick him to death, the dirty blood hound ! "

Before I can come to his assistance I get a blow in the face that makes me stagger. " You son of a bitch ! " I cough and with all my weight plant my boot in my assailant's stomach. He sighs and topples over. Immediately three others fall on me and drag me down. " Lights out, knives out ! " cries the woman.

Between the trampling legs I can see Ludwig with his free left hand throttling one sailor, whom he has brought down by giving him a crack behind the knees. He still hangs on, though the others are hoeing into him with all their might. Then someone swipes me over the head with a belt-buckle and another treads on my teeth. Wolf promptly seizes him by the calf of his leg, but still we are unable to rise ; they knock us down again every time and would tread us to pulp. Wild with rage I try to get at my revolver. But at that moment one of the attackers crashes backwards to the pavement beside me. A second crash—another fellow unconscious—and straightway a third—this can have only one meaning : Willy is on the job.

He came storming up at top gallop, flung off his pack as he ran and now is standing over us, raging. He seizes them in twos by the nape of the neck, one in each hand, and bashes their heads together. Both are knocked out on the instant—when Willy gets mad he is a living sledge hammer. We break free. I jump up, but the attackers make off. I just manage to land one of them a blow in the small of his back with my pack and then turn to look after Ludwig.

But Willy is in full pursuit. He saw the two sailors who made the first attack on Ludwig. One now lies there in the gutter, blue and groaning—and like a flying hurricane with red hair he is hot on the heels of the other.

Ludwig's arm has been trodden on and the blood is oozing through the bandage. His face is smeared with mud and his forehead torn by a heel. He wipes himself down and rises slowly. "Hurt much?" I ask him. Deathly pale he shakes his head.

In the meantime Willy has captured the sailor and is lugging him along like a sack. "You bloody cow!" he storms. "There you've been sitting in your ships taking the summer air all the war and never have heard so much as a shot fired; and now you think it's time for you to open your beer trap and attack front-line soldiers, do you? You let me catch you! Kneel down, you malingering sod! Kneel down and ask his pardon!"

He thrusts the fellow down before Ludwig with an air ferocious enough to put the fear of God into any man. "I'll massacre you!" he snarls. "I'll tear you to bits! Kneel! Down on your knees!"

The man whimpers. "Let him alone, Willy," says Ludwig, picking up his things.

"What?" says Willy incredulously. "Are you mad! After they've trampled all over your arm!"

Ludwig is ready to go. "Ach, let him go——"

For a moment Willy continues staring at Ludwig; then with a shake of his head he releases the sailor. "Right you are, then. Now, run like hell!" But he cannot resist letting fly at the last moment and giving the fellow a kick that sends him through a double somersault.

We go on our way. Willy curses—he must talk when he is angry. But Ludwig is silent.

Suddenly we see the gang of runaways coming back round the corner of Beer Street. They have gathered reinforcements.

Willy unslings his rifle. " Load, and prepare to fire ! " says he, his eyes narrowing. Ludwig draws out his revolver and I also put my gun in readiness. Until now it has merely been a free fight ; but this time is going to be earnest. We do not mean to be set upon a second time.

We deploy across the street at intervals of three paces so as not to form one single compact target ; then we advance. The dog understands at once what is afoot. He slinks along growling in the gutter beside us. He too has learned at the Front to advance under cover.

" At twenty yards we fire ! " threatens Willy.

The crowd facing us moves anxiously. We advance farther. Rifles are pointed at us. With a click Willy slips his safety-catch and from his belt takes the hand-grenade he still carries as an iron ration. " I count up to three——"

An older man, wearing an N.C.O.'s tunic from which the badges of rank have been removed, now steps out from the gang. He advances a few paces. " Are you comrades, or not ? " he calls.

Willy gasps ; he is outraged. " Well ! I'll be damned ! That's what we're asking you, you white-livered calf ! " he retorts indignantly. " Who was it started attacking wounded men ? "

The other stops short. " Did you do that ? " he asks of the fellows behind him.

" He wouldn't take down his shoulder-straps," answers one of the group.

The man makes an impatient gesture and turns toward us again. "They shouldn't have done that, Comrades. But you don't seem to understand what is the matter. Where have you come from, anyway?"

"From the Front, of course; where else do you think?" snorts Willy.

"And where are you going?"

"Where you've been all the war—back home."

"Comrade," says the man showing an empty sleeve, "I didn't lose that at home."

"That doesn't make it any better," says Willy unmoved. "In that case you ought to be ashamed to be seen with that push of upstart toy soldiers."

The sergeant comes nearer. "It's revolution," he says quietly, "and who isn't for us is against us."

Willy laughs. "Bloody fine revolution, no mistake! with your Society for the Removal of Shoulder-Straps! If that's all you want——" He spits contemptuously.

"Not so fast, mate," says the one-armed man now walking swiftly toward him. "We do want a lot more! We want an end of war, an end of all this hatred! an end of murder! That's what we're after. We want to be men again, not war machines!"

Willy lowers his hand-grenade. "A damned fine beginning that was, I must say," he says, pointing to Ludwig's trampled bandage. Then with a few bounds he makes for the mob. "Yes, you cut along home to your mothers, you snotty-nosed brats!" he roars as they give back before him. "Want to be men, do you? Why, you aren't even decent soldiers yet! To see the way you hold your rifles, it makes a man scared, you'll be breaking your fingers next!"

The gang starts to run. Willy turns round and stands towering before the sergeant. "And now I

have something to say to you ! We've had as much
a bellyful of this business as you ; and there's going to
be an end of it, too, that's certain. But not your way.
What we do we do of ourselves ; it is a long time now
since we have taken orders from any man. But see
now ! "

Two rips, and he has torn off his shoulder-straps.
" I'm doing this because I myself wish it ; not at all
because you wish it. It's my business—understand?
But that chap," he points to Ludwig, " he's our
lieutenant, and he's keeping his—and God help any
man who says he's not ! "

The one-armed man nods. Something in his face
quickens. " I was there, too, mate," he blurts out,
" I know what is what, as well as you do. Here . . ."
he shows his stump excitedly, " Twentieth Infantry
Division, Verdun."

" So were we," says Willy laconically. " Well—
good luck."

He puts on his pack and slings his rifle once more.
We march on. As Ludwig passes him, the sergeant
with the red armband suddenly brings his hand to his
cap, and we understand his meaning. He is saluting
not a uniform, not the war—he is saluting his mates
from the Front.

Willy's home is nearest. He waves gaily across the
street in the direction of the little house. " Hullo,
you old horse-box !—Home is the sailor ! "

We propose to wait for him but Willy refuses. " We'll
see Ludwig home first," he says spoiling for fight.
" I'll be getting my potato-salad and my curtain
lectures quite soon enough."

We stop a while on the road to spruce ourselves up so

that our parents shall not see we have come fresh from a fight. I wipe Ludwig's face and we take off his bandage to cover up the traces of blood, so that his mother may not be alarmed. Later, of course, he will have to go to the hospital and get his bandages renewed.

We arrive without further disturbance. Ludwig still looks rather the worse for his drubbing. "Don't let that worry you," I say, shaking him by the hand. Willy puts a great paw on his shoulder. "Sort of thing might happen to anyone, old boy. If it hadn't been for the wound you'd have made mincemeat of them."

Ludwig nods to us and goes indoors. We watch to see that he manages the stairs all right. He is already halfway up when another point suddenly occurs to Willy. "Kick, next time, Ludwig," he shouts after him, "just kick, that's all! Don't let 'em get near you, understand me?" Then, well content, he slams to the door.

"I'd like to know what's been up with him the last few weeks," say I.

Willy scratches his head. "It'll be the dysentery," he suggests. "Why otherwise—well, you remember how he cleaned up that tank at Bixchoote! On his own too. That was no child's play, eh?"

He settles his pack. "Well, good luck, Ernst! Now I'll be after seeing what the Homeyer family's been doing the last six months. One hour of sentiment, I expect, and then full steam ahead with the lectures. My mother—Oh boy, but what a sergeant-major she would have made! A heart of gold the old lady has —in a casing of granite."

I go on alone, and all at once the world seems to have altered. There is a noise in my ears as if a river ran under the pavement, and I neither see nor hear anything till I am standing outside our house. I go slowly up the stairs. Over the door hangs a banner : *Welcome Home*, and beside it a bunch of flowers. They have seen me coming already and are all standing there, my mother in front on the stairs, my father, my sisters. I can see beyond them into the dining-room, there is food on the table, everything is gay and jubilant. " What's all this nonsense you've been up to ? " I say. " Flowers and everything—what's that for ? it's not so important as all that.—But, Mother ! what are you crying for ? I'm back again—and the war's ended—surely there is nothing to cry about——" then I feel the salt tears trickling down my own nose.

2

We have had potato-cakes with eggs and sausage— a wonderful meal. It is two years since I last saw an egg; and potato-cakes, God only knows.

Comfortable and full we now sit around the big table in the living-room drinking coffee with saccharine. The lamp is burning, the canary singing, the stove is warm, and under the table Wolf lies asleep. It is as lovely as can be.

" Now tell us all about your experiences, Ernst," says my father.

" Experiences——" I repeat, and think to myself, I haven't experienced anything—It was just war all the time—how should a man have experiences there ?

No matter how I rack my brains, nothing suitable occurs to me. A man cannot talk about the things out there with civilians, and I know nothing else.

E   65

" You folk here have experienced much more, I'm sure," I say by way of excusing myself.

That they have, indeed ! My sisters tell how they had to scrounge to get the supper together. Twice the gendarmes took everything from them at the station. The third time they sewed the eggs inside their cloaks, put the sausages into their blouses and hid the potatoes in pockets inside their skirts. That time they got through——

I listen to them rather absently. They have grown up since last I saw them. Or perhaps I did not notice such things then, so that I find it the more remarkable now. Ilse must be over seventeen already. How the time goes——

" Did you know Councillor Pleister was dead ? " asks my father.

I shake my head. " When was that ? "

" In July—about the twentieth, I think. . . ."

The water is singing in the kettle. I toy with the tassels along the fringe of the tablecloth. So— July, I think to myself—July—we lost thirty-six men during the last five days of July. And I hardly remember the names of three of them now, there were so many more joined them as time went on.—" What was it ? " I ask, feeling sleepy from the unaccustomed warmth of the room, " H.E. or machine-gun ? "

" But he wasn't a soldier, Ernst," protests my father rather mystified. " He had inflammation of the lung."

" Oh, yes, of course," I say, setting myself upright in my chair again, " I forgot about that."

They recount all the rest that has happened since my last leave. The butcher at the corner was half killed by a mob of hungry women. At one time, the end of August, there had been as much as a whole

66

pound of fish to a family. The dog at Doctor Knott's has been taken away, to be worked up into soap, like as not. Miss Mentrup is going to have a baby. Potatoes are dearer again. Next week, perhaps, one may be able to buy some bones at the slaughter-yard. Aunt Grete's second daughter was married last month —and to a captain, too !

My sister stops short. "But you aren't listening at all, Ernst!" she says in astonishment.

"O yes, yes," I reassure her, and pull myself together, "a captain, quite, she married a captain, you said."

"Yes, just think of it ! Such luck !" my sister runs on eagerly, "and her face simply covered with freckles, too ! What do you say to that now ? "

What should I say ?—if a captain stops a shrapnel bullet in the nut, he's a gonner, same as any other sort of man.

They talk on. But I cannot marshal my thoughts, they will keep wandering.

I get up and look out the window. A pair of underpants are dangling on the line. Grey and limp they flap to and fro in the twilight. The dim, uncertain light in the drying-yard flickers—then suddenly, like a shadow, remote, another scene rises up away beyond it—fluttering linen, a solitary mouth organ in the evening, a march up in the dusk—and scores of dead negroes in faded blue greatcoats, with burst lips and bloody eyes : gas. The scene stands out clearly for a moment, then it wavers and vanishes ; the underpants flap through it, the drying-yard is there again, and again behind me I feel the room with my parents, and warmth and security. That is over, I think to myself with a sense of relief, and turn away.

"What makes you so fidgetty, Ernst?" asks my father. "You haven't sat still for ten minutes together."

"Perhaps he is overtired," suggests my mother.

"No," I answer a little embarrassed, "it's not that. I think perhaps I've forgotten how to sit on a chair for so long at a stretch. We didn't have them out at the Front; there we just lay about on the floor or wherever we happened to be. I've lost the habit, I suppose, that's all."

"Funny," says my father.

I shrug my shoulders. My mother smiles. "Have you been to your room yet?" she asks.

"Not yet," I reply, getting up and going over. My heart is beating fast as I open the door and sense the smell of the books in the darkness. I switch on the light hastily and look about me. "Everything has been left exactly as it was," says my sister behind me.

"Yes, yes," I reply in self-defence; for I would rather be left alone now. But already the others have come too, and are standing there in the doorway watching me expectantly. I sit down in the armchair and place my hands on the top of the table. It is smooth and cool to the touch. Yes, everything just as it was. The brown marble letter-weight that Karl Vogt gave me—there in its old place beside the compass and the inkstand. But Karl Vogt was killed at Mount Kemmel.

"Don't you like your room any more?" asks my sister.

"O yes," I say hesitantly, "but it's so small——"

My father laughs. "It's just the same size that it used to be."

" Of course, it must be," I agree, " but I had an idea it was so much bigger, somehow——"

" It is so long since you were here," says my mother.

I nod. " The bed is freshly made," she goes on— " but you won't be thinking of that yet."

I feel for my tunic pocket. Adolf Bethke gave me a packet of cigars when he left us. I must smoke one of them now. Everything around me seems to have come loose, as if I were a bit giddy. I inhale the smoke deep into my lungs and begin to feel better already.

" Smoke cigars, do you ? " asks my father in surprise and almost reprovingly.

I look at him with a certain wonderment. " But of course," I reply. " They were part of the ration out there. We got three or four every day. Will you have one ? "

He takes it, shaking his head meanwhile. " You used not to smoke at all, before."

" O yes, before——" I say, and cannot help smiling that he should make such a song about of it. There are a lot of things I used not to do, before, that's a fact. But up the line there one soon lost any diffidence before one's elders. We were all alike there.

I steal a glance at the clock. I have only been here a couple of hours, yet it feels like a couple of weeks since I last saw Willy and Ludwig. I should like to get up and go to them at once. I am quite unable to realise that now I must stay here in the family for good. I still have the feeling that to-morrow, or maybe the next day, but surely some time we shall be marching again, side by side, cursing or resigned, but all together.

At last I get up and fetch my greatcoat from where it hangs in the passage.

"Aren't you going to stay with us this evening?" asks my mother.

"I have to go and report myself yet," I lie—I have not the heart to tell her the truth.

She comes with me to the stairs. "Wait a moment," she says, "it is very dark; I'll bring a light."

I stop in surprise. A light! For those few steps? Lord, and through how many shell-holes, along how many gloomy duckboard walks have I had to find my way at night all these years without light and under fire? And now a light for a few stairs! Ah, mother! But I wait patiently till she comes with the lamp and holds a light for me, and it is as if she stroked me in the darkness.

"Be careful, Ernst, that no harm comes to you out there," she calls after me.

"But what harm could come to me at home here, mother, in peace time?" I say smiling, and look up at her. She leans over the banister. Her small, timorous face has a golden light upon it from the lamp shade. The lights and shadows dance fantastically over the wall behind her. And suddenly a strange agitation takes hold on me, almost like pain—as if there were nothing like that face in all the world, as if I were a child again that must be lighted down the stairs, a youngster that may come to some harm out on the street—and as if all else that has been between were but phantasm and dream.

But the light of the lamp concentrates to a flashing point in the buckle of my belt. The moment has passed. I am no child, I am wearing a uniform. Quickly I run down the stairs, three steps at a time, I fling open the outer door and hurry out, eager to come to my comrades.

I call first on Albert Trosske. His mother's eyes are red from weeping; but that is merely because of to-day, it is not anything serious. But Albert is not his old self either, he is sitting there at the table like a wet hen. Beside him is his elder brother. It is an age since I saw him last; all I know is that he has been in hospital a long time. He has grown stout and has lovely, red cheeks.

"Hullo, Hans, fit again?" I say heartily. "How goes it? Nothing like being up on your pins again, eh?"

He mumbles something incomprehensible. Frau Trosske bursts into sobs and goes out. Albert makes me a sign with his eyes. I look around mystified. Then I notice a pair of crutches lying beside Hans's chair. "Not finished with yet?" I ask.

"Oh, yes," he replies. "Came out of hospital last week." He reaches for the crutches, lifts himself up and with two jerks swings across to the stove. Both feet are missing. He has an iron artificial foot on his right leg and on the left just a frame with a shoe attachment.

I feel ashamed at my stupid talk. "I didn't know, Hans," I say.

He nods. His feet were frost-bitten in the Carpathians, then gangrene set in, and in the end they both had to be amputated.

"It is only his feet, thank God," says Frau Trosske, bringing a cushion and settling it under the artificial limb. "Never mind, Hans, we will soon put it right, you'll soon learn to walk again." She sits down beside him and strokes his hands.

71

"Yes," I say, only to say something, "you still have your legs, anyway."

"That's what I say," he answers.

I offer him a cigarette. What should one do at such moments?—anything seems brusque, however well it is meant. We talk a while, halting and painfully, but whenever Albert or I get up and move about, we see Hans watching our feet with a gloomy, anguished gaze, and his mother's eyes following his in the same direction—always only at the feet—back and forth.—You have feet—I have none——

He still thinks of nothing else—and his mother is wholly taken up with him. She does not see that Albert is suffering under it.—No one could stick that for long.

"Albert, we ought to be going along to report now," I say, to give him a pretext for escape.

"Yes," he says eagerly.

Once outside, we begin to breathe again. The night reflects softly in the wet pavement. Street lights flicker in the wind. Albert stares straight ahead. "There's nothing I can do about it," he begins; "but when I sit there between them like that and see him and my mother, in the end I get to feel as if it were all my fault, and am ashamed at still having my two feet. A man begins to think he is scum just for being whole. Even an arm-wound like Ludwig's would do; then perhaps one wouldn't seem such an eyesore standing about there."

I try to console him; but he will not have it. What I say does not convince him, but it gives me at least some relief. It is always so with comfort.

We go to find Willy. His room is a wilderness. The

bed has been dismantled and stands up-ended against the wall. It has to be made larger—Willy has grown so much in the army he does not fit it any more. Planks, hammers, saws lie strewn all around. And on a chair there glistens an immense dish of potato salad. He is not there himself. His mother explains that he has been out in the scullery a whole hour scrubbing himself clean.

Frau Homeyer is on her knees before Willy's pack, rummaging through it. Shaking her head she hauls out some dirty rags that were once a pair of socks. "Dreadful holes!" she murmurs, looking up at Albert and me disapprovingly.

"Cheap stuff," I say with a shrug.

"Cheap, indeed!" she protests bitterly. "Shows how little you know about it! It's the best wool, let me tell you, young man. Eight days I was running up and down before I got it. And now see! through already! And you won't find their like anywhere." She contemplates the ruins with an aggrieved air. "I'm sure there must have been time at the war just to pull on a pair of clean socks quickly at least once a week! Four pairs of them he had last time he went out. And now he has brought back only two—and look at them!" She passes her hand through the holes.

I am just about to take up his defence when he himself enters in triumph, announcing at the top of his voice: "Here's a piece of luck for you! Another aspirant for the Order of the Dixie! There's going to be fricasseed chicken to-night, lads!"

Waving in his hand like a flag is a fat cock. The green-golden tail feathers gleam, its comb glows crimson and from its beak there hang a few drops of blood.

Though I have had a good meal, water begins to gather in my mouth.

Willy swings the creature to and fro blissfully. Frau Homeyer straightens up and utters a shriek. " Willy ! But where did you get it from ? "

Willy announces with pride that he saw it behind the shed, caught it and killed it, all inside two minutes. He slaps his mother on the back. " We did learn something out there, you see. Willy wasn't acting-deputy-chief-cook for nothing, I tell you."

She looks at him as if he had murdered a child. Then she calls to her husband. " Oscar ! " she moans in a broken voice, " come and look at this.—He has killed Binding's pedigree cock ! "

" Binding ? What Binding ? " asks Willy.

" The cock belongs to Binding, the milkman next door. O my God, how could you do such a thing ? " Frau Homeyer sinks down on a chair.

" I wasn't going to leave a fine roast like that just running about," says Willy in astonishment, " not when I had him as good as in my hand already."

Frau Homeyer is not to be comforted. " There'll be trouble about it, I know. That Binding man has such a terrible temper."

" But what do you take me for ? " asks Willy, beginning to feel really slighted. " Do you think I let so much as a mouse see me ? I'm no novice, you know. This makes just the tenth I've swiped now. A jubilee bird, you might say. We can eat him in perfect comfort, and your Binding won't know one thing about it." He shakes it affectionately. " You certainly will taste good ! Do you think I should boil him or roast him ? "

" Do you imagine I would eat one little bit of it ? "

cries Frau Homeyer beside herself. "You take it back at once."

"I'm not quite balmy," explains Willy.

"But you stole it!" she laments desperately.

"Stole it?" Willy bursts into laughter. "That's a nice thing to say! Commandeered, this was. Boned. Picked up, if you like. But stolen? When a man takes money, then perhaps you can talk of stealing, but certainly not when he just bags a little bit of something to eat. In that case we would have stolen a lot in our time, eh, Ernst?"

"Sure, Willy," I say. "He just ran out to meet you, I dare say. Same as the one at Staden that belonged to the O.C. No. 2 Battery. Remember? And you made fricasseed chicken for the whole company out of it. Half and half—to one hen add one horse—that was the recipe, wasn't it?"

Willy beams and pats the stove plate with his hand. "Cold!" he says disappointed, and turns to his mother. "Haven't you any coal, then?"

Frau Homeyer cannot speak for agitation, she can only shake her head. Willy reassures her with a wave of the hand. "Never mind, I'll scrounge some to-morrow. We'll make do for the moment with this old chair here—it's pretty wobbly, you see, not much good for anything any more really."

Frau Homeyer looks at her son uncomprehendingly. She snatches the chair and then the fowl out of his very hands and makes off with it to milkman Binding's.

Willy is righteously indignant. "So, off he goes and sings no more!" he says sadly. "Do you understand that, Ernst?"

I understand well enough that we may not take

75

the chair—though up the line we once burned a whole piano to make a dapple-grey horse come tender ; and that at home here we must not yield to every involuntary twitching of our fingers—though out there everything eatable was looked on as a gift from God and by no means as a problem in morals —perhaps I can understand that also. But that a fowl that is already dead should be taken back to where the merest recruit knows it can only cause a lot of unnecessary trouble—that seems to me just plain madness.

" If it isn't the custom, then we must starve, that seems to be the way of it, eh ? " says Willy, quite nonplussed. " And to think we might have been having fricasseed chicken inside half an hour, if only we'd been on our own with the boys ! And I meant to serve it with white sauce, too ! "

His eye wanders from the stove to the door and back again. " The best thing for us to do would be to make ourselves scarce," I suggest. " Looks to me as if there's a strafe brewing."

But Frau Homeyer is back again already. " He isn't at home," she says out of breath, and, all excitement, is about to open her mind further when suddenly she notices that Willy has put on his things. Immediately it all is forgotten. " You aren't going away already ? "

" Just for a little bit of a patrol, mother," he says, laughing.

She starts to weep. Willy, rather embarrassed, slaps her lightly on the shoulder. " I'll be back all right. We'll always be coming back now. A bit too often, perhaps, I shouldn't wonder——"

Side by side, our hands in our pockets, we set off at a swinging pace down Castle Street. " Shouldn't we collect Ludwig ? " I ask.

Willy shakes his head. " No, let him sleep. That's better for him."

The town is disturbed. Motor-lorries filled with sailors go roaring through the streets. Red flags are flying.

Bundles of handbills are being unloaded and distributed in front of the Town Hall. The people snatch them from the hands of the sailors and glance through them eagerly. Their eyes shine. A gust of wind swoops down upon the packages and sends the broadsheets whirling up into the air like a flock of pigeons. The sheets catch in the bare branches of the trees and hang there rustling. " Comrades," says an old chap in a field-grey overcoat, " things will be better now, comrades." His lips are quivering.

" Hullo ! Looks as if there's something doing here," I say.

We set off at the double. The nearer we approach to the Cathedral Square, the denser is the throng. The square itself is crammed with people. A soldier is standing on the theatre steps and making a speech. The chalky light of a carbide lamp is flickering on his face. We cannot understand properly what he is saying, for the wind sweeps over the square in spasmodic, long-drawn gusts, each time bringing with it a wave of organ music in which the thin, halting voice almost drowns.

A vague, tense excitement is hanging over the place. The crowd stands like a wall—almost all are soldiers, some of them with their wives. Their silent faces have the same grim expression as when they

77

peered out across No Man's Land from under their steel helmets. But something more is in their look now—hope for a future—elusive expectancy of a new life.

Shouts come from the direction of the theatre, and are answered by a subdued roar. " That's the stuff ! " cries Willy joyfully. " Now for some fun ! " Arms are raised. A sudden tremor passes over the crowd, the ranks begin to move. A procession forms itself. Shouts, cries : " Forward, comrades ! " Like an immense deep sigh the sound of marching rustles over the pavement. We swing into line automatically. On our right is an artilleryman ; ahead, an engineer. We form up squad by squad. Few of us are known to the other, yet at once we trust each other. They are our comrades, that is enough. " Come, Otto, join in ! " shouts the engineer in front of us to one who as yet has not moved.

He hesitates. His wife is with him. She slips her arm into his and looks at him. He smiles awkwardly : " Afterwards, Franz."

Willy pulls a wry face. " When petticoats appear comradeship's finished, you take it from me ! "

" Ach, rot ! " protests the engineer, giving him a cigarette. " Women are one half of life.—But there's a time for everything, of course."

Involuntarily we fall into step. But this is another kind of marching from that we have been used to. The pavement echoes, and like lightning a wild breathless hope sweeps over the column, as though the road would now lead us straight on into the new life of freedom and justice.

But already, after only a few hundred yards, the

procession stops. It has halted in front of the Mayor's house. Some workers rattle at the outer door. All remains quiet ; but the pale face of a woman is seen a moment behind the shut windows. The rattling increases ; a stone is thrown at the window. A second follows. Splintered glass falls clashing into the front garden.

Then the Mayor shows himself on the balcony of the first floor. He is greeted with shouts, he tries to protest but none will hear him. " Come out ! Come with us ! " cries somebody.

The Mayor shrugs his shoulders and nods assent. A few minutes later he is marching at the head of the procession.

The next to be hauled out is the chief of the Food Control Office. Then a bewildered, bald-headed fellow who has been profiteering in butter. We missed nabbing a corn dealer—he shut himself up just in time when he heard us coming.

The procession now marches to the Castle and piles up before the entrance to the District Headquarters. A soldier dashes up the steps and goes inside. We wait. The windows are all alight.

At last the door opens again. We crane our necks. A man with a portfolio comes out. He turns out some sheets of paper from his case and in a monotonous voice begins reading a speech. We listen intently. Willy puts both hands to his great ears. Being a good head taller than anyone else, he follows the sentences more easily and repeats them aloud. But the words prattle away over our heads. They echo and die away, but they do not touch us ; they do not sweep us away, they do not stir us, they only prattle and prattle away.

We begin to grow restive. We do not understand this. We are accustomed to act ; but the fellow up there only talks and talks. Now he is exhorting us to calmness and prudence. But then nobody has been imprudent as yet !

At last he goes off. " Who was that ? " I ask disappointedly.

The artilleryman beside us knows everything. " President of the Workers' and Soldiers' Council. Used to be a dentist, I believe."

" Aha ! " growls Willy, turning his red head uncomfortably from side to side. " What a frost ! And me thinking we were off to the station and then straight to Berlin ! "

Shouts begin to come from the crowd ; they multiply. " The Mayor—let the Mayor speak ! " He is pushed up the steps. In a calm voice he explains that the whole matter is being thoroughly looked into. Beside him, stuttering, stand the two profiteers. They are sweating with fright. But nothing is done to them either. They come in for some abuse, but that is all, no one takes the trouble to lift a hand against them.

" Well," says Willy, " the Mayor has his courage with him, anyway, I'll say that much."

" Pooh ! he's used to it," says the artilleryman. " They drag him out like this every few days——"

We look at him in astonishment. " You mean this happens often ? " asks Albert.

The other nods. " There are always fresh troops coming back, you see, who think they must put matters right. And—well that's all that comes of it——"

" Damned if I understand that," says Willy.

" Nor me either," adds the artilleryman yawning largely. " Expected something different myself, I admit. Well, cheero ! I'll be trotting along to my flea-bag, I guess. That's the most sensible thing to do."

Others follow suit. The square has emptied perceptibly. A second delegate is talking now. He also advises calm. The leaders will see to it all. They are on the job already. He indicates the lighted windows. The best thing would be for us to go home.

" Well ! damn my eyes ! So that is all ? " I say peevishly.

We begin to feel rather absurd for having joined in with the mob. What did we want exactly when we came here ? " Ach, shit ! " says Willy disenchanted. We shrug our shoulders and slope off.

I walk home with Albert and then return alone. It is very strange—now that my comrades are with me no longer, everything around me begins to sway gently and become unreal. A while back it was all matter of fact and sure ; and now it has suddenly come loose. It is so perplexingly new and strange that I hardly know whether I may not be dreaming it all.—Am I here ? Am I really here again, home ?

There are the streets, cobbled and sure; smooth, gleaming roofs, nowhere the gaping holes and gashes of shells ; undamaged the walls tower into the blue night, gables and balconies silhouetted against it, making dark shadows. Nothing here has suffered the teeth of war, window-panes are intact, and behind the bright clouds of their curtains lives a hushed world, very different from that howling place of death where till now I have made my home.

I come to a stand before a house where there is light in the lower windows. Muffled music is coming from it. The curtains are but half drawn and I can see inside.

A woman is seated at a piano, playing. She is alone. The only light is from a standard lamp and it falls on the white page of the music. The rest of the room is lost in a colourful gloom. A sofa, a couple of armchairs and cushions suggest a peaceful life there. On a settle a dog lies asleep.

I gaze like one enchanted. Only when the woman stands up and moves noiselessly to the table do I step back hastily. My heart is beating fast. In the wild light of the rockets, and among the shattered ruins of front-line villages, I had almost forgotten such things existed—such street-long, walled-in peace of carpets and warmth and women. I should like to open the door and go in and curl myself up on the settle ; I should like to stretch out my hands to the warmth there and let it flood over me ; I should like to talk and to thaw out there the hardness, the violence, all the past ; to leave it behind me, peel it off like a dirty shirt.

The light in the room goes out. I walk on. But suddenly the night is full of dark cries and indistinct voices, full of faces and things gone by, full of questions and of answers. I wander far out beyond the limits of the city, and stand at last on the slope of the Kloster-berg. Below lies the town all silver. The moon is reflected in the river. The towers seem afloat in the air, and all is unbelievably still.

I stand a while and then go back to the streets and the houses. Quietly I grope my way up the stairs that lead to my home. My parents are already asleep.

I hear their breathing—the soft breathing of my mother, and my father's, heavier—and feel ashamed I have come back so late.

In my room I make a light. In the corner is the bed with fresh linen sheets, the covers turned back. I sit down on it and so remain for some time, lost in thought. At last I feel tired. Mechanically I stretch out and make to pull up the blanket. I sit up again suddenly—I had quite forgotten to undress. At the Front we always slept in our clothes just as we were. Slowly I take off my uniform, put my boots in a corner. Then, hanging over the end of the bed, I perceive a nightshirt. I hardly recognise the thing. I put it on. And all at once, while I am still pulling it over my naked, creeping body, my senses overwhelm me. I stroke the sheets, I bury myself in the pillows, I hug them to me, press myself down into them, into the pillows, into sleep, into life once again, and I know one thing and one only : I am here—I am here.

3

Albert and I are sitting in the Café Meyer by the window. Before us on the marble table are two glasses of cold coffee. We have been here three hours now without yet being able to make up our minds to drink such bitter brew. We have made the acquaintance of most varieties at the Front, but this stuff is straight stewed coal.

Three tables only are occupied. At one a couple of profiteers are making a deal over a truck-load of food-stuff ; at another is a married couple reading newspapers ; and at the third we are sprawling our ill-mannered backsides all over the red plush settle.

The curtains are grimy, the waitress is yawning, the air is sticky, and altogether there is not much to be said for it—and yet to our mind there is a great deal to be said for it. We squat there contentedly —we have loads of time, the orchestra is playing, and we can see out the window.

So we remain, until at last the three musicians pack up their things and the waitress moves sourly in ever diminishing circles round our table. Then we pay and move off into the evening. It is marvellous to pass so idly from one shop window to the next, not to have to trouble about anything, just to be freed men.

At Struben Street we call a halt. " What about going in to see Becker ? " I say.

" Good idea," agrees Albert. " Let's. That will make him talk, I bet ! "

We spent a good part of our school days in Becker's shop. One could buy every imaginable thing here : note-books, drawing materials, butterfly nets, acquariums, collections of postage stamps, antique books and cribs with the answers to algebraical problems. We would sit for hours in Becker's—it was here we used to smoke cigarettes on the sly, and here too that we had our first stolen meetings with the girls from the City School. He was our great confidant.

We go in. A couple of schoolboys in a corner hastily conceal their cigarettes in the hollow of their hands. We smile and put on airs a little. A girl comes and asks what we want.

" We would like to speak to Herr Becker, if you

please," I say. The girl hesitates. " Can I not attend to you ? "

" No, Fräulein," I reply, " that you can't ! Just call Herr Becker, will you ? "

She goes off and we spruce ourselves up, thrusting our hands deep into our trousers pockets with a swaggering air. That should fetch him !

We hear the old familiar tinkle of the office door opening, and out comes Becker, little, grey, and unkempt as ever. He blinks a moment. Then he recognises us. " Well! Birkholz and Trosske ! " says he. " Back again, eh ? "

" Yes," we say quickly, awaiting the outburst.

" That's fine ! And what will you have ? " he asks. " Cigarettes ? "

We are taken aback and feel rather sheepish. We didn't want to buy anything, that was not our idea. " Yes," I say at last, " ten, please."

He gives us them. " Well, till next time ! " says he and shuffles off. We stand there a moment. " Forgotten something ? " he calls from where he stands on the few steps.

" No, no," we answer and go.

" Well ! " I say once we are outside. " He seems to think we've just been off on a bit of a walk ! "

Albert makes a listless gesture. "Civilian beetle——"

We stroll on. Late in the evening we run into Willy and set off together for the barracks.

En route Willy suddenly springs to one side, and I crouch down likewise. The unmistakable howl of a shell coming—then we look round mystified and laugh. It was merely the screech of an electric tram.

Jupp and Valentin, looking rather forlorn, are

squatting in a great empty room meant to accommodate a whole platoon. Tjaden has not come back yet apparently. He is still at the brothel, no doubt. At sight of us their faces beam with satisfaction—now they will be able to make up a game of skat.

The short time has sufficed for Jupp to become a Soldiers' Councillor. He just appointed himself, and now continues to be one for the reason that the confusion in the barracks is such that no one knows any difference. It will do to keep him for the moment, his civil occupation having gone west. The solicitor for whom he used to work in Cologne has written to tell him that women are now doing the work excellently and more cheaply, whereas Jupp during his time in the army will have grown out of office requirements, no doubt. He deeply regrets it, so he says ; the times are hard. Best wishes for the future.

"It's a cow ! " says Jupp glumly. "All these years a man has been living for just one thing—to get clear of the Prussians—and now he has to be thankful if he is able to stay on.—Well, it's six of one and half a dozen of the other—I'll go eighteen."

Willy has a corker of a hand. "Twenty," I answer for him. "And you, Valentin ? "

He shrugs his shoulders. "Twenty-four."

As Jupp passes forty Karl Bröger appears. "Just thought I'd look in and see what you were doing," he says.

"So you looked in here, eh ? " says Willy with a smirk, settling himself down large and comfortable. "Well, I suppose barracks are the soldier's real home, if it comes to that. Forty-one ! "

"Forty-six," advances Valentin, defiantly.

"Forty-eight," Willy thunders back.

"Christ! This is big bidding!" We draw in closer. Willy leans back luxuriously against the locker and shows us privately a Grand. But Valentin is grinning ominously—he has the still more powerful Nul Ouvert up his sleeve.

It is wonderfully cosy in the barracks here. A stump of candle stands flickering on the table and the bedsteads loom dimly in the shadows. Then the great chunks of cheese that Jupp has scrounged up from somewhere. He proffers each his portion on the end of a bayonet. We munch contentedly.

"Fifty!" says Valentin.

The door flings open and in bursts Tjaden. "Se—Se——" he stutters and in his excitement develops a terrible hiccough. We lead him with upraised arms round the room. "Did the whores pinch your money?" asks Willy sympathetically.

He shakes his head. "Se—Se——"

"Halt!" shouts Willy, in a voice of command.

Tjaden springs to attention. The hiccough has gone.

"Seelig—I've found Seelig," he cries jubilantly.

"Boy," roars Willy, "if you lie, I'll pitch you clean out the window!"

Seelig was our company sergeant-major, a pig of the first water. Unfortunately two months before the Revolution he was transferred, so that we have not as yet been able to get track of him. Tjaden explains that he is running a pub, the "König Wilhelm," and keeps a marvellous good drop of beer.

"Let's go!" I shout, and we troop out.

"But not without Ferdinand," says Willy. "We

must find him first."—Ferdinand has an account to settle with Seelig on Schröder's behalf.

In front of Kosole's house we whistle and cat-call until at last he comes fuming to the window in his nightshirt. "What the hell's up with you—at this hour of night?" he growls. "Don't you know I'm a married man?"

"Plenty of time for that," shouts Willy. "Shake a leg, come down out of it, we've found Seelig."

Ferdinand now shows signs of interest. "Honest?" he asks.

"As true as I'm standing here," Tjaden assures him.

"Righto, I'm coming!" he answers. "But God help you if you're pulling my leg——"

Five minutes later he joins us below and learns how matters stand. We push off.

As we turn into Hook Street, Willy in his excitement bumps into a chap and sends him head over heels. "You great rhinoceros!" the man on the ground shouts after him.

Willy turns about sharply and stands over him threateningly. "Pardon! did you speak?" he asks touching his cap. The other picks himself up and looks at Willy. "Not that I can remember," he answers sullenly.

"Just as well for you!" says Willy. "You haven't the right build to be insulting."

We cut across the park and pull up outside the "König Wilhelm." The name has already been painted over. It is now called the *Edelweiss*. Willy reaches for the latch.

"Half a mo'!" Kosole lays hold of his great paw. "Willy," he says, almost imploringly, "if it comes to

88

a dust up, I do the dusting ! Is that right ? Give
us your hand on it."

" Right you are," agrees Willy, and throws open
the door.

Noise, light and thick smoke come out to meet us.
The clinking of glasses. An orchestrion is thundering
the march from *The Merry Widow*. The taps along
the counter sparkle. An eddy of laughter is swirling
about the bar-sink where two girls are rinsing the
froth from the empty glasses. A swarm of men
stands clustered around them. They are exchanging
jokes. Water slops over, mirroring the faces, tattered
and distorted. An artilleryman orders a round of
schnapps, at the same time pinching the girl's behind.
" Good pre-war stuff, this, eh, Lina ? " he roars
jovially.

We elbow our way in. " So ! there he is ! " says
Willy.

With sleeves rolled up, shirt unbuttoned, sweating,
with moist red neck, behind the counter stands the
host drawing off the beer, that streams down brown
and golden from under his fat hands into the glasses.
Now he looks up. A broad grin spreads over his
face. " Hullo ! You here ! What's it to be, light
or dark ? "

" Light, Herr Sergeant-Major," replies Tjaden
impudently. He counts us with his eyes.

" Seven," says Willy.

" Seven," repeats Seelig with a glance at Ferdinand,
" six—and Kosole, by Jove ! "

Ferdinand pushes up to the counter. He leans
with both hands against the edge of it. " Say,
Seelig, have you got any rum ? "

Seelig fusses about behind his row of nickle pump-handles. "Rum? Why, yes, of course I've got rum."

Kosole looks up at him. "You're rather partial to it, if I remember?"

Seelig is filling a row of cognac glasses. "Yes, I do rather like it, as a matter of fact."

"Happen to remember the last time you got tight on it?"

"No, can't say I do——"

"But I do!" shouts Kosole, standing at the counter like a bull glaring over a hedge. "Ever hear the name Schröder?"

"Schröder?—It's a very common name, Schröder," says Seelig casually.

That is too much for Kosole. He gets ready to spring. But Willy seizes him and pushes him down into a chair. "Drink first!—Seven light!" he repeats over the bar.

Kosole is silent. We sit down at a table. Seelig brings us the pints himself. "Good health!" says he.

"Good health!" answers Tjaden, and we drink. Tjaden leans back. "There now, didn't I tell you?"

Ferdinand's eyes follow Seelig as he goes back behind the counter. "My God," he mutters fiercely, "and to think how that swob stank of rum the night we buried Schröder——"

He breaks off.

"Now don't come unstuck," says Tjaden gently.

Then, as though Kosole's words had suddenly plucked aside a curtain that until now had but lightly swayed and shifted, a grey, ghostly desolation begins to unfold there in the bar-room. The windows disappear, shadows rise up through the floor-boards and memory hovers in the smoke-laden air.

There had never been any love lost between Kosole and Seelig, but it was not until August of 1918 that they became deadly enemies. We were holding a stretch of battered trench at the time just in rear of the front line and had to work all the night digging a common grave. We were unable to make it very deep, because the water in the ground soon began to seep in. At the end we were working knee deep in mud.

Bethke, Wessling, and Kosole were kept busy shoring up the sides. The rest of us gathered the corpses that lay about in the area ahead of us, and placed them side by side in a long row till the grave should be ready. Albert Trosske, our section corporal, removed any identity discs or paybooks that they still had on them.

A few of the dead had already black, putrefied faces—putrefaction was rapid during the wet months. On the other hand they did not stink quite so badly as in summer. Some of them were soaked and sodden with water like sponges. One we found lying flat, spread-eagled on the ground. Only when we took him up did we see that there was practically nothing left of him but the rags of his uniform, he was so pulped. His identity disc was gone too. We only recognised him finally by a patch in his trousers. Lance-Corporal Glaser, it was. He was light to carry, for almost half of him was missing.

Such stray arms, legs or heads as we found we set apart on a waterproof sheet by themselves. " That'll do," said Bethke, when we had brought up Glaser, " we won't get any more in."

We fetched a few sandbags full of chloride of lime. Jupp scattered it about the wide trench with a flat shovel. Max Weil turned up soon after with a few crosses that he had brought from the dump. Then to our astonishment Serjeant-Major Seelig also appeared out of the darkness. As there was no padre handy and both our officers were sick, he had been told off, apparently, to pronounce the prayer for the dead. He was feeling rather sore about it ; he could not bear the sight of blood—and besides he was so fat. He was nightblind, too, and could hardly see in the dark. All this together made him so jumpy that he over-stepped the edge of the grave and fell in. Tjaden burst out laughing, and called in a subdued voice : " Shovel, boys ! Shovel him in ! "

Kosole, as it happened, was digging in the trench just at that spot and Seelig landed square on the top of his head—a good two hundredweight of live meat ! Kosole swore blue murder. Then he recognised the sergeant-major, but being an old hand—this was 1918—he did not let that deter him. The S.M. picked himself up, saw Kosole in front of him, exploded, and began to abuse him. Kosole yelled back. Bethke, who was also down there, tried to part them. But the sergeant-major spat with rage, and Kosole, justly regarding himself as the aggrieved party, returned as good as he got. Willy now jumped in also to lend Kosole a hand. A terrific uproar arose from the grave.

" Steady," said someone suddenly. Though the voice was quiet, the din ceased immediately. Seelig, puffing and blowing, clambered out of the grave.

His uniform was white with the soft chalk, he looked for all the world like a ginger-bread baby covered in icing sugar. Kosole and Bethke climbed out likewise.

On top, leaning on his walking-stick, stood Ludwig Breyer. Until now he had been lying out in the open before the dugout, with two greatcoats over him—he was suffering then his first bad attack of dysentery.

"What's the trouble?" he asked. Three men tried to tell him at once. Wearily Ludwig checked them. "Anyway, what does it matter?"

The S.M. insisted that Kosole had struck him on the chest. At this Kosole flared up again.

"Steady," said Ludwig once more. There was silence again. "Have you got all the identity discs, Albert?" he then asked. "Yes," replied Trosske, adding softly, so that Kosole should not hear it: "Schröder's among them."

For a moment each looked at the other. Then Ludwig said: "Ah, then he wasn't taken prisoner? Which is he?"

Albert led him along the line, Bröger and I following—Schröder was our schoolfellow. Trosske stopped before a body, the head of which was covered with a sandbag. Breyer stooped. Albert pulled him back. "Don't uncover, Ludwig," he implored. Breyer turned round. "Albert," he said quietly.

Of the upper part of Schröder's body nothing was recognisable. It was as flat as a flounder. The face was like a board in which a black, oblique hole with a ring of teeth marked the mouth. Without a word Breyer covered it over again. "Does he know?" he asked, looking toward where Kosole was digging. Albert shook his head. "See to it that the S.M. clears off," said he, "otherwise there'll be trouble."

93

Schröder had been Kosole's friend. We had never understood it quite, for Schröder was delicate and frail, a mere child, and the direct opposite of Ferdinand. Yet Ferdinand used to look after him like a mother.

Behind us stood someone puffing. Seelig had followed us and was standing there with staring eyes. "I never saw the like of that before," he stammered. "However did it happen?"

No one answered. Schröder should really have gone home on leave eight days ago. But because Seelig disliked him and Kosole, he bitched it for him. And now Schröder was dead.

We walked off. We could not bear to see Seelig at that moment. Ludwig crawled in under his greatcoats once more. Only Albert remained. Seelig stared at the corpse. The moon came out from behind a cloud and shone down upon it. The fat body stooped forward. The sergeant-major stood there and peered down into the pallid face below, upon which an inconceivable expression of horror was frozen to a stillness that almost screamed.

"Better say the prayer now and get back," said Albert coldly.

The sergeant-major wiped his forehead. "I can't," he murmured.—The horror had caught him. We had all had that experience: for weeks together a man might feel nothing, then suddenly there would come some new, unforeseen thing and it would break him under.—With green face he stumbled off to the dugout.

"He imagined they pelted you with jujubes up here," said Tjaden drily.

The rain fell more heavily. The sergeant-major did not return. At last we fetched Ludwig Breyer

94

from under his overcoats once again. In a quiet voice he repeated a Paternoster.

We passed the dead down. Weil lent a hand below, taking them from us. I noticed that he was trembling. Almost inaudibly he was whispering : " You shall be avenged." Again and again. I looked at him, astonished.

" What's got you ? " I asked him. " These aren't the first, you know. You'll have your work cut out avenging them all." Then he said no more.

When we had packed in the first rows, Valentin and Jupp came stumbling up with a stretcher.

" This bloke's alive still," said Jupp, setting down the waterproof.

Kosole gave it a glance. " Not for long, though," said he. " We might wait for him."

The man on the stretcher choked and gasped inter- mittently. At each breath the blood ran down over his chin.

" Any use carrying him out ? " asked Jupp.

" He'd only die just the same," said Albert, pointing to the blood.

We turned him over on his side, and Max Weil attended to him while we went on with our work. Valentin was helping me now. We passed Glaser down. " My God ! think of his wife ! " murmured Valentin.

" Look out, here comes Schröder," Jupp called to us as he let the waterproof slide.

" Shut your mouth ! " hissed Bröger.

Kosole still had the body in his arms. " Who ? " he asked uncomprehending.

" Schröder," repeated Jupp, supposing Ferdinand knew already.

"Don't be funny, you bloody fool! he was captured," growled Kosole angrily.

"It is, Ferdinand," said Albert Trosske, who was standing near-by.

We held our breath. Kosole gathered up the body and climbed out. He took his torch from his pocket and shone it upon the corpse. He stooped down close over what was left of the face and examined it.

"Thank God, the S.M.'s gone," whispered Karl.

We stood motionless through the next seconds. Kosole straightened himself up. "Give's a shovel," said he sharply. I handed him one. We expected bloody murder. But Kosole merely began to dig. Allowing none to help him he made a grave for Schröder apart. He placed him in it himself. He was too stricken to think of Seelig.

By dawn both graves were finished. The wounded man had died in the meantime, so we put him in with the rest. After treading the ground firm we set up the crosses. With a copying-pencil Kosole wrote Schröder's name on one that was still blank, and hung a steel helmet on top of it.

Ludwig came once more. We removed our helmets and he repeated a second Paternoster. Albert stood pale beside him. Schröder used to sit with him at school. But Kosole looked terrible. He was quite grey and decayed, and said never a word.

We stood about yet a while and the rain fell steadily. Then the coffee fatigue came and we sat down to eat.

As soon as it was light the sergeant-major came up out of a dugout near-by. We supposed he had been gone long ago. He stank of rum for miles and now only wanted to get back to the rear. Kosole let out a bellow when he saw him. Luckily Willy was by.

He sprang at Kosole and held him fast. But it took four of us all our strength to keep him from breaking loose and murdering Seelig. It was a full hour before he had sufficiently recovered his senses to see that he would only make trouble for himself if he went after him. But by Schröder's grave he swore to get even with Seelig.

Now there stands Seelig at the bar, and not five yards from him sits Kosole. But neither is a soldier any longer.

For the third time the orchestrion thunders out the march from *The Merry Widow*.

"Another round of schnapps, mate," cries Tjaden, his little pig's eyes sparkling. "Coming up!" answers Seelig, bringing the glasses. "Health, comrades!"

Kosole looks at him scowling.

"You're no comrade of ours," he grunts. Seelig takes the bottle under his arm. "No? Very well then—that's that," he retorts and goes back behind the bar.

Valentin tosses down the schnapps. "Soak it up, Ferdinand," says he, "that's the main thing."

Willy orders the next round. Tjaden is already half tight. "Well, Seelig, you old blighter," he bawls, "no more field punishment now, eh? Have one with me!" He slaps his former superior officer so heartily on the back that it nearly chokes him. A year ago that would have been enough to land him for court-martial, or in a mad-house.

Kosole looks from the bar to his glass and from his glass back again to the bar, and at the fat, obsequious fellow behind the beer pumps. He shakes his head.

" It's not the same man, you know, Ernst," he says.

So it seems to me also. I hardly recognise Seelig now. In my mind he was so much of one piece with his notebook and his uniform, that I could hardly even have imagined what he would look like in his shirt, to say nothing of this bar-tender. And now here he is fetching a glass for himself, and letting Tjaden, who used to be of less account to him than a louse, slap him on the back and call him " Old fellow-my-lad ! "—Damn it, but the world is clean upside-down !

Willy gives Kosole a dig in the ribs to stir him up. " Well ? "

" I don't know, Willy," says Ferdinand bewildered. " Think I ought to give him a smack over the mug, or not ? I didn't expect it would be like this. Just get an eyeful of the way he is running about serving, slimy old shit ! I just haven't the heart to do it."

Tjaden orders and orders. To him it is a hell of a joke to see his superior officer go hopping about at his bidding.

Seelig also has got outside of a good many by this time, and his bull-dog cranium glows again, partly from alcohol and partly from the joys of good business.

" Let's bury the hatchet," he suggests, " and I'll stand a round of good pre-war rum."

" Of what ? " says Kosole stiffening.

" Rum. I've still a spot or two left in the cupboard there," says Seelig innocently, going to fetch it. Kosole looks as if he had been struck in the face and glares after him.

" He's forgotten all about it, Ferdinand," says Willy. " He wouldn't have risked that else."

Seelig comes back and pours out the drinks. Kosole glowers at him.

" I suppose you don't remember getting tight on rum from sheer funk once, eh? You ought to be a night watchman in a morgue, you ought!"

Seelig makes a pacifying gesture. "That was a long time ago," says he. "That doesn't count any more."

Ferdinand lapses into silence again. If Seelig would but once speak out of his turn the fun would begin. But this compliance puzzles Kosole and leaves him irresolute.

Tjaden sniffs at his glass appreciatively, and the rest of us lift our noses. It is good rum, no mistake.

Kosole knocks over his glass. "You're not standing me anything!"

"Ach, man!" cries Tjaden, "you might have given it to me, then!" With his fingers he tries to save what he can; but it is not much.

The place empties little by little. "Closing time, gentlemen!" cries Seelig, and pulls down the revolving shutter. We get up to go.

"Well, Ferdinand?" I say. He shakes his head. He cannot bring himself to it. That waiter there, that's not the real Seelig at all.

Seelig opens the door for us. "Au revoir, gentlemen! pleasant dreams!"

"Gentlemen!" sniggers Tjaden. "Gentlemen! — ' Swine' he used to say."

Kosole is already almost outside when, glancing back along the floor, his eyes light on Seelig's legs, still clad in the same ill-omened leggings as of old. His trousers, too, have the same close-fitting military cut with piping down the seams. From the waist up he is inn keeper ; but from the waist down sergeant-major. That settles it.

Ferdinand swings round suddenly. Seelig retreats, and Kosole makes after him. " Now, what about it ? " he snarls. " Schröder ! Schröder ! Schröder ! Do you remember him now, you dog, damn you ? Take that one, from Schröder!" His left goes home. " Greetings from the common grave ! " He hits again. The inn keeper dodges, jumps behind the counter and grabs a hammer. It catches Kosole across the face and glances off his shoulder. But Kosole does not even wince, he is so enraged. He grasps hold of Seelig, and bashes his head down on the counter—there is a clatter of glass. He turns on the beer taps. " There, drink, you bloody rum keg ! Suffocate, drown in your stinking pigs'-wash."

The beer pours down Seelig's neck, it streams through his shirt into his breeches, making them swell out on his legs like balloons. Seelig bellows with rage.—It is no easy thing to get such beer in these days.—At last he manages to free himself and seizes a glass, with which he drives upwards against Kosole's chin.

" Foul ! " cries Willy, from where he stands in the doorway watching. " He should have butted him in the guts, and then pulled his legs from under him ! "

None of us interferes. This is Kosole's show. Even if he were to get a hiding, it would not be our business to help him. We stand by merely to see that no one tries to help Seelig. But Tjaden has already explained the matter in half a dozen words, and nobody is now disposed to take his part.

Ferdinand's face is bleeding fast ; he now gets

properly mad and quickly makes short work of Seelig. With a hook to the jaw he brings him down, he straddles over him and bashes his head on the floor a few times till he feels he has had enough.

Then we go. Lina, looking as pale as a cheese, is standing over her gasping master. " You'd better cart him away to the hospital," Willy shouts back. " Looks to me like a matter for two or three weeks. Not a very bad case, though."

Kosole is smiling, as happy as a child—Schröder, so he feels, is avenged. " That was fine," says he, wiping the blood from his face. " Well, now I must be trotting back to my missus, or the neighbours will be thinking things, what ? "

At the market-place we separate. Jupp and Valentin go off to the barracks and their boots clatter over the moonlit pavement.

" I wouldn't mind going along with them," says Albert suddenly.

" I know," agrees Willy, thinking of his fowl, no doubt. " They're a bit pedantic, the people here, don't you find ? "

I nod. " And we'll have to be starting school again soon, I suppose——"

We stand still and grin. Tjaden cannot contain himself for joy at the mere thought of it. Still laughing, he trots off after Valentin and Jupp.

Willy scratches his head. " Think they'll be very pleased to see us ? We're not quite so docile as we used to be, you know."

" We were more to their liking as heroes," says Karl, " and a long way off for preference."

"I'm rather looking forward to the fun," explains Willy. "What with our present temper—hardened in the bath of steel and all, as they used to say——"

He lifts one leg a trifle and lets off a terrific fart. "Twelve-point-five," he announces with evident satisfaction.

4

When our company was disbanded we had to take our rifles along with us. The instructions were to give them up on arrival at our home town, so now we have come to the barracks and passed in our arms. At the same time we received our demobilisation pay—fifty marks discharge money per man, and fifteen as sustenance allowance. In addition to that we are entitled to one greatcoat, a pair of boots, a change of underclothes and a uniform.

We climb up to the top floor to take delivery of the goods. The quarter-master makes a perfunctory gesture : "Look something out for yourselves."

Willy sets off on a hasty tour, nosing through all the things displayed. "Listen here, you," he then says in parental fashion, "you keep this for the recruits. This stuff came out of the ark with Noah. Show us something new."

"Haven't got any," retorts the Q.M. in a surly tone.

"Is that so ? " says Willy and considers a while. He brings out an aluminium cigar-case. "Smoke ? "

The other shakes his bald pate.

"Chew, is it ? " Willy gropes in his tunic pocket. "No——"

"Good, then you drink ? " Willy has overlooked

nothing—he feels toward a protuberance on his chest.

"Nor that either," replies the quarter-master off-hand.

"Well, there's nothing for it but to swipe you a couple on the snout," explains Willy amiably. "Anyway we're not leaving here without a decent set of new togs, get me?"

Fortunately at this moment Jupp appears, who, being a Soldiers' Councillor, now carries some weight. He tips the Q.M. a wink. "Pals of mine, Heinrich. Old foot sloggers. Show 'em into the salong, won't you?"

The quarter-master brightens up. "Why couldn't you say so at first?"

We accompany him to a room at the back and there the new things are hanging. We hastily discard our old gear and put on new. Willy submits that he needs two greatcoats, explaining that his blood has got very thin under the Prussians. The Q.M. hesitates. Jupp takes him by the arm into a corner and has a talk with him about sustenance allowance. When the two return the quarter-master is pacified. He casts an eye over Tjaden and Willy who have grown noticeably stouter. "Very good," he growls, "it's all one to me. A lot of them don't even trouble to collect their stuff. Have enough brass of their own, I suppose. The main thing is, my invoice must be in order."

We sign that we have received everything. "Didn't you say something about smoking a while back?" says the Q.M. to Willy.

Willy is taken by surprise and produces his case with a grin.

"And chewing?" the other persists.

Willy turns out his tunic pocket. "But you don't drink, I believe," essays Willy.

"On the contrary," says the Q.M. calmly, "that's the one thing the doctor has ordered me. I'm a bit anæmic myself, as a matter of fact. Just leave the bottle here, will you?"

"Half a mo'!" says Willy, and takes a long pull at the flask so that something at least may be rescued. Then he hands over a half-empty bottle to the astonished storeman. A moment ago it was full!

Jupp accompanies us to the barracks gate. "Guess who else is here," says he. "Max Weil! On the Soldiers' Council!"

"That's where he belongs, too," says Kosole. "Nice soft job, I should say, eh?"

"Not so bad," answers Jupp. "Valentin and I are in the same line, for the time being. If ever you want anything—railway passes or the like—I'm at the fountain-head, don't forget."

"Give me a pass then," I say, "and I can go and see Adolf to-morrow."

He takes out a block and tears off a pass. "Fill it in yourself. You travel second, of course."

"Sure."

Outside Willy unbuttons his greatcoat. There is another beneath it. "It's better I should have it, than that it should be sold off later by some swindler or other. And anyway, the Prussians owe it to me for my half-dozen shell splinters."

We set off down the High Street. Kosole is telling us that he proposes to repair his pigeon-loft this afternoon. He used to breed carrier-pigeons and black-

and-white tumblers before the war, and is thinking of starting again now. That had been his one idea out at the Front.

" And what then, Ferdinand ? " I ask.

" Look for work," says he bluntly. " I'm a married man, you know. Always got to keep the pot boiling now."

Suddenly from the neighbourhood of St. Mary's Church comes a sound of shots. We listen. " Rifles and service revolvers," says Willy professionally, " two revolvers, by the sound of it."

" Anyway," laughs Tjaden gaily, swinging his new boots by the laces, " it's a bloody sight more peaceful than Flanders."

Willy stops short in front of a gentlemen's outfitters. In the window is exhibited a garment made out of paper and stinging nettle instead of cloth. But that interests him little. On the other hand a row of faded fashion plates set out behind the suit of clothes holds him spellbound. He points excitedly to one picture of an elegant gentleman with a goatee beard, lost in eternal converse with a huntsman of sorts. " Know what that is ? "

" A shot-gun," says Kosole, looking at the sportsman.

" Rot ! " interrupts Willy impatiently. " That's a cut-away, that is. A swallow-tail, you know. Absolutely the latest thing. And do you know what's just occurred to me ? I'll have one of them made for myself from this overcoat here. Take it to pieces, you see, and dye it black, remodel it, cut away the bottom part here—bong, I tell you ! "

He is obviously in love with his idea. But Karl damps his ardour. " Have you the striped trousers to go with it ? " says he loftily.

Willy is nonplussed a moment. "I know, I'll pinch the old man's," he decides at last. "And his white waistcoat for weddings as well. What will you think of Willy then, eh?" Beaming with pleasure he surveys the whole row of us. "We'll see life yet, lads, eh? damn it all."

I return home and give half of my demobilisation pay to my mother. "Ludwig Breyer's in there," says she. "He's waiting in your room."

"He's a lieutenant, too!" adds my father.

"Yes," I reply, "didn't you know?"

Ludwig seems rather better. His dysentery has improved. "I just wanted to borrow some books from you, Ernst," he says, and smiles at me.

"Take whatever you like, Ludwig," I say.

"Won't be wanting them yourself, then?" he asks.

I shake my head. "Not at the moment, anyway. I tried to read a bit only yesterday. But it's queer, you know—I don't seem to be able to concentrate properly any more. By the time I've read two or three pages I find I'm thinking of something else altogether. As if one were looking at a blank wall, you know. But what is it you want, novels?"

"No," says he, selecting a few books for himself. I glance at the titles. "Heavy stuff, eh, Ludwig?" I say. "What are you going to do with that?"

He smiles, a little embarrassed; then hesitatingly he says: "Well, Ernst, you know, out there a lot of things would keep coming into my head, and I could never get the rights of them somehow. But now it's all over, there's a heap I'd like to understand —I'd like to know, for instance, what mankind is up to that such a thing could happen, and how it all came about. That raises a lot of questions. Questions for us, too. We had a very different notion of what manner of thing life was, before, if you remember. There's a lot I'd like to know, Ernst——"

I point to the books. " Think you'll find it in there ? "

" I mean to try anyway. I read from morning till night now."

He soon takes his leave and I still sit on, lost in thought. What have I been doing all this time ? With a feeling of shame I reach for a book. But soon I have let it fall again and am gazing out the window. I can do that for hours together, just look out into vacancy. It used to be different, before ; I always knew then what I would do.

My mother comes into the room. " Ernst, you are going to Uncle Karl's to-night, aren't you ? "

" Yes, I suppose so," I reply, rather disgruntled.

" He has often sent us things to eat," she says prudently.

I nod. From the window I can see the twilight beginning outside. Blue shadows lurking in the branches of the chestnuts. I turn round. " Did you often go down by the poplars in the summer-time, mother ? " I ask suddenly. " That must have been beautiful——"

" No, Ernst—not once all this year."

" Why not, mother ? " I ask in surprise. " You used to go there every Sunday before."

" We gave up going for walks altogether," she replies quietly ; " one is always so hungry afterwards. And, you see, we had nothing to eat."

" Ah, so——" I say slowly, " but Uncle Karl, he always had enough, I suppose ? "

107

" He often sent us some too, Ernst."

All at once I feel utterly dejected. " What was the good of it all, mother ? " I say.

She strokes my hand. " It must have been for some good, Ernst. The Father in heaven knows, you may be sure of that."

Uncle Karl is the famous member of our family. He has a villa and was Chief Paymaster during the war.

Wolf accompanies me to the house, but he must stay outside—my aunt dislikes dogs of any sort. I ring.

An elegant man in a dress-suit opens to me. " Good evening, sir," I say, rather taken aback. Then it occurs to me, he must be a domestic. I had quite forgotten such things in the army.

The fellow looks me over, as if he were a battalion commander in civvies. I smile, but he does not smile back. When I take off my greatcoat he raises his hand as if to help me. " Why," I say, to regain his favour, " surely an old soldier can do that much for himself, eh ? " and I hook my things up on a peg.

Without a word he takes them down again and with a superior air solemnly hangs them on a peg near by. " Poor worm ! " I think to myself, and pass in.

Uncle Karl comes toward me, spurs clinking. He greets me condescendingly. I merely belong to the ranks. I look at his flashing regimentals in astonishment. " What's on to-day ? " I ask, by way of making a joke, " roast horse ? "

" Horse ? how do you mean, horse ? " he asks, mystified.

"Well, you wearing spurs to dinner," I reply, laughing.

He gives me a sour look. Without meaning to, I seem to have touched a sore spot with him. It is often so with these army-office pen-pushers—they are prone to swords and spurs.

Before I can explain to him that I meant no offence, my aunt comes up rustling. She is still as she used to be, flat as an ironing board, and her little, black eyes shining as ever, as though they had been newly polished on a button stick. While she is showering me with a flood of words, her quick eyes are glancing continually here, there, and everywhere about the room.

I am rather embarrassed. Too many people for me, too many women and, worst of all, too much light. The most we ever had up the line was an oil lamp. But these chandeliers here, they are as merciless as bailiffs. One can hide nothing from them.—I scratch my back uncomfortably.

"But what are you doing?" says my aunt, interrupting her talk.

"Oh, it's probably just a louse that has escaped," I explain. "We had so many of them, you know, it will take at least a week before a man is rid of them all——"

She steps back, horrified. "Nothing to be frightened of," I reassure her. "They don't hop. They're no fleas."

"For heaven's sake!" She puts a finger to her lips and makes a face, as if I had uttered God only knows what obscenity.—But then they are like that. Heroes we may be, but one mustn't mention one word about lice.

I have to shake hands with a lot of people and begin to perspire. The men here are quite different from us out there. I feel as cumbersome as a tank in comparison. They behave as if they were sitting in a shop window, and talk as if they were on the stage. I try cautiously to hide my hands ; the grime of the trenches is ground into them like poison. I dry them off surreptitiously on my trousers ; but they are immediately wet again when I have to shake hands with a lady.

I work my way round and come on a group where a chartered accountant is airing his views. " Just think of it ! " he is saying, all worked up. " A saddler ! A saddler, mind you, and President of the Empire ! Imagine it, a court levée and a saddler giving audience ! It would make a cat laugh ! "

It makes him cough, he is so excited. " What do you think about it, my young warrior ? " he says, patting me on the shoulder.

As a matter of fact I have never given the matter a thought. I shrug my shoulders doubtfully. " Perhaps he knows a thing——"

The accountant looks at me fixedly a moment. Then he chuckles. " I should say he does know a thing or two ! No, no, my young friend, these things are inborn ! A saddler ! If so, then why not a tailor or a cobbler even ? "

He turns again to the others. I dislike his talk ; it goes against my grain to hear him speak so contemptuously of cobblers. They made as good soldiers as the finer folk, anyway. Adolf Bethke was a cobbler, for that matter—and he knew a sight more about war than a good many majors. It was the man that counted with us, not his occupation.—I eye the accountant dispraisingly. He is throwing about quotations now, and it may well be that he has ladled in culture with a spoon—but if it ever came to that again and someone had to bring me in under fire, I would sooner put my trust in Adolf Bethke.

I am glad when at last we sit down to table. Beside me is a young girl with a swan's-down boa round her neck. I like the look of her, but have not the faintest idea what I should talk to her about. As a soldier one did not talk much, and to ladies not at all. The others are conversing freely, so I try to listen in the hope of picking up an idea or two.

Further up the table the accountant has just been explaining how, if only we had held out a bit longer, the war would have been won. Such bilge makes me almost sick ; any soldier knows that we had no more munitions and no more men—and that's all there is about it. Opposite him is a woman talking about her husband who was killed, and from the way she goes on one might think it was she had been killed and not he. Lower down they are talking about securities and peace terms, and all of them, of course, know much better what should be done than the people who actually have to deal with the matter. A fellow with a hook nose is talking scandal about the wife of a friend of his, but with an air of such sanctimonious sham sympathy, I should like to pitch my beer into his face as a reward for such ill-concealed malice.

All the talk makes me stupid in the head, and I am soon quite unable to follow it any longer. The girl with the swan boa asks scornfully whether I became dumb out at the Front.

"Not entirely," I answer, and think to myself: I only wish Kosole and Tjaden could sit here among you. How they would laugh, to hear the flapdoodle you peddle and so pride yourselves on! All the same it riles me not to be able to show them in one telling thrust what I think. It would not rile Kosole though. He would know well enough what to say. It would be pat and to the point.

At this moment, God be praised! crisp, grilled chops appear on the table. I sniff. Real pork chops they are, fried in real fat, too. The sight of them consoles me for all the rest. I lean over and secure a good one and begin chewing with relish. It tastes marvellous.—It's a power of time since I last ate a fresh chop. In Flanders it was—we bagged a couple of sucking pigs—we ate them down to the very ribs, one lovely mild summer evening—Katczinsky was alive then—ach, Kat—and Haie Westhus—a sight better they were than these fellows at home here— I prop my elbows on the table and forget everything around me, so clearly do I see them before me. Such tender little beasts, too—we made potato-cakes to go with them—and Leer was there and Paul Bäumer—yes, Paul—I neither hear nor see anything now, I have lost myself in memories——

A giggle awakes me. About the table is dead silence. Aunt Lina has a face like a bottle of vitriol. The girl beside me is stifling a laugh. Everybody is looking at me.

Sweat breaks out on me in streams. There I sit, just as we did then out in Flanders, absent-minded, both elbows on the table, the bone in my two hands, my fingers covered in grease, gnawing off the last scraps of the chop. But the others are eating cleanly with knife and with fork.

Red as a beetroot I look straight ahead and put down the bone. How could I so have forgotten myself ? But, to tell the truth, I hardly know now how else to go about it. We always ate that way at the Front ; at the best of times we had only a spoon or a fork, certainly never a plate.

But there is anger too in my embarrassment— anger against this Uncle Karl now beginning to talk so loudly of war loans ; anger against all these people here that think so much of themselves and their smart talk ; anger against this whole world living here so damned cocksure with their knick-knacks and jiggery-pokery, as though the monstrous years had never been, when one thing and one thing only, mattered —life or death, and beyond that nothing.

Grimly, in silence, I stuff in all I can. I mean at least to be full. Then as soon as I can I make my way out.

In the lobby is the servant in the dress-suit. I reach down my things. " We should have had you up the line, too, you lacquered ape ! " I spit. " You and the whole bunch here ! " Then I slam to the door.

Wolf has waited for me outside the house. He leaps up on me. " Come, Wolf," I say, and suddenly know that it was not the affair with the chop that made me feel so bitter ; but the fact that the same vapid, self-satisfied spirit as of old should still be lording it here and giving itself airs.—" Come, Wolf," I repeat, " those are not our sort. We would get along better with any Tommy, with any front-line Froggy, than with them. Come, let's go to our pals.

It's better there, even if they do belch and eat with their hands. Come ! "

We trot along, the dog and I, we run as hard as we can, faster and faster, panting, barking, we run like mad, with shining eyes. To hell with them all ! But we live, eh ? Wolf ! We live !

5

Ludwig Breyer, Albert Trosske and I are on our way to school. Lessons are to begin again.

We were students at the Teachers' College when the war came, but no special examination was granted to us. The men of the Grammar School who went fared much better. Most of them were able to take a special exam., either before they enlisted or when they came home on leave. The remainder, who did neither the one nor the other, have now to start their schooling again like the rest of us. Karl Bröger is one of these.

We pass by the cathedral. The green sheets of copper that once covered the spire have been taken away and replaced by strips of grey felt. They look mildewed and shabby, so that the church has almost the air of a factory. The sheets of copper were melted down to make shells.

" The Lord God never dreamed of that, I'll bet," says Albert.

In a winding alley to the west of the cathedral stands the two-storeyed Teachers' College. Almost opposite is the Grammar School ; behind it the river and the embankment with the lime trees. Before we enlisted these buildings made up our world.

After that it was the trenches. Now we are here again. But this is no longer our world ; the trenches ousted it.

In front of the Grammar School we meet our old chum, Georg Rahe. He was a lieutenant and had charge of a company, but on leave he only got drunk and loafed about, and took no thought for his Finals. So now he is going back into Upper Second again, where already he has been twice left behind.

" Is it true, Georg," I ask him, " that you've become such a crack Latin scholar up the line ? "

He laughs and stalks off on his long legs to the Grammar School.

" Watch out you don't get a bad conduct mark," I shout after him.

He was an airman for the last six months, and brought down four Englishmen. But I don't believe he can still demonstrate Pythagoras' theorem.

We go on to the Teachers' College. The whole lane is teeming with uniforms. Faces suddenly loom up that one has almost forgotten ; names one has not heard of for years. Hans Walldorf hobbles along. We carried him out with a shattered knee in November '17. His leg has been amputated at the hip ; now he wears a heavy, jointed, wooden leg, and thumps along on it noisily. Kurt Leipold appears, and introduces himself, laughingly : " Godfrey of the Iron Hand, gentlemen ! " He has an artificial right arm. Then someone comes out at the gate and says in a gurgling voice : " You don't recognise me perhaps, eh ? "

I study the face, if such it can still be called.—Across

the forehead is a broad, red scar that runs down into the left eye. There the flesh has grown over, so that the eye lies buried, deep and small. But it is there still. The right eye is fixed, that is glass. The nose is clean gone, a black patch covers the place. The scar continues below it and splits the mouth in two. The mouth itself is bulbous ; the parts have grown together askew—hence the unintelligible speech. The teeth are artificial. A bracket is visible across them. In doubt still, I continue to look at him.— " Paul Rademacher," says the gurgling voice.

I recognise him now. Why yes, of course, the grey suit with the stripes. " Well, Paul ! and what have you been doing to yourself ? "

" Can't you see ? " he says, trying to straighten his lips. " Two cuts with a trenching tool.—And these went with the rest." He shows a hand from which three fingers are missing. His one eye is blinking distressfully. The other looks straight ahead, fixed and unconcerned. " Wish I knew if I could still be a school teacher. My speech is pretty bad, isn't it ? Can you understand me ? "

" Sure," I answer. " And it will improve, too, as time goes on. Besides, they'll be able to operate on it again later, of course."

He shrugs his shoulders and says nothing. He does not seem very hopeful. If it were possible at all, they would have done so already, no doubt.

Willy barges his way through to us to give us the latest news. Borkmann, we hear, died of his lung-wound after all. He developed consumption. Henze, too—he shot himself when he found out his spine injury could only end in an invalid's chair for life. No wonder—he used to be our best footballer.

Meyer was killed in September; Lichtenfeld in June. Lichtenfeld was only out there two days.

We stop suddenly. A diminutive little figure is standing before us.

" No? not Westerholt? " says Willy incredulously.

" The very same, you old mushroom," he answers.

Willy is staggered. " But you're dead ! "

" Not yet," retorts Westerholt amicably.

" But I saw it in the newspaper ! "

" That was just a misprint," says Westerholt with a grin.

" A man can't rely on anything these days ! " says Willy, shaking his head. " I thought the worms had eaten you long ago! "

" After you, Willy," answers Westerholt complacently. " You'll be the first. Red-haired people never live long."

We go in. The quadrangle, where we used to eat our bread-and-butter at ten o'clock; the class-rooms with the desks and the forms; the corridor with the rows of hat-pegs—all just the same; and yet to us it seems somehow as if they belonged to another world. Only the smell of the gloomy rooms is familiar —not so rank, but still similar to that of the barracks.

The great organ with its hundreds of pipes is gleaming in the hall. To the right stand the masters in a group. On the Principal's desk are two pot plants with coarse, leathery leaves. In front of it hangs a laurel wreath tied with a big ribbon. The Principal is in his frock-coat. So—there's to be a ' Welcome ' !

We pile up together in a heap. Nobody wants to be in the front rows. Only Willy takes up his place there unembarrassed. In the semi-darkness of the hall his head is glowing like the red lamp outside a brothel.

I look at the group of masters.—For us they were once more than other men ; not merely because they were in charge of us, but because, however much we may have made fun of them, we still believed in them. To-day we see them merely as so many somewhat older men, and of whom we feel mildly contemptuous.

There they stand now and propose to teach us again. But we expect them to set aside some of their dignity. For after all, what can they teach us ? We know life now better than they ; we have gained another knowledge, harsh, bloody, cruel, inexorable. We could teach them for that matter—but who would be bothered ? If a sudden raid were to be made on the hall just now, they would all be rushing about like a bunch of poodles, frightened out of their wits, without a ghost of an idea what to do, whereas not a man of us would lose his head. As the first thing to be done—merely that they should not be in the way—we should quietly lock them all up, and then begin the defence.

The Principal is clearing his throat for a speech. The words spring round and smooth from his mouth ; he is an excellent talker, one must admit that. He speaks of the heroic struggle of the troops, of battles, of victories, and of courage. But for all the fine words, I feel there is a snag in it somewhere ; perhaps just because of the fine words. It was not so smooth and round as all that—I look at Ludwig ; he looks at me ; Albert, Walldorf, Westerholt, it does not suit any of them.

The Principal is getting into his stride. He celebrates not only the heroism out there, but now the quieter heroism at home, also. "We at home here have done our duty, too ; we have pinched and gone hungry for our soldiers ; we have agonised ; we have trembled. It was hard. Sometimes perhaps it has been almost harder for us than for our brave lads in field-grey out yonder——"

"Hopla !" says Westerholt. Murmurs begin to be heard. The Old Man casts a sidelong glance in our direction and goes on : "But indeed such things are not to be weighed and nicely balanced. You have looked into the brazen face of Death without fear, you have discharged your great task. And though final victory has not accompanied our arms, yet all the more will we now stand together, united in passionate love of our afflicted Fatherland ; in defiance of all hostile powers we will rebuild it ; rebuild it in the spirit of our ancient teacher, Goethe, whose voice rings out now so commandingly across the centuries to our own troubled time : ' Let Might assail, we live and will prevail.' "

The Old Man's voice sinks to a minor. It puts on mourning, it drips unction. A sudden tremor passes over the black flock of masters. Their faces show self-control, solemnity.—" But especially we would remember those fallen sons of our foundation, who hastened joyfully to the defence of their homeland and who have remained upon the field of honour. Twenty-one comrades are with us no more ; twenty-one warriors have met the glorious death of arms ; twenty-one heroes have found rest from the clamour of battle under foreign soil and sleep the long sleep beneath the green grasses——"

There is a sudden, booming laughter. The Principal stops short in pained perplexity. The laughter comes from Willy standing there, big and gaunt, like an immense wardrobe. His face is red as a turkey's, he is so furious.

"Green grasses!—green grasses!" he stutters, "long sleep? In the mud of shell-holes they are lying, knocked rotten, ripped in pieces, gone down into the bog—— Green grasses! This is not a singing lesson!" His arms are whirling like a windmill in a gale. "Hero's death! And what sort of a thing do you suppose that was, I wonder?—— Would you like to know how young Hoyer died? All day long he lay out in the wire screaming, and his guts hanging out of his belly like macaroni. Then a bit of shell took off his fingers and a couple of hours later another chunk off his leg; and still he lived; and with his other hand he would keep trying to pack back his intestines, and when night fell at last he was done. And when it was dark we went out to get him and he was full of holes as a nutmeg grater.—Now, you go and tell his mother how he died—if you have so much courage."

The Principal is pale. He is hesitating whether to enforce discipline or to humour us. But he arrives at neither the one nor the other.

"Mr. Principal," begins Albert Trosske, "we have not come here that you should tell us we did our job well, though unfortunately, as you say, we were not victorious. Shit to that——"

The Principal winces, and with him the whole college of masters. "I must request you, at least in your expressions——" he begins indignantly.

"Shit! I say; Shit! and again Shit!" reiterates

Albert. " That has been our every third word for years ; and it's high time that you knew it. But you don't seem to realise how things stand. We are none of your brave scholars ! we are none of your good schoolboys, we are soldiers ! "

" But, gentlemen," cries the Old Man almost imploringly, " there is a misunderstanding—a most painful misunderstanding——"

But he does not finish. He is interrupted by Helmuth Reinersmann, who carried his brother back through a bombardment on the Yser, only to put him down dead at the dressing-station.

" Killed," he says savagely, " they were not killed for you to make speeches about them. They were our comrades. Enough ! Let's have no more wind-bagging about it."

The place is in wild confusion. The Principal stands there horrified and utterly helpless. The college of masters looks like a lot of scandalised old hens. Only two of the teachers are calm and they have been soldiers.

The Old Man decides to humour us at all costs. We are too many, and Willy stands there too formidably trumpeting before him. And who can say what these undisciplined fellows may not be doing next ; they may even produce bombs from their pockets. He beats the air with his arms as an archangel his wings. But no one listens to him.

Then suddenly comes a lull in the tumult. Ludwig Breyer has stepped out to the front. There is silence. " Mr. Principal," says Ludwig in a clear voice. " You have seen the war after your fashion—with flying banners, martial music, and with glamour. But you saw it only to the railway station from which we set off. We do not mean to blame you. We, too, thought as you did. But we have seen the other side since then, and against that the heroics of 1914 soon wilted to nothing. Yet we went through with it—we went through with it because there was something deeper that held us together, something that only showed up out there, a responsibility perhaps, but at any rate something of which you know nothing, and about which there can be no speeches."

Ludwig pauses a moment, gazing vacantly ahead. He passes his hand over his forehead and continues. " We have not come to ask a reckoning—that would be foolish ; nobody knew then what was coming.— But we do require that you shall not again try to prescribe what we shall think of these things. We went out full of enthusiasm, the name of the ' Fatherland ' on our lips—and we have returned in silence, but with the thing, the Fatherland, in our hearts. And now we ask you to be silent too. Have done with fine phrases. They are not fitting. Nor are they fitting to our dead comrades. We saw them die. And the memory of it is still too near that we can abide to hear them talked of as you are talking. They died for more than that."

Now everywhere it is quiet. The Principal has his hands clasped together. " But, Breyer," he says gently, " I—I did not mean it so——"

Ludwig has done.

After a while the Principal continues : " But tell me then, what is it that you do want ? "

We look at one another. What do we want ? Yes, if it were so easy a thing to say in a sentence. A vague, urgent sense of it we have—but for words ?

We have no words for it, yet. But perhaps later we shall have.

After a moment's silence Westerholt pushes his way to the front and plants himself in front of the Principal. "Let's hear something practical," says he, "that's what we're here for now. Here we are, seventy soldiers, and we have to go back to school again. What do you propose to do with us? And I may as well tell you at once—we know as good as nothing now of all your bookish stuff, and what's more we've no wish to stay here longer than need be."

The Principal checks his displeasure. He explains that as yet he has had no instructions in the matter from the authorities. For the present we must go back to the several classes from which we went out. Then later, of course, we shall see what arrangements can be made.

This is received with mutterings and laughter.

"Don't you run away with any idea," says Willy indignantly, "that we're going to perch on forms along with kids who never saw the war, and put up our hands nicely whenever we know anything.— We're staying together."

We are beginning to see now how funny it all is. For years they have let us shoot, and stab, and kill; and now it is a matter of grave importance whether it was from the Second Form or from the Third Form that we went off to do it. In this one they do equations with two unknowns, and in the other with only one. These are the differences that matter here.

The Principal promises to ask that a special course be granted for soldiers.

" We can't wait for that," says Albert Trosske
curtly. " We had better see about it ourselves."

The Principal does not reply ; he walks to the
door in silence.

The masters follow, and we traipse out after them.
But Willy, for whom it has all gone much too
smoothly, first takes the two pot plants from the
lecture desk and smashes them on to the floor. "I
never could stomach vegetables anyway," he says
viciously. The laurel wreath he plants askew on
Westerholt's head. " Make yourself soup out of
it——"

The smoke of cigars and pipes fills the room. We
are sitting in council with the Returned Men
of the Grammar School—more than a hundred
soldiers, eighteen lieutenants, thirty warrant-officers
and non-coms.

Westerholt has brought a copy of the old School
Regulations and is reading aloud from it. Progress
is slow, for almost every paragraph is received with
roars of laughter. We can hardly believe that such
rules once applied to us.

Westerholt is particularly amused to discover that
before the war we were not allowed to be on the
streets after nine o'clock at night without permission
of a form-master. But Willy deals with him. " Don't
you be too fresh, Alwin," he shouts across at him.
" You've flouted your form-master worse than any
of us—what with saying you were killed, and getting
yourself a funeral oration off the Principal, and
him saying you were a hero and a model scholar !
and then after that you have the damned cheek to
come back alive ! Nice predicament you've landed

the Old Man in! Now he'll have to take back all
the credit he gave to your corpse—for if I know
anything, you're just as rotten at algebra and
composition as ever you were."

We elect a Students' Council; for, though our
schoolmasters may do, perhaps, to pump a few facts
into us for examination purposes, we are certainly
not going to let them govern us any more.—For
ourselves we appoint as representatives, Ludwig
Breyer, Helmuth Reinersmann and Albert Trosske;
for the Grammar School, Georg Rahe and Karl
Bröger.

Then we settle on three delegates to start next
morning for the Provincial Authorities and the
Ministry, to set out our demands regarding the
syllabus and the examination. For this purpose we
choose Willy, Westerholt and Albert. Ludwig cannot
go, as he is still not well enough. The three are
then duly equipped with passes and free railway
vouchers, of which we have whole blocks in hand.
And we have, of course, plenty of Lieutenants and
Soldiers' Councillors to countersign them.

Helmuth Reinersmann looks to it that the delega-
tion shall have the appropriate outward appearance
also. He requires Willy to leave at home the new
outfit that he pinched from the quartermaster, and
to put on for the journey a soiled and tattered one
instead.

"But why?" asks Willy, disappointed.

"That will tell with the pen-pushers more than a
hundred good reasons," explains Helmuth.

Willy protests, for he is very proud of his tunic,
and thought to make rather a hit with it in the

cafés of the capital. "If I thump good and hard on the inspector's table, won't that do just as well?" he suggests.

But Helmuth is not to be dissuaded. "It's no good, Willy," says he. "We can't knock them all on the head. We have need of these people for once. But if you thump on the table in a ragged tunic, then, I say, you'll get more out of them for us than you would in your new one.—That is the sense of the meeting, I take it?"

Willy gives way, and Helmuth now turns his attention to Alwin Westerholt. He seems to him rather too naked, so Ludwig Breyer's decoration is pinned on his chest. "Your arguments will sound much more convincing to an Under Secretary that way," adds Helmuth.

In Albert's case this is not necessary; he has enough to hang out on his own account. At length the three are satisfactorily furnished, and Helmuth surveys his handiwork. "Superb!" says he. "Now for it! And for once show the bloody turnip-eaters what a real front-line man-eater looks like."

"Make your mind easy on that score," says Willy, now quite himself again.

The smoke of pipes and cigars fills the room. Desires, thoughts, ambitions in seething confusion. God only knows what will come of them. A hundred young soldiers, eighteen lieutenants, thirty warrant-officers and non-coms., all sitting here, wanting to start to live. Any man of them could take a company under fire across No Man's Land with hardly a casualty. There is not one who would hesitate for an instant to do the right thing when the cry:

" They are coming ! " was yelled down into his dugout. Every man has been tempered through countless, pitiless days ; every man a complete soldier, no more and no less.

But for peace? Are we suitable? Are we fit now for anything but soldiering ?

PART III

I

I AM on my way from the station to visit Adolf Bethke. I know his house at once—he has described it to me so often out there.

A garden with fruit trees. The apples have not all been picked yet. There are a lot lying in the grass under the trees. On an open space before the door is an immense chestnut tree and the ground beneath it is covered over and over with russet leaves, the stone table below and the bench also. The pinkish white of the burst, spikey husks, the lustrous brown of the fallen nuts gleams among the leaves. I take up one or two and look at the lacquered, veined, mahogany rind and the lighter coloured, germinal spot underneath. To think such things exist ! I look about me.—To think that there is still all this—these gay trees ! blue, misty woods— yes, woods, not mere shattered tree-stumps ; and this wind over the fields, without fume of powder or stink of gas ; this greasy, glistening, ploughed earth with its pungent smell ; horses pulling ploughs, not gun-limbers now ; and following behind them, without rifles, the ploughmen, home again, plough- men in soldiers' uniforms.

The sun is hidden by clouds floating above a little copse, but pencils of silver light shoot out from behind them. Children's gaily coloured kites sway-

ing high up in the air. Lungs breathing deeply, the
cool air streaming in and out—no guns, no trench-
mortars now ; no pack cramping the chest, no belt
hanging heavy at the belly ; gone from the neck the
taut sense of wariness and watching, gone too the
half-slinking gait that may be changed within the
second to falling and lingering and horror and death.
I walk free and upright with swinging shoulders
and feel the strength and the richness of this moment
—to be here, to be visiting Adolf, my comrade !

The door of the house stands half open. On the
right is the kitchen. I knock. No one answers.
" Good day ! " I call. Nothing stirs. I go in
farther and open yet another door. Somebody is
seated alone at the table—now he looks up,
dishevelled, an old uniform, a glance : Bethke !

" Adolf ! " I exclaim, happily, " didn't you hear
me ? Asleep, were you, eh ? "

Without shifting his position he gives me his hand.

" Thought I'd come over and see you, Adolf."

" That's good of you, Ernst," he says gloomily.

" Something the matter, Adolf ? " I ask in surprise.

" Ach, don't ask, Ernst——"

I sit down beside him. " But, Adolf, old man,
what's the matter with you ? "

He parries. " Nothing, I'm all right ; leave us
alone, Ernst, can't you ?—It's good, though—it's
good one of you has come at last." He stands up.
" It makes a man crazy, being alone here like this——"

I look around. There is no sign of his wife
anywhere.

He remains silent a while, then suddenly says
once again : " It's good you have come." He

I   129

hunts about for some schnapps and some cigarettes. We have a spot out of two thick glasses with a pink inset underneath. Before the window lies the garden and the path with the fruit trees. There is a gust of wind and the garden gate rattles. Out of the corner a dark, weighted grandfather-clock sounds the hour.

" Good health, Adolf ! "   " Good health, Ernst ! "

A cat steals across the room. It jumps up on the sewing-machine and begins to purr. After a while Adolf begins to talk. "They come here and talk, my people and her people—and they don't understand me, and I don't understand them. It's as if we weren't the same persons any more." He props his head in his hands. " You understand me, Ernst, and I you—but with these people, it's as if there were a stone wall between us."

Then at last I hear the whole story.

With his pack on his back and a whole sack full of good things, coffee, chocolate, and a length of silk even, enough to make a whole dress, Bethke came home.

He meant to come softly and give his wife a surprise, but the dog starts barking like mad, almost upsetting his kennel. Then Bethke can restrain himself no longer. He runs down the path between the apple trees—his path, his trees, his house, his wife ! His heart is thudding in his throat like a sledge-hammer. He flings open the door, a great sigh, and then in—" Marie——"

Now he sees her. With his very glance he embraces her. It overwhelms him with joy—home, the dim light, the clock ticking, the table, the big armchair, and there, his wife!—he makes toward her. But she retreats before him, staring at him as if he were a ghost.

He suspects nothing. "Did I frighten you?" he asks, laughing.

"Yes," she says nervously.

"That will soon pass, Marie," he answers, trembling in his excitement.—Now at last that he is here again in the room, his whole being is trembling. He has been away from it so long, too long!

"I didn't know you were coming so soon, Adolf," says his wife. She is standing with her back to the cupboard and gazing at him with great wide eyes. For an instant something cold suddenly grips him, it takes his breath away. "Aren't you even a little bit glad, then?" he asks awkwardly.

"Yes, Adolf, of course——"

"Has something happened?" he goes on, still holding all his traps in his hand.

Then the trouble begins. She puts her head down on the table and starts to blub.—He might as well know it at once—the others would only tell him, anyway.—She had an affair with a man! It just came over her; she didn't mean any harm; she had never thought of anyone but him.—Now let him kill her if he will.

Adolf stands there and stands. At last he notices that he still has his sack perched like a monkey on his shoulder. He looses it and starts to unpack; he is trembling; he keeps thinking to himself: "It can't be true, though, it can't be."—He goes on unpacking, merely to do something, not to have to be still. The silk crackles in his hand, he holds it out: "I wanted to bring this for you," he says,

and is still thinking: " It can't be, it can't be true."—
Helplessly he holds out the red silk, and still nothing
of what has happened sinks into his skull.

But she is weeping and will hear nothing. He
sits down to think, and suddenly is conscious of a
terrible hunger. On the table are some apples
from the trees in the garden, good russets they are ;
he takes them and eats, he must do something. Then
his hands become limp, and he has understood it.
A raging fury rises in him. He must murder someone.—He runs out in search of the man.

But he does not find him. Then he goes to the
ale house. There the men greet him, but there is an
air of constraint ; they talk warily, looking past him,
choosing their words. So they know it.—Bethke
behaves as if nothing were wrong—but no man could
keep that up.—He drinks off his pint and goes,
just as somebody asks : " Been home yet ? " And
when he has left the bar-room there is silence behind
him. He ranges hither and thither until it is late,
and at last is standing again before his own house.
What should he do ? He goes in. The lamp is
burning ; there is coffee on the table, and fried
potatoes in a pan on the hearth. " Ah, but how
good, if only the other weren't true ! " he thinks
miserably. " Even a white cloth on the table !
But now it only makes it the harder."

His wife is there, and she is crying no longer. As
he sits down, she pours out the coffee, and puts the
potatoes and sausages on the table. But she has
laid no place for herself.

He looks at her. She is pale and thin. It all
surges up once again, it sweeps over him, sinks him

in utter meaningless misery. He wants to know no more—he wants only to lock himself in, to lie down on his bed, to turn into stone. The coffee is steaming. He pushes it away, the pan too. The woman shrinks back. She knows what is coming.

But Adolf does not get up, he cannot. He merely shakes his head and says : " Go, Marie."

She makes no protest. She casts her shawl about her shoulders, edges the pan a little toward him again, says in a timid voice : " At least, eat, Adolf——" and then goes. She is going, she is going, her soft tread, soundless. The door shuts. Outside the dog barks, the wind moans at the window. Bethke is alone.

And then the night——

A few days like that alone in a house eat into a man come straight from the trenches.

Adolf tried to catch the fellow, but he always saw Adolf in time and made himself scarce. Adolf lay in wait and hunted for him everywhere—but he could not get him, and that quite destroyed him.

Then her people came and talked. He should reconsider it, they said ; his wife had been straight again for a long time now ; and then, to be alone for four years—that is no small thing ; the man was to blame ; and after all, people did a lot of strange things during the war.

" What's a fellow to do, Ernst ? "—Adolf looks up.

" God, I don't know," I say. " It's a bloody shame."

" Worth coming back home for, Ernst, eh ? "

I refill the glasses and we drink. Adolf has no cigars in the house and does not want to go himself to the store, so I offer to fetch some. He is a heavy smoker ; it might help matters if he had a few cigars. So I take a whole box full of " Woodman's Joy "— fat, brown stumps, that have not been misnamed, for they are pure beech leaf. Still, they are better than nothing.

When I re-enter the house someone else is also there, and I see at once that it is his wife. She carries herself upright, though her shoulders are frail.—There is something pathetic about a woman's neck and shoulders. They are childlike in some way. One could never really bring oneself to be harsh with them.—I don't mean the fat ones, of course, the ones with necks like hams.

" Good day," I say and take off my cap. She does not reply. I put the cigars in front of Adolf, but he does not touch them. The clock is ticking. Leaves of the chestnut tree fall spinning down past the window. Sometimes one will strike on the pane and the wind holds it there. The five earth-brown leaves all joined on one stem, look like outspread, clutching hands threatening from outside there into the room—brown, dead hands of autumn.

Adolf moves at last, and in a voice I do not know, says : " Go now, Marie."

She rises obediently like a school child, and looking straight before her, she goes. The slim neck, the frail shoulders—how can it be possible ?

" Every day she comes like that and sits there and says nothing, and waits and looks at me," says Adolf morosely. I am sorry for him, but I feel sorry now for the woman, too.

" Come back to town with me, Adolf. There's no point in your squatting here," I suggest.

But he will not. Outside the dog starts to bark.
His wife is going out at the garden gate now, back
to her parents.

"Does she want to come back again, then?" I
ask. He nods. I say no more. He must settle
that for himself. "Won't you come with me?"
I try once again.

"Later, Ernst."

"Well, have a cigar, anyway." I shove the box
toward him and wait until he takes one. Then I
shake hands with him. "I'll come and see you
again, Adolf."

He comes with me as far as the gate. I turn again
after a little while and wave to him. He is still
standing in the little doorway, and behind him is
the darkness of evening again, just as when he first
climbed out and left us. He ought to have stayed
with us. Now he is alone and unhappy, and we
unable to help him, glad though we would be if we
could.—Yes, things were much simpler at the Front
—there, so long as a man was still alive, all was well.

2

I lie outstretched on the sofa, my head against the
arm, and my eyes closed. My thoughts move
through my drowse in fantastic confusion. Consciousness hovers between waking and dream, and weariness
like a shadow rides through my brain. Beyond,
indistinctly, distant gun-fire floats in, shells pipe
over softly, and the tinny ringing of gongs sounds
nearer, announcing a gas-attack. But before I
can grope for my gas-mask the darkness recedes

without sound, the earth, against which my face is pressed, dissolves before a feeling of warmth, more bright; it turns again into the plush sofa-cover on which my cheek rests. Dimly, deep down, I am aware it is home. The gas-alarm of the trenches resolves into the subdued clatter of dishes which my mother is setting out cautiously on the table.

Then the darkness glides up swiftly again, and with it a rumble of artillery. And only out of the far distance, as if they came up over forests and seas, I hear words dropping down, words that gradually sort themselves to a meaning and then penetrate in to me. " Uncle Karl sent the sausage," says the voice of my mother amid the faint roll of the guns.

The words reach me on the very edge of the shell-hole into which I am sliding, and with them there appears a smug, self-satisfied face, and disappears. " Ach, him," I say sourly, and my voice sounds as though I had a mouth full of wadding, weariness is swilling round and about me so—" that—silly—arsehole——" Then I fall, fall, fall, and the shadows leap toward me, sweep over me in long rollers, dark and darker.

But I do not fall asleep. Something has gone that was there before—that steady, light, metallic clinking. Slowly I grope my way back into consciousness and open my eyes.—There is my mother, pale and horrified, staring down at me.

" What's the matter, mother? " I cry, jumping up in alarm. " Are you ill? "

She shakes her head. " No, no—but to think you would say such a thing——"

I reflect. What did I say then? Ah, yes, that

about Uncle Karl——— "Come, mother, you mustn't be so touchy," I laugh in relief. "After all, Uncle Karl is a profiteer, you know, isn't he now?"

"That is not what I mind at all," she answers quietly, "but that you should use such expressions———"

Then I remember what I did say in my drowse, and I feel ashamed that it should have happened before my mother. "It just popped out of me, mother," I explain apologetically. "It takes a while, you know, to get used to not being at the Front any longer. Our language was a bit rough out there, mother, I know.—Rough, but honest."

I smooth down my hair and button my tunic. I start to hunt for a cigarette and observe incidentally that my mother is still looking at me. Her hands are trembling!

I give up my search. "But, mother!" I say in astonishment, putting my arm about her shoulders. "There's really nothing so very bad in that! Soldiers are always like that."

"Yes, yes, I know," she protests, "but you—you too———"

I laugh. Me too? Why, of course! I am about to exclaim; but check myself and remove my arm, for something has suddenly dawned on me. I sit down on the sofa to sort myself out.

There she stands before me, an old woman with an anxious, care-worn face. Her hands are clasped; weary, toil-worn hands, with a soft, wrinkled skin, where the veins stand out bluish; hands become so for my sake. I never thought of that before. There is a lot I did not think of before—I was too young. But now I understand how it is that for this withered, little woman I am something different from any other soldier in the world : I am her child.

To her I have always remained so, even as a soldier. In the war she has seen only a pack of wild beasts threatening the life of her child. It has never occurred to her that this same threatened child has been just such another wild beast to the children of yet other mothers.

My gaze drops from her hands to my own. In May, '17, I stabbed a Frenchman with these hands. The blood ran nauseatingly hot over my fingers, and in a panic of fear and of rage I stabbed again and again. And when the Frenchman, choking, clapped his hands to the wound I could not stop myself, but stabbed through his hands too, till he sagged down like an emptying tube. And afterwards I vomited and the whole night through I wept. Only next day was Adolf Bethke able to comfort me—I had just turned eighteen then, and that was the first attack I was in.

I turn my hands over slowly. In the big push at the beginning of July, I shot three men with these hands. They remained the whole day long hanging on the barbed-wire. Their limp arms would fling upward with the blast of the shell-explosions as if they still threatened us, and sometimes too, as if imploring us for help. One of them had snow-white hair and his tongue lolled out of his mouth.—And again later, I once threw a bomb at twenty yards that tore the legs off an English captain. He screamed terribly. He threw back his head, his mouth wide open, and, propping himself on his rigid arms, his trunk reared like a seal ; then rapidly he bled to death.

Now I sit here before my mother, and she is on

the verge of tears because she cannot understand that I should have become so coarse as to make use of an improper expression.

" Ernst," she says gently, " I have been meaning to say this to you for some time :   You have changed. You have become very restless."

Changed ! I think bitterly ; yes, I have changed !—What is it you know of me now, mother ?   A mere memory, nothing but the memory of a quiet, eager youth of the days that are gone.   You must never know, mother, never know of these last years ; never even wonder what they were like, and much less what has become of me.   A hundredth part would break your heart—you, who tremble and are shocked by the impact of a mere word, one word that has been enough to shatter your picture of me.   " Things will be better soon," I say rather helplessly, and try to comfort myself with that.

She sits down beside me and strokes my hands. I take them away.   She looks at me grieved.   " You are quite strange to me sometimes, Ernst," she says. " Then you have such a look that I hardly recognise."

" I must get used to things first, mother," I say. " I still keep feeling as if I were merely here on a visit."

Twilight is gathering in the room.   My dog comes in from the passage and lies down on the floor in front of me.   His eyes shine as he looks up at me. He, too, is restless still ; he has not settled down yet either.

My mother leans back in her chair.   " Just to think you have come back again, Ernst——"

" Yes, that's the main thing," I say and stand up.

She remains seated in her corner, a little figure in

the twilight; and with strange tenderness I see how all at once our rôles have been interchanged. Now it is she has become the child.

I love her—when did I ever love her more than now? now, though I know I may never come to her and sit beside her and tell her it all, and so perhaps regain peace. I have lost her. Suddenly I feel how alien and alone I really am.

She has closed her eyes. "I'll get dressed now and go out for a bit," I whisper, so as not to disturb her. She nods. "Yes, my boy," says she—and after a while, softly—"my good boy."

It pierces me like a stab. Gently I pull the door to.

3

The meadows are wet and from the pathways and tracks the water runs gurgling. In the pocket of my greatcoat is a small pickle-jar and I walk along the brook by the poplars. As a youngster I used to catch fish and butterflies here, and here I used to lie down under the trees and dream.

In springtime it would be full of water-weeds and frog spawn. Bright green bushes of water-weed flickered to and fro in the little, clear waves, long-legged skaters zig-zagged between the stalks of the sedge, and shoals of tittlebats in the sun cast their swift, slim shadows on the golden-spotted sand.

But now it is cold and damp. The poplars stand beside the stream in a long line. Their branches are bare but a soft blue bloom is on them. One day they will be green again and rustling, and the sun will lie warm and blessed over this stretch of ground that holds so many memories of my childhood. And then I shall have forgotten the war and all will be again as it used to be.

I stamp my foot on the sloping edge of the bank. A couple of fish dart out from under it. At sight of them I can contain myself no longer. Where the stream narrows so that I can bestride it with my legs, I wait watching, and at last scoop up two tittlebats in my hollowed hand. I drop them into my jar and examine them.

They dart to and fro, lovely and perfect with their three spines, their slender, brown bodies and quivering pectoral fins. The water is clear as crystal and spangles of light on the glass are reflected in it. Suddenly my breath is quite taken away, so piercingly do I see how beautiful it is, this water in the glass, the lights and the reflections.

I hold it carefully in my hand and wander farther ; I carry it cautiously and look into it often, with beating heart, as if I had caught my childhood in it and now would take it back home with me. I squat on the edge of the pool where dense layers of duckweed are floating and see the blue-marbled salamanders, like little mines, dangling vertical as they come up for air. Caddis-fly larvæ creep slowly through the mud, a beetle paddles lazily along the bottom, and from under a decaying root the astonished eyes of a motionless pond-frog look up at me. I see everything, and more is there even than can be seen— memory is there, and hopes and past happiness.

Cautiously I take up my jar and go on, searching, hoping—— The wind blows and the mountains lie blue along the skyline.

Suddenly a spasm of alarm sweeps over me——

Down, man! Down! Under cover! You're in full view there!—I crouch down in mad fear, I spread my arms ready to sprint forward and take shelter behind a tree, I tremble and pant.—Now I breathe again. It is over—and I look round foolishly—no one has seen me. It is a moment before I am calm again. Then I make a dive for my pickle-jar that has fallen out of my hand. The water is all spilled, but the little fish are still flapping about inside it. I stoop down to the stream and let fresh water pour in.

I push on slowly, absorbed in my thoughts. The wood is nearer now. A cat stalks across the pathway. There the railway embankment cuts through the fields and is lost again in the thicket. One could build dugouts there, I think to myself, good deep ones with concrete roofs—then extend the line of trench to the left, with cover-saps and listening-posts—and over there a few machine-guns—no, two would be enough, the rest in the wood—then practically the whole terrain would be under cross-fire. The poplars would have to come down, so as not to give the enemy artillery a point to register on—and behind there, on the hill, a couple of trench-mortars.—Then let them come!

A train whistles and I look up. What is this I am doing? I came here to recover the scene of my childhood, and I am drawing a system of trenches across it! It has become a habit, I say to myself: We see no countryside now, only terrain—terrain for attack and defence. The old mill on the top there is no mill, but a strong point—the wood is no wood, it is artillery cover. Such things will always creep in.

I shake it off, and try to remember past times, but

I do not succeed very well. And I no longer feel so happy as I did. I have no wish to go farther. I turn back.

In the distance I see a solitary figure approaching. It is Georg Rahe.

" What are you doing here ? " he asks in surprise.

" What are you ? "

" Nothing," he says.

" Same here," I reply.

" And the pickle-jar ? " he asks and looks at me a trifle mockingly.

I turn red.

" Nothing to be ashamed of," he says. " Been trying to catch fish again ? "

I nod. " And then what ? " he asks.

I shake my head.

" Yes, hardly goes with a uniform, eh ? " he says meditatively.

We sit down on a log and begin to smoke. Rahe takes off his cap. " Remember how we used to exchange postage stamps here ? "

" Yes, I remember." And how the timber-yard in the sun smelt of resin and tar ; how the poplar trees shimmered, and the wind blew up cool from the water—I still remember it all—how we hunted for green frogs ; how we used to read books here together ; how we would talk of the future and of life, where it lay waiting for us there beyond the blue horizon, alluring as soft music.

" It all turned out rather differently, eh, Ernst ? " says Rahe and smiles—this smile that we all have, something bitter and something weary—" Why we even caught fish differently out there ! One bomb into the water and then up they would come floating to the surface, with burst swimming-bladders and white bellies. It was more practical, there's no denying."

"How is it, do you suppose, Georg," I ask, "that we just sit around here like this and don't know even what we should begin to do?"

"You find there's something missing, Ernst, eh?"

I nod. He taps me on the chest. "I think I can tell you—I've been thinking about it, too. You see this here," he points to the meadows before us, "that was life, it flowered and grew, and we grew along with it. And that behind us—" he motions with his head backwards into the distance, "that was death; it killed and destroyed, and destroyed something of us along with the rest." He smiles again. "We're in need of repairs a little, my boy."

"Perhaps things would be better if only it were summer," I say. "Everything is easier in summer."

"No, it's not there the trouble lies," he answers, blowing the smoke before him. "It's something very different from that, I think."

"What then?" I ask.

He shrugs his shoulders and stands up. "Let's be going, Ernst. Would you care to know what I've decided to do?" He stoops down to me. "I think I'm going to become a soldier again."

"You're crazy, Georg!" I say in consternation.

"Not at all," he retorts, and for an instant is deadly earnest, "perhaps merely logical."

I stop. "But, good God, Georg——"

He walks on. "Well, you see, I've been here now a couple of weeks longer than you," he says and starts talking of other things.

When the first houses appear I take my jar with the

tittlebats and empty it back into the brook. With a flick of the tail they are gone. The jar I leave standing on the bank.

I take leave of Georg and he walks off slowly down the street. In front of our house I stand still and look after him. His words have strangely troubled me. A vague, threatening something seems to be sneaking upon me ; it retreats when I try to grapple with it, it disperses when I advance upon it, and then it gathers again behind me and watches.

The sky hangs like lead over the low shrubbery of the Luisenplatz, the trees are bare, a loose window is clashing in the wind, and amid the frowsy alder-bushes in the garden of the square squats the November twilight, dank and cheerless.

I peer over into it ; and suddenly it is as if I saw it all to-day for the first time, so unfamiliar that I hardly know it again. This dirty, damp patch of grass, was this really the setting of those years of my childhood, so radiant and winged in my memory ? This waste, dreary square with the factory yonder, can this be that quiet corner of earth we called " Home," and which alone amid the waters of destruction out there meant hope to us and salvation from perishing in the flood ? Or was it not rather a vision of some far other place than this grey street with its hideous houses, that rose up there over the shell-holes like some wild, sad dream in the grudging intervals between death and death ? In my memory was it not far more shining and lovely, more spacious and abounding with ten thousand things ? Is that no longer true, then ? Did my blood lie and my memory deceive me ?

K   145

I shiver.—It is different, yet without having changed. The clock in the tower of Neubauer's factory is still going ; it strikes the hours still, as in the days when we used to stare up at its face to see the finger move. The black boy with the clay pipe is still sitting over the tobacconist's shop where Georg Rahe bought us our first cigarettes ; and in the grocer's opposite is the same picture advertising the same soap-powder. Otto Vogt and I scorched its eyes out with a burning-glass one sunny time. I peer in through the window—the seared spots are still visible even now. But the war lies between, and Otto Vogt was killed at Kemmel long ago.

I do not understand how it can be that I should stand here, and yet no longer feel about it as I did then in the barracks and out there in the shell-holes. What has become of all its riches, the thrill, the brightness, the glamour, and that other that is unnameable ? Had my memory more of life in it than the reality itself ? Or has that become reality, while this has shrunk and shrivelled up, till now nothing is left of it but bare scaffolding where gay banners once waved ? Did the splendour detach itself from these things and places, now only to float over them like a forlorn cloud. Did the years out there burn the bridges that lead back into the past ?

Questions, questions—but no answer.

4

The orders regulating the attendance at school of the returned soldiers have arrived. Our delegates have achieved what we wanted—a shortened course, a separate syllabus for the soldiers and an easing of the examination requirements.

It was no simple matter to put through, despite the Revolution ; all this commotion has been nothing but a mere rippling of the surface. It has not gone under. What is the good of merely changing the occupants of a half a dozen of the top posts ? Any soldier knows that a company commander may have the best of intentions, but if his non-coms. are against him, he is powerless to effect anything. So too, even the most progressive minister must shipwreck if he has a block of reactionary bureaucrats against him. And in Germany the bureaucrats all have their jobs still. These pen-pushing Napoleons are invincible.

It is the first hour of lessons, and we are seated again at our desks. Almost all are in uniform, three have full beards, and one is married.

On my desk I discover my name neatly carved with a penknife and picked out in ink. I can remember doing it one history lesson ; yet it seems it must have been a hundred years ago, so strange is it to be sitting here again. This sets the war back into the past ; things have gone full circle.—But we are no longer in it.

Hollermann, our Literature teacher, comes in and at once sets about what he considers his first duty. He must return to us such things of ours as still remain here from the days before the war. They have too long been a burden on his orderly schoolmaster's soul. He opens the class-locker and turns out the stuff— writing materials, drawing boards and, most important of all, the fat, blue note-books full of essays, dictations, and class exercises. A great pile they tower up beside him on the left of his desk. The names are called out, we answer and receive our goods. Willy tosses them over and blotting papers go flying.

" Breyer—— " " Here—— "

" Bücker—— " " Here—— "

" Detlefs—— "

Silence. " Dead," cries Willy.

Detlefs—little, fair, bandy, was plucked in his exam. once and left behind. A lance-corporal, killed, 1917, at Mount Kemmel. The note-book goes to the right of the master's desk.

" Dirker—— " " Here—— "

" Dierksmann——" " Dead."

Dierksmann—a farmer's son, a good skat player, but a rotten singer ; killed at Ypres. The note-book passes to the right.

" Eggers—— "

" Not back yet," calls Willy. Ludwig supplements : " Lung-wound, in the Reserve Hospital at Dortmund, to go from there to the Sanatorium at Lippspring for three months."

" Friederichs—— " " Here—— "

" Giesecke—— " " Missing."

" No, he's not," says Westerholt.

" Well, he was reported missing," says Reinersmann.

" I know," replies Westerholt, " but he's been in the asylum here for the last three weeks. I've seen him myself."

" Gehring I—— " " Dead."

Gehring I—a First, wrote verses, used to give coaching lessons, and bought books with his earnings. Killed at Soissons, along with his brother.

" Gehring II," the master merely murmurs and himself puts the note-book with the others on the right.

"He wrote really excellent essays," he says meditatively, turning the pages of Gehring I's exercise book once more.

Yet many another book goes to the right, and when at last all have been called, there still remains a big pile of unclaimed exercises. Professor Hollermann looks at them irresolutely. His feeling for order rebels, yet he does not know what to do with them. At last he hits on a solution.—Let the note-books be sent to the dead men's parents.

But Willy does not agree. "Think their parents will be glad to see exercise books so full of mistakes?" he asks, "and with your comments : *Unsatisfactory, Incompetent, Poor.* Better leave it alone rather ! "

Hollermann looks at him with round eyes. "Yes, that's so ; but what else can I do with them ? "

"Let them stay where they are," says Albert.

Hollermann is almost offended. "But that won't do at all, Trosske," he says. "These note-books, you see, they don't belong to the school, they cannot just be left where they are."

"Oh, God ! what a fuss you do make ! " groans Willy, running his fingers through his hair. "Give them to us then, we'll see to them." Hollermann hands them over reluctantly. "But "—he begins nervously, for, of course, it is other men's property.

"Oh, quite, quite," says Willy, "anything you like, all in order, properly stamped and addressed, only for Christ's sake don't fret yourself, whatever you do. One must have order, even though it may cause other people pain." He winks at us and touches his forehead.

When the lesson is over we turn through the pages of our exercise books. The last theme on which we

wrote is entitled : *Why Must Germany Win the War ?*
That was the beginning of 1916. There must be an
introduction, six reasons, and a conclusion. Point
four—" The religious reasons," I appear not to have
resolved very successfully. In the margin in red ink
there is written : *Scamped and unconvincing.* My
seven-page effort was rewarded with a grand total of
minus two—a very fair result, if one takes present
facts into consideration.

Willy is reading over his notes on Natural History :
" The Windflower and its rooting system ! " he
exclaims, and looks about him with a grin. " Well, I
think the gentlemen will agree that that little matter
has lapsed—no ? "

" Agreed ! " says Westerholt.

Yes, it has lapsed, indeed. We have forgotten it
all, and by that fact alone the whole system stands
condemned. What Bethke and Kosole taught us,
that we do not forget.

During the afternoon Albert and Ludwig call
round for me. We want to see how things are going
with our old schoolmate, Giesecke. On the way we
meet Georg Rahe who accompanies us, as he also
was a friend of Giesecke.

The day is clear, and from the hill-top, where the
building stands, one can see far out across the fields
to where the lunatics in their blue-and-white striped
jackets are at work in gangs under the supervision
of uniformed warders. From a window in the right
wing of the building we hear a voice singing : *On
the lovely banks of Saale . . .* That will be a patient.
It sounds strangely from a window with iron bars :
And the clouds go sailing by——

Giesecke is lodged in a large room with several other patients. As we enter one cries out shrilly: "Cover! Cover!" and crawls under the table; but the others take no notice of him. Giesecke comes at once to meet us. He has a narrow, yellow face; with his sharp chin and prominent ears he looks much younger than he used to do. Only his eyes are restless and old.

Before we can greet him, someone else buttonholes us: "Anything new out there?" he asks.

"New? no, nothing new," I reply.

"And what about the Front? Have we got Verdun yet?"

We look at each other. "But it's peace long ago," says Albert reassuringly.

The man laughs, an unpleasant, bleating laughter. "Don't you kid yourself! They're only trying to fool you. They're just waiting for us to come out, and then tara, before you know where you are, they've nabbed you and you're off back up the line." And he adds slyly: "But they won't catch me again!"

Giesecke shakes hands with us. This rather takes us aback; we imagined he would be hopping about like a monkey, and raving and pulling faces, or at any rate, shivering all the time, like the shakers at the street corners. But instead he only smiles at us with a wry, poor mouth, saying: "Didn't expect it to be like this, eh?"

"But you're quite fit!" I protest; "What's up with you, then?"

He passes his hand over his brow. "Headaches," says he. "A sort of steel band round the back of my head. And then Fleury——"

He was buried during the fighting at Fleury, and

for several hours he lay with another fellow, his face clamped by a beam against the other man's crutch that was ripped up as far as the belly. The other had his head free and kept crying out, again and again, and each time he yelled a stream of blood would well out over Giesecke's face. Then gradually the intestines pressed themselves out of the belly and threatened to suffocate Giesecke, so that he had to squash them back to get air, and each time, as he dug into them, he would hear the other man bellow.

He tells us all this quite clearly and consequently. " And now every night it comes again, and I suffocate, and the room is full of slimy white snakes and of blood."

" But when you know what it is, can't you fight against it ? " asks Albert.

Giesecke shakes his head. " It's no good, even though I may be wide awake. As soon as it gets dark, they are there." He shudders. " You don't see them, but I see them. I jumped out of a window at home and broke my leg. Then they brought me here."

" But how about you ? what are you doing now ? " asks Giesecke. " Had your exams. yet ? "

" Soon," says Ludwig.

" I suppose that's all over for me," says Giesecke sadly. " They wouldn't let a chap like me loose among children ! "

The man who had cried " Cover " as we entered now sneaks up behind Albert and digs him in the back of the neck. Albert swings round, but he remembers in time. " A.1.," sniggers the man, " A.1.," and he roars with laughter. Then suddenly he is solemn again and goes softly into a corner.

"Couldn't you write to the major?" asks Giesecke.

"What major?" I ask mystified. Ludwig gives me a prod. "What should we say to him?" I add hastily.

"Tell him he should let me go back to Fleury again," answers Giesecke excitedly. "That would help me, I'm sure it would. It is all quiet there now; but I only know it as it was then, when everything was going up. You see, I'd go down by Death Valley, past Cold Earth, and so to Fleury; and not a shot would fall and everything would be over. Then, I believe, I couldn't help but get peace and quiet again. Don't you think so yourself, too?"

"It will pass all right, anyway," says Ludwig, putting his hand on Giesecke's arm. "You've only to make it all perfectly clear to yourself."

Giesecke stares ahead gloomily. "But you will write to the major? Gerhard Giesecke, that's my name, spelled with ck." His eyes are fixed and blind. "Couldn't you bring me some apple sauce though? I should so like to taste apple sauce again."

We promise him everything, but he hears us no longer, he has suddenly lost all interest. As we go he stands up and clicks his heels to Ludwig. Then with vacant eyes he sits down again at the table.

At the door I look toward him once again. He jumps up suddenly as if he had just waked, and runs after us. "Take me with you," he says in a queer, high-pitched voice. "They are coming again!" He huddles against us in terror. We don't know quite what to do. But then the doctor comes in, and seeing us, puts a hand cautiously on Giesecke's shoulder. "Now we'll go into the garden," he says to him gently. And submissively Giesecke allows himself to be led away.

Outside the evening sun lies over the fields. From the barred window the voice sounds singing still—
"*The castles are in ruin—but the clouds—go sailing by——*"

We walk out in silence, side by side. There is a splendour on the furrowed fields. Slender and pale the sickle moon hangs among the branches of the trees.

"I believe," says Ludwig after a while, "I believe we all have a touch of it——"

I look at him. His face is lit with the glow of sunset. He is solemn and pensive. I am about to answer, but a light shudder suddenly creeps over my skin—whence I know not, nor why.

"Let's not talk of it," says Albert.

We go on. The sunset fades and twilight begins. The crescent moon shows clearer. The night wind blows up from the fields and in the windows of the houses first lights are appearing. We re-enter the town.

Georg Rahe has not said a word the whole way. Not until we stop to take leave of each other does he appear to waken out of his thoughts. "Did you hear what he wanted?" he says. "To go to Fleury—back to Fleury——"

I do not want to go home yet. Nor does Albert. So we stroll along the embankment, the river flowing softly below. We halt by the mill and lean over the railing of the bridge.

"It's queer that we can't bear to be alone, Ernst, isn't it?" says Albert.

"Yes," I say. "One doesn't seem to have any idea where one belongs here."

He nods. "Yes, that's it. But one just has to belong somewhere."

"Perhaps if we had a job," I hazard.

He does not agree. "That's no good either. What we need is something living, Ernst. A human being, you know——"

"A human being!" I protest. "Why, that's the least sure thing in the world. God knows we've seen often enough how easily they can snuff it. You'd need ten or a dozen at least to be sure there would still be one left at roll-call."

Albert studies the silhouette of the cathedral attentively.

"I don't mean that way," says he. "I mean a human being to whom one really belongs. Sometimes I think—well, a wife——"

"Good Lord!" I exclaim, and cannot help thinking of Bethke.

"Oh, don't be funny now!" he fires at me suddenly. "A man has to have something he can put faith in. Can't you see that? What I want is someone that will love me; she would have me and I her. Otherwise a man may just as well go hang himself!"

"But, Albert," I say soothingly, "you've got us, haven't you?"

"Yes, yes, but this is different——" and after a while he whispers, almost as if he were in tears: "Children, that's what a man needs—children, who know nothing about it——"

I do not quite follow his meaning; but I cannot ask him more questions.

PART IV

I

WE had pictured it all otherwise. We thought that with one accord a rich, intense existence must now set in, one full of the joy of life regained—and so we had meant to begin. But the days and the weeks fly away under our hands, we squander them on inconsiderable and vain things, and when we look round nothing is done. We were accustomed to think swiftly, to act on the instant—another minute and all might be out for ever. So life now is too slow for us ; we jump at it, shake it, and before it can speak or resound we have already let go again. We had Death too long for companion ; he was a swift player, and every second the stakes touched the limit. It is this that has made us so fickle, so impatient, so bent upon the things of the moment ; this that now leaves us so empty, because here it has no place. And this emptiness makes us restless ; we feel that people do not understand us, that mere love cannot help us. For there is an unbridged gulf fixed between soldiers and non-soldiers. We must fend for ourselves.

But occasionally into our restless days there intrudes something, a strangely growling, muttering something, like the distant menace of gun-fire, some indistinct warning from beyond the horizon which we do not know how to interpret ; which we do not wish to hear ; from which we turn away always in a curious fear lest we may miss something—as if something were trying to escape us. Too much has escaped us already —and for not a few it was no less than life itself.

Karl Bröger's lodgings are in a terrible mess. The bookcases are all empty and piles of books are strewn over the tables and floor.

Karl was a bibliomaniac before the war ; he collected books as we did butterflies and postage stamps. Eichendorff was his special weakness. He had three separate editions of his works, and knew most of his poetry by heart. But now he means to sell up his library, to get enough capital to set up in the schnapps business. According to him there is a lot of money to be made in such things. So far he has merely been agent for Ledderhose, but now he proposes to start on his own account.

I turn the pages of the first volume of one of the editions of Eichendorff that is bound in a beautiful, soft, blue leather. Sunset, Woods and Dreams— Summer Nights, Desire, Exile—— What a time that was !

Willy has the second volume. He looks at it appraisingly. " You ought to offer them to a shoe-maker," he suggests.

" How so ? " asks Ludwig smiling.

" The leather ! " answers Willy. " The shoemakers haven't a square inch of decent leather these days. Here"— he takes up the Works of Goethe—" Twenty volumes ! They would make at least six pairs of topping leather shoes. A shoemaker would give a sight more for them than a bookseller, believe me. They're absolutely crazy for real leather ! "

" Would any of you like some yourselves, perhaps ? "

says Karl. "I'll let you have them at reduced prices." But nobody wants them.

"Think it over though, Karl," says Ludwig. "It won't be so easy to buy them back again later."

"What's it matter?" laughs Karl. "Live first, that's more important than reading. As for the exam., well, to hell with it! It's all bunk, anyway. To-morrow I start in with the schnapps samples. Ten bob on a bottle of smuggled brandy—not much wrong with that, eh, my lads? Money's what you want, then you can get everything else."

He ropes up the books in great bundles. There was a time, I remember, when he would have gone without food rather than sell one of them. "What are you pulling such a face about?" he says scornfully. "One must be practical! Dump all the old stuff and start in afresh."

"Yes, that's right," agrees Willy. "I'd sell mine too—if I had any."

Karl pats him on the shoulder: "Half an inch of business is better than a mile of culture, Willy. I sat in the muck out there long enough—I mean to see a bit of life now."

"He's right, you know," I say. "What are we going to do about it, lads? a little bit of schooling— what does it amount to, anyway? Damn all——"

"Yes, you pull out too, boys," advises Karl. "What do you want with pen-pushing?"

"God knows; it is a lot of tripe," replies Willy. "But at least we are all together still. And then, it's only a couple of months now to the examination, it would be a pity not to go through with it. One can always have a look round afterwards."

Karl shears off some brown paper from a roll.

" Get away with you !—you'll always have some couple of months or other about which it would be a pity—and in the end you will wake up and find yourself an old man——"

Willy grins. " Yes, and won't you have a cup of tea while you're waiting, Mr. Homeyer, eh? "—Ludwig stands up.

" What does your father say about it ? "

Karl laughs. " What all the frightened old people say. But one can't take that seriously. Parents always overlook the fact that one has been a soldier. . . ."

" What would you have been if you hadn't been a soldier ? " I ask.

" Bookseller probably, poor fool," answers Karl.

Karl's decision has made a profound impression on Willy. He is in favour of our giving up all this useless grind and taking joy where it is to be had.

But man easiest tastes the joys of life eating. So we settle on a scrounging expedition. The ration-cards allow only half a pound of meat, three-quarters of an ounce of butter, an ounce and a half of margarine, three ounces of pearl-barley and some bread each week per person.—No man can get a square feed off that.

The foragers begin to assemble at the station in the evening and during the night, in readiness to go out into the villages first thing in the morning, so we must set off by the first train if they are not to be there before us.

Grey misery sits sullen in the compartment as we move off. We fix on an outlying spot and there leave the train, separating, always in pairs, to scrounge systematically over the countryside. We have sufficiently studied this art of patrolling.

Albert and I are together. We come on a large farmstead; the dung-heap is steaming in the yard and cows stand in long rows in the stalls. A warm odour of cattle and of milk comes out to greet us. There are hens cackling too. We look at them covetously, but restrain ourselves as there are people in the barn. "Good day," we say. No one takes any notice. We continue to stand about. At last a woman shrieks at us : "Get out of the yard, you damned gypsies ! "

The next place. The farmer is standing outside. He has a long military greatcoat and is lightly flicking a whip. "Like to know how many have been here already ? " says he. "Just a dozen ! " We are surprised, after all we came out with the first train. They must have come last evening and passed the night in barns or out in the open. "A hundred come in a day sometimes," the farmer persists. "What can a man do ? I ask you."

We see his point. Then his eye suddenly fastens on Albert's uniform. "Flanders ? " he asks. "Flanders," replies Albert. "Me too," says he, and goes within. He comes back with two eggs apiece for us. We fumble with our pocket-books. He shakes his head. "You can keep that. We'll call it a bargain, eh ? "

"Well, thanks, mate."

"Not at all—— But don't spread it about, or half Germany will be here to-morrow."

The next house. A notice plastered with cow-dung on the hedge. "No scroungers. Beware of the dog." That is practical.

We push on. A spacious field and a large farm-house. We go into the kitchen. In the middle is a cooking-range of the latest model that would more than serve an hotel. On the right a piano, on the left a piano. Facing the cooking-range is a superb bookcase with fluted columns and books with gilt bindings. And in front the same old table and three-legged wooden stools. It looks comical. Especially the two pianos.

The farmer's wife appears. " Have you got any yarn ? But it must be real."

We look at each other. " Yarn ? No ! "

" Silk then ? Silk stockings ? "

I look at the woman's massive calves. Slowly it dawns on us—she wants to exchange, not to sell.

" No, we haven't any silk," I say. " But we will gladly pay you for anything."

She dismisses the idea. " Money ! Pooh ! It's not good even to wipe the floor with ! It's worth less every day." She ambles off. Two buttons are missing from the back of her flaming red, silk blouse.

" May we have a drink of water, anyway ? " Albert calls after her. She turns round ungraciously and pours us out one glass.

" Now, be off ! I haven't time to waste standing about," she snaps. " You ought to be at work instead of stealing other people's time."

Albert takes the glass from her and smashes it down on the floor. He is speechless with rage. So I speak for him. " May you get cancer, you old slut ! " I roar. But now the woman turns on us and lets fly, hammer and tongs, like a tinsmith in full swing. We take to our heels. The strongest man could not stand up to that.

We trudge on. As we go we meet whole hordes of scroungers. They circle about the farmsteads like hungry wasps round a piece of plum-tart. We begin to see now how the farmers must be driven almost mad by it, and why they become so abusive. But we persist all the same, get fired out here, perhaps score something there, are cursed by other foragers and curse again in return.

During the afternoon we all foregather at the pub. Our booty is not much—a few pounds of potatoes, some meal, a few eggs, apples, a couple of head of cabbage and some meat. Only Willy is sweating. He comes in last of all with half a pig's head under his arm. Other packages are bulging from his pockets. But as against that, he no longer has any greatcoat. He has exchanged it, because he has another at home that Karl gave him, and then, he thinks that after all Spring must come again sometime.

We have still two hours before the train leaves, and they bring me luck. In the bar-room is a piano of sorts, on which I give a performance of *The Maiden's Prayer*, all pedals down. This brings out the landlady, who listens a while and then beckons me to go outside with her. I elbow my way into the lobby, where she explains to me that she is very fond of music, but unfortunately no one who can play ever comes there. Then she asks me if I would not be willing to come again, and passes me half a pound of butter, saying that there is more where that came from. I fall in with the proposal of course, and undertake to play two hours each time for as much. I return to the piano and as the next item do my best with the *Heidegrab* and *Stolzenfels am Rhein*.

Then we set off for the station. On the way we meet a lot more foragers, all intending to return by the same train as ourselves. But they are frightened of the gendarmes. At last a whole troop has collected and they stand outside in the windy darkness, hiding in a corner some little distance from the station so as to escape observation before the train shall arrive. Once aboard there is less risk of being caught.

But we are out of luck. Two gendarmes with bicycles suddenly appear before us. They have ridden up silently from behind.

" Halt ! All remain where you are ! "

There is a terrible commotion. Everyone begging and praying. " Let us go, quick ! We have to catch the train ! "

" The train won't be here for a good quarter of an hour yet," says the fatter of the two, unperturbed. " This way, all of you." He indicates a street lamp. They will be able to see better there. One stands guard to see that nobody sneaks off, while the other conducts the examination. Nearly all are women, children or old folk ; most of them stand silent and resigned—— They are used to being treated so, and never dared really to hope they might have the luck to get home with a half-pound of butter.

I take a good look at the gendarmes—yes, there they are, just the same, just as snotty and superior in their green uniforms, their red faces, their swords and their revolvers as they used to be up the line—— Might ! I say to myself, Might, always Might—and be it no more than an inch it is merciless.

One woman has some eggs taken from her. Just as she is about to make off, the fat fellow calls her back. " Hey ! what have you got there ? " He points to her skirt. " Out with it ! " She is obstinate and squats on the ground. " Quick, out with it ! " From under her skirt she produces a piece of bacon. He puts it with the rest. " Thought you'd get away with it, did you ? " She can hardly believe what has happened and keeps on making grabs to get it again. " But I paid for it !—every bit of my money it cost me ! "

He shoves her hand away, at the same time hauling out a length of sausage from inside a woman's blouse. " Scrounging's forbidden, you know that yourself."

The woman is quite willing to forgo the eggs, but she pleads to have back the bacon. " Well, give me the bacon, at least. Whatever shall I say when I get home ? It's for my children ! " She kneels in the mud.

" Go to the Food Office and see about getting extra ration-cards ! " snarls the gendarme. " That's none of our business. Next ! " The woman staggers away, vomits and shrieks : " Is that what my man was killed for !—that my children should starve ! "

A young girl who is next, crams, gulps, chokes down her butter ; her face is smothered in grease, her eyes goggle, she wolfs and gorges, so as to have at least a little before it is taken away from her. But it is small comfort—she will only be sick after and probably get diarrhœa as well.

" Next ! " No one moves. The gendarme, who is stooping down, calls again : " Next ! " He straightens up wrathfully and meets Willy's eyes. Perceptibly calmer, " Are you next ? " he asks.

" Am I hell ? " answers Willy unamiably.

" What have you got in that parcel ? "

" Half a pig's head," explains Willy frankly.

" Well, hand it over."

Willy does not move. The gendarme hesitates, and then gives a glance at his colleague who promptly takes up a station beside him.—That is a bad mistake. Neither of them seems to have had much experience in these things, nor to be used to any resistance. The second fellow ought to have seen long ago that we are together, even though we have not spoken a word to one another. He should have stood off to one side and covered us with his gun. Not that that would have troubled us much—what's a revolver, after all? But instead of that, he goes and plants himself right alongside his colleague, lest Willy should cut up rough.

The consequence becomes clear immediately. Like a lamb Willy passes up his half a pig's head. The astonished gendarme takes it from him, and so becomes as good as unarmed, both hands being full. At the same instant Willy calmly lands him one on the mouth, and knocks him over. Before the second can collect himself Kosole butts him upward under the chin with his bony skull, and Valentin is already behind him, squeezing so hard on his wind-pipe that his mouth comes wide open. Kosole swiftly rams a newspaper into it. Both the gendarmes are now gurgling and gulping and spitting, but it is no good; there is paper in their throats, and their arms are being twisted behind them and made fast with their own cross-straps. It was quick business. Now, where to put them?

Albert has the idea—fifty yards off he has found a lonely little house, in the door of which a heart has been cut—the station privy. We set off at a trot. We shove the two in. The door is oak, and the bolts thick and strong. It will be a good hour before they are out again. Kosole is most considerate—he has even piled their bicycles in front of the door.

The other foragers have watched us apprehensively. " Grab your things ! " says Ferdinand grinning. Already the train is whistling in the distance. They look at us timidly, but do not need telling twice. One old woman is quite panic-stricken.

" Oh, God," she wails, " you have assaulted the gendarmes—that's terrible—terrible ! "

Apparently she thinks it is a capital offence. The others, too, are rather worried about it.—Fear of uniforms and policemen is in their very bones.

Willy grins. " Don't carry on, mother—even though the whole government were here, we wouldn't let them take anything from us ! Old soldiers and their mess-mates hand over their grub ?—A nice state of affairs that would be ! "

It is fortunate that village railway stations so often lie far from the houses, for no one has seen anything of what we have done. The station-master now comes out of his office, yawning and scratching his head. We march up to the barrier, Willy with his half a pig's head again under his arm. " Me give you up ? " he murmurs, stroking it fondly.

The train starts. We wave from the window. The astonished station-master thinks it is intended for him and waves back. But we mean the privy. Willy leans far out, watching the red cap of the station-master.

" He's gone back into the office ! " he announces triumphantly. " The gendarmes will be able to keep themselves busy a long time, now."

The tension relaxes in the faces of the foragers. They venture to talk again. The woman with the bacon laughs with tears in her eyes, so grateful is she. Only the girl who swallowed the butter is still weeping inconsolably. She was too hasty; and besides, she is already beginning to feel sick. But now Kosole shows what he is made of. He gives her the half of his sausage which she tucks away in her stocking.

As a precaution we dismount at a station well without

166

the town, and cut across the fields to gain the road. We had meant to do the last stretch on foot but encounter a motor-lorry loaded with cans. The driver is wearing an army greatcoat. He lets us ride with him, and so we tear along through the darkness. The stars are shining. We squat one beside the other and from our parcels there is issuing a rare smell of pork.

2

The High Street is under a wet, silvery, evening mist. The street lamps have big yellow courtyards of light about them and the people are walking on cotton-wool. Shop windows show up to right and left like mysterious fires. Wolf swims up through the fog and dives into it again. The trees gleam black and wet under the street lamps.

With me is Valentin Laher. He is not complaining exactly, but he cannot forget the famous acrobatic turn with which he made such a hit in Paris and Budapest. " That's all finished now, Ernst," he says. " My joints creak like a stiff shirt and I've got rheumatism, too. I've rehearsed and rehearsed till I've dropped. It is no use trying it any more."

" What will you do, then, Valentin ? " I ask. " The State should give you a pension really, the same as it does retired officers."

" Ach, the State ! " answers Valentin contemptuously. " The State only gives those anything that open their mouths wide enough. I'm working up a couple of turns with a dancer just now, a bit of a leg-show, you know. It promises well enough as regards a public, but it's not much—a decent artist ought to be ashamed

167

of doing such a thing really. But then what's a man to do ? he must live."

Valentin is going for a rehearsal now, so I decide to accompany him. At the corner of Hamken Street a black bowler hat goes trundling past us in the fog, and beneath it a canary-yellow mackintosh and a portfolio.—" Arthur ! " I shout.

Ledderhose stops. " My hat ! " exclaims Valentin, " But you have got yourself up swell ! " With the air of a connoisseur he fingers Arthur's tie, a handsome affair in artificial silk with lilac spots.

" Oh yes, not so bad, not so bad," says Ledderhose flattered and in haste.

" And the lovely Sunday-go-to-meeting lid, too ! " says Valentin with renewed astonishment, examining the bowler.

Ledderhose is in a hurry. He taps his portfolio. " Business ! Business——"

" Don't you run the cigar shop any more ? " I ask.

" Sure," he replies. " But one extends gradually. You don't happen to know of any offices to let, I suppose ? I pay any price."

" Offices ? Can't say we do," says Valentin. " We haven't got so far yet. But how does the missus suit you these days ? "

" How do you mean ? " asks Ledderhose cautiously.

" Well, you used to moan about it out there enough. She was grown too scraggy for you, so you said, and now you were all out for fat ones."

Arthur shakes his head. " I don't remember to have said that." And he vanishes.

Valentin laughs. " How they do change, eh, Ernst ? What a miserable poor worm he was up the line ; and now look, what a swell business man !

Remember how the blighter used to pig it out there?
But he won't hear of it any more! He'll be President
of some League or other for the Promotion of Pure
Morals yet, you see!"

"Things do seem to be going bloody well with
him though," I say meditatively.

We stroll on. The fog drifts and Wolf plays with
it. Faces come and go. Suddenly in the white-clear
light I see a glistening, red patent-leather hat, and
beneath it a face softly bloomed with the dampness
that makes the eyes shine the more brightly.

I stand still. My heart is beating fast. That was
Adele! Swiftly memories spring up of other evenings when we sixteen-year-olds would hide outside the
doors of the gymnasium, waiting till the girls should
come out in their white sweaters; and then we would
run after them down the streets, and overtake them,
only to stand before them, breathing hard, silent,
staring at them—till they would break away and the
chase start all over again.—And the afternoons when,
if we happened to meet them somewhere, we would
walk shyly and stolidly after them, always a few paces
behind them, much too embarrassed to speak to them,
and only as they turned in at some house, would we
suddenly summon up all our courage and shout after
them, "See you again!" and run away.

Valentin looks round. "I have to go back for a
moment," I say hastily. "I want to speak to someone.
I'll be here again in a minute." And I run off in
search of the red hat, the red glow in the mist, the
bright days of my youth before uniforms and trenches.

"Adele——"

She looks round. "Ernst! You back again!"

We walk side by side. The mist flows between us. Wolf jumps up about us and barks, the trams are ringing, and the world is warm and soft. The old feeling is there once again, full, tremulous, wavering; the years are blotted out, an arch has flung over into the past, a rainbow, a bright bridge through the mist—

I have no idea what we are talking about—what does it matter?—the point is that we are walking side by side; that this sweet, inaudible music of other days is here again, a cascade of dreams and desire, beyond which shimmers silken the green of meadows; beyond which sings the silver chatter of the poplar trees and the smooth horizon of youth shows clear like the dawn.

Were we walking long?—I do not know. I run back alone. Adele has said Good-bye. But still like a big, many-coloured banner there waves within me joy, and hope and fullness; the little room where I was once a boy, Summer, the green spires and the open wide world.

As I run back I bump into Willy and we go on together in search of Valentin. We overtake him. With every appearance of joy, he is darting off after some fellow whom he gives a resounding slap on the back. " Hullo, Kuckhoff, old son ! where have you sprung from ? " He holds out his hand. " This is a bit of luck, eh ? Fancy meeting again like this."

The other looks at him a while deprecatingly.

" Ah, Laher, I think ? "

" Sure, why we were together on the Somme, don't you remember ? and how, right in the middle of the bloody stunt, we polished off those fritters Lilly sent me ? It was Georg brought them up, with the mail. A damned risky thing to do, you know, what ? "

" Yes, indeed," says the other.

Valentin is quite excited by his memories. " He

170

got it properly later on, though," he continues—
"You'd gone then of course. Lost his right arm, he
did. Stiff luck on a coachman like him. I suppose
he's had to start something else now too.—And where
have you been hiding all this time, eh?"

The other makes an evasive answer, then says
patronisingly:

"Nice to have met you.—And how are you getting
along now, my man?"

"Eh?" retorts Valentin in astonishment.

"How are you getting along? What are you doing
now?"

Valentin has still not recovered. "My man?"
For a moment he continues to stare at the other as he
stands there before him in his elegant raincoat.
Then he glances down at his own things, goes fiery
red and pushes off. "Skunk!"

I feel sorry for Valentin. It is the first time
apparently that the idea of a difference has struck
him. Until now in his mind we had all been just
plain soldiers. And with one single "My man,"
this conceited puppy has now shattered his simple
faith.

"Don't let that worry you, Valentin," I say. "It's
the likes of him that pride themselves on how much
their fathers earn. That's their business."

And Willy supplements with a few forceful
expressions.

"Fine sort of pal he is, anyway," says Valentin at
last sullenly.—But that does not take the taste away.—
It works on chokingly within him.

Fortunately at that moment we run into Tjaden.
He is as grey as a floor-cloth. "Say!" says Willy.

" The war's over now, you know ! Couldn't you give yourself a good wash once in a while ? "

" Not just now," explains Tjaden solemnly. " But next Saturday I will. I'm even going to have a bath then, and to get deloused, too, what's more."

We start in surprise. Tjaden have a bath ! What ever's the matter with the man ? He must have stopped something, surely, that time he was buried last August. Willy, who is quite floored, puts a hand to his ear. " I'm afraid I haven't understood you properly. What did you say you are going to do on Saturday ? "

" Have a bath ! " says Tjaden proudly. " I'm getting engaged next Saturday night."

Willy stares at him as if he were some strange kind of parrot, then gently he puts his great paw on Tjaden's shoulder and says in a fatherly tone : " Say, Tjaden, do you sometimes have a stabbing pain in the back of the head ? Or a funny buzzing sort of noise in your ears ? "

" Only when I'm half starved," Tjaden reassures him ; " and then I have a regular bombardment in my belly, too—an awful feeling that is, I tell you ! But to come back to my fiancée : she isn't beautiful, mind you, she has two left legs and she squints a bit ; but she makes up for it with a heart, and then, you see, her father's a butcher."

A butcher ! The light begins to dawn. Tjaden volunteers yet more information. " You'd be surprised, she's just crazy about me. And, well, it's catch as catch can these days. Times are bad, you know, so a man has to make some sacrifices. But a butcher will be the last man to starve. And anyway, engaged is after all still a long way from married."

Willy listens with growing interest. "Tjaden," he begins, "you know we have always been good friends——"

"Certainly, Willy," interrupts Tjaden, "you may have a few sausages. And chops too, to go with them, for mine. Come round next Monday. We are having a white sale on Monday."

"White sale? What do you mean?" I ask mystified. "Have you a drapery business, as well?"

"No, not that, but you see, we are killing a white horse."

We promise faithfully to be there, and go on our way.

Valentin turns in at the Altstädter Hof, where the artists put up. A group of Lilliputians are already sitting at supper as we enter. There is turnip soup on the table and beside each is a piece of bread.

"Let's hope they at least can get a square meal off their ration-cards," growls Willy. "They'll have smaller bellies, I suppose, wouldn't you think?"

Pasted on the walls there are play-bills and photographs—vari-coloured patches, some of them half-torn, and pictures of weight-lifters, and female lion-tamers, and clowns. They are old and faded. The front-line has been the arena for weight-lifters, crack riders and acrobats during the past few years, and there they had no need of placards.

Valentin points to one of them. "That was me once." In the picture is a fellow with a pouter's chest turning a somersault from a horizontal bar away up the dome of a circus. But with the best will in the world one could not recognise Valentin in it any more.

The dancer with whom he proposes to work is already waiting. We pass on into the little hall at the back of the restaurant. Some stage scenery is leaning in a corner. It belongs to the farce : *Fly Little Pineapple, a humorous piece from the lives of our lads in field-grey, with songs for all,* which had a great run for over two years.

Valentin sets a gramophone on a chair and looks out some records. A hoarse melody issues croaking from the horn. The thing has been played to death, but one can still detect in it a vestige of wildness, like the used-up voice of a disconsolate woman who once was beautiful. " Tango ! " Willy whispers to me with the air of an adept that does not betray the fact that he has just read the inscription on the record.

Valentin is wearing blue pants and a shirt, the woman is in tights. They practise an apache dance, and a fancy number where the girl finally hangs by the legs about Valentin's neck, while he gyrates as fast as he can.

The two rehearse in silence with grim faces. Only occasionally is a half-audible word spoken. The dim light of the lamp flickers. The gas hisses softly. The shadows of the dancers move immense across the scenery for the *Pineapple.* Willy ambles back and forth like a bear, to wind up the gramophone.

Valentin finishes. Willy claps his applause. Valentin, ill-satisfied, makes a gesture to desist. The girl changes without even noticing us. Deliberately she unbinds her dancing shoes beneath the gas-light. The back arches lithely under the faded tights. She straightens up and raises her arms to draw over some garment. Lights and shadows play on her shoulders. She has beautiful, long legs.

Willy goes nosing round the room. He discovers a programme for the *Pineapple*. On the back are some advertisements. A confectioner, for instance, recommends bombs and shells made of chocolate, all ready packed to send off to the trenches. And a Saxon firm is offering paper knives made from shell-splinters, and closet paper with sayings of great men about the war—also two sets of picture postcards : —*The Soldier's Farewell* and *I stand in the Darkest Midnight*.

The dancer has dressed. In cloak and hat she looks quite strange. Before she was a lithe animal ; now she is like all the others again. One would hardly believe that it is necessary only to put on a few bits of clothing to make so much difference. Most strange it is, how clothes do change people ! And uniforms more than all.

3

Willy goes every evening to Waldman's.—That is a resort not far from the town where there is dancing in the afternoons and evenings.—I am going to-night, too, for Karl Bröger has told me that Adele is there sometimes. I should like to see her again.

All the windows of the garden ballroom at Waldman's are lit up. The shadows of the dancers move lightly across the drawn curtains. I take up a position at the bar and look round for Willy. Every table is occupied, there is not a chair free.—There has been a perfect frenzy for amusement these last few months since the war.

My eye suddenly lights on a dazzling white belly and the majestical claw-hammer of a swallow-tailed coat.

Willy in his new cut-away ! I stand there and blink. The coat is black, the vest white, and the hair red—a living flag-pole.

Willy receives my astonishment affably as admiration. " You might well stare ! " says he, turning himself round like a peacock. " My Kaiser-William-Memorial Cut-away ! How do you like it ? You never would have thought that could come out of an army greatcoat, now, would you ? "

He pats me on the shoulder. " But it's grand that you've come. There's a dance tournament to-night, we're all in for it, topping prizes ! It starts in half an hour."

Until then one may still try out one's paces. Willy has a sort of female pugilist for a partner, a great hefty creature, as powerful as a shire stallion. At the moment he is practising a one-step with her in which speed is the most noticeable feature. Karl, on the other hand, is dancing with a girl from the Food Office, all tricked out with rings and chains like a sleigh-horse. In this way he combines business and pleasure most agreeably. But Albert—Albert is not at our table. A trifle shyly he salutes us from a corner where he is sitting with a fair-haired girl.

" We've seen the last of him," says Willy prophetically.

I take a stroll around in the hope of picking up a good dancer. That is no simple matter. Many who at table appear light-footed as a doe, turn out afterwards to dance no better than an elephant in pup. And good dancers are much coveted, of course.— However, I do at last succeed in bespeaking a little seamstress.

The orchestra sounds a flourish. A chap with a

chrysanthemum in his buttonhole comes to the front
and explains that a couple will now give a demonstra-
tion of the latest thing from Berlin—a Fox-trot! That
is unknown here as yet ; we have only heard tell of it.

We gather round curiously. The orchestra strikes
up a syncopated measure and the pair begin to skip
round each other like a couple of spring lambs. Sometimes they will retreat from one another ; then they
will link arms again and twirl limping in a circle.
Willy is craning his neck, his eyes as big as saucers.
Here at last is a dance after his own heart.

The table with the prizes is brought in. We barge
across. There are three prizes each for the One-step,
the Boston, and the Fox-trot. The Fox-trot rules us
out, we cannot do that ; but like old Blücher, we mean
to knock off the other two.

The first prize in each case is ten gull's eggs or a
bottle of schnapps. Willy inquires suspiciously
whether gull's eggs are edible. Reassured he comes
back. The second prize is six gull's eggs, or an all-
wool Balaclava cap ; the third, four eggs, or two
packets of *Germany's Heroic Fame* cigarettes. " We're
not having them anyhow," says Karl, who knows about
such things.

The competition begins. We have entered Karl and
Albert for the Boston ; Willy and me for the One-step.
But we have not very high hopes of Willy. He can
win only if the judges have a sense of humour.

In the Boston, Karl and Albert with three other
couples reach the final round. Karl has the advantage
—the high collar of his swagger uniform, his new
patent-leather shoes, the chains and rings of his sleigh-
horse make a picture of dazzling elegance that none
could hope to rival. In style and deportment he is

matchless, but in rhythm and sympathy Albert is at least as good. The judges are making notes solemnly, as though the elimination rounds for the Last Judgment were in progress at Waldman's. Karl wins and takes the ten gull's eggs—he knows the brand of schnapps too well, having sold it to the house himself. He very nobly presents us with the booty—he has better at home. Albert takes second prize. With an embarrassed glance in our direction he carries off his six gull's eggs to the fair-headed girl. Willy whistles.

With my little seamstress I sail away on the one-step, and also come to the final round. To my surprise I see that Willy has just remained seated, he will not even try. I distinguish myself with a peculiar variant of the knee-bend and backward chassé that I have not shown off before, and the little girl is dancing like thistle-down. We carry off the second prize and share it between us.

Full of pride I go back to our table with the silver medal of the National Union for Dancing pinned on my chest.

" Willy, you old putty-head ! " I say, " why didn't you have a cut at it, anyway ? You might even have got the bronze medal ! "

" Yes, that's right," says Karl supporting me, "why didn't you, now ? "

Willy stands up, stretches himself, adjusts his swallow-tail coat, looks down on us loftily and answers only the one word—" Because ! "

The chap with the chrysanthemum then calls for competitors in the fox-trot. Only a few couples enter. Willy does not go, he strides out on to the floor.

" But he hasn't the faintest notion of it ! " snorts Karl.

Fascinated, we hang over the backs of our chairs to see what he will do. The female lion-tamer is coming out to meet him. With a sweeping gesture he offers his arm. The orchestra begins.

On the instant Willy is transfigured. He has turned into a runaway camel with an attack of St. Vitus's dance. He leaps in the air and he limps ; he skips and he circles ; he lashes out with his legs and tosses his lady to and fro ; then with a sort of pig's gallop he goes careering down the room, the lion-tamer not before, but beside him, so that she is giving an exhibition of the bent-arm hang from his outstretched right arm, while he has full liberty on his other side to do his worst, without having to worry lest he tread on her feet. Then he is an impersonation of a roundabout, till his coat-tails stand off at right angles ; next moment he sets off with fancy skippings slantwise across the dance floor, bucking like a billy-goat with pepper under its tail ; he thunders and spins and rages, and finally winds up with a weird pirouette in which he whirls his lady high through the air.

Not a soul in the hall doubts but that he is watching a hitherto unknown, professional exponent of some super fox-trot. Willy had seen his chance and made the most of it. His victory is so convincing that after him there is a long pause, and then the second prize. He holds up the bottle of schnapps to us in triumph. But he has sweated to such an extent that the dye in his cut-away has run badly ; his shirt and waistcoat are quite black, while his swallow-tail seems decidedly paler.

The competition is over, but the dancing continues. We sit round the table and drink up Willy's win.

Only Albert is missing—wild horses would not drag him from his fair-headed girl.

Willy gives me a prod : " Say, you, there's Adele."

" Where ? " I ask quickly.

He points with his thumb toward the throng on the dance floor. And sure enough there she is, waltzing with a tall, dark fellow.

" Has she been here long ? " I ask—I should like to think she had witnessed our triumph.

" Came about five minutes ago," answers Willy.

" With the stork ? "

" With the stork."

Adele, as she dances, carries her head tilted backward a little. One hand is on the dark fellow's shoulder. As I catch a glimpse of her face from the side my breath catches, so like is she under the shaded lights of the ballroom to my memory of those evenings of before the war. But from the front her face is fuller, and when she laughs it is quite strange to me.

I take a long pull from Willy's bottle. The little seamstress is just dancing by. She is slimmer and neater than Adele. I did not notice it in the fog the other night on the High Street, but Adele has grown now to a woman, with full breasts and stalwart legs. I cannot recall if she was like that before ; probably I did not give it any attention then.

" Grown to a proper tough little bit, what ? " says Willy, as if he had read my thoughts.

" Ach, you shut up ! " I retort sourly.

The waltz is over. Adele is leaning against the door. I go over to her. She greets me, and goes on talking and laughing with her dark-haired chap. I stand there and look at her. My heart is beating fast, as if I were about to make a great decision.

" What are you looking at me like that for ? " she asks.

" Oh, nothing," I say. " What about a dance ? "

" Not this, the next one," she replies and goes off with her partner to the dance floor.

I wait for her and we dance a Boston together. I do my utmost and she smiles appreciatively :

" You learned to dance at the Front, of course."

" Not there exactly," I answer. " But we won a prize just now."

She looks up quickly. " Oh ! what a pity ! we might have done that together.—What was it ? "

" Six gull's eggs and a medal," I reply, and the colour mounts into my hair. The violins are playing so softly that the shuffle of many footsteps can be heard.

" Anyway, we're dancing together now," I say. " Do you remember the evenings when we used to race along here one after the other from the Gym. Club ? "

She nods. " Yes, we were rather childish in those days. But just look over there ! the girl with the red dress—those loose blouses are the latest thing. Chic, don't you think ? "

The violins relinquish the melody to the 'cello. Tremulous, like suppressed weeping, they quiver above the golden brown tones.

" The first time I spoke to you we both ran away," I say. " June it was, on the old wall of the town—I remember it as if it were yesterday——"

Adele is waving to someone. Now she turns to me again.

" Yes, weren't we silly ? And can you really dance the tango ? The dark boy over there is a gorgeous tango dancer ! "

I do not reply. The music is silent. " Would you care to come to our table for a bit ? " I ask.

She looks across. " Who's the slim boy with the patent-leather shoes ? "

" Karl Bröger," I answer. She sits down with us. Willy offers her a glass and makes some joke or other. She laughs and looks across at Karl. Off and on she shoots a glance at Karl's sleigh-horse—that is the girl with the latest-fashioned blouse. I observe her in astonishment, she is so changed.—Has memory played me false here too, then ? Did it grow and grow too, until it has outgrown the reality ?—This rather loud girl sitting here at the table and talking much too much, is a stranger to me. But concealed under that manner must there not be, perhaps, someone that I do know better ? Does a thing become so distorted then, just because one gets older ?— Perhaps it is the years, I say to myself. It is more than three years now—she was sixteen then and a child ; now she is nineteen and grown up—— And suddenly I am conscious of the nameless sadness of Time that runs and runs on and changes, and when a man returns he shall find nothing again.—Yes, it is a hard thing to part ; but to come back again, that is sometimes far harder.

" What are you making such a long face about, Ernst ? " asks Willy. " Got the gripes ? "

" He is dull, isn't he ? " says Adele laughing. " But then he was always like that. Why don't you be a bit frisky, Ernst ? The girls like that much better than sitting around there like a sad pudding."

" So that is over," think I to myself ; " so that is over too ! " Not because she thinks me dull ; not because she has altered—no, not for any of these things, but because I see now that it has all been in vain.—I have been running about and about, I have knocked again at all the doors of my youth and desired to enter in there; I thought, surely it must admit me again, for I am still young and have wished so much to forget—but it fled always before me like a will-o'-the-wisp, it fell away without sound, it crumbled like tinder at my lightest touch. And I could not understand.—Surely here at least something of it must remain? I attempted it again and again, and as a result made myself merely ridiculous and wretched. But now I know, I know now that a still, silent war has ravaged this country of my memories also; I know now it would be useless for me to look farther. Time lies between like a great gulf; I cannot get back. There is nothing for it; I must go forward, march onward, anywhere, it matters nothing, I have no goal.

I grip my schnapps glass tightly and look up. Yes, there is Adele still questioning Karl as to where one may best buy smuggled silk stockings—and the dance goes on as before, the orchestra is still playing the same waltz from the *House of the Three Maidens*—and here I sit too, just as before, on the same chair, and I breathe and am alive still. Was there no flash of lightning then that tore me away? Did no country suddenly founder and go down about me, leaving me only surviving, all else this moment perished and lost to me for ever?

Adele gets up and takes leave of Karl. "At Meyer and Nickel's then?" she says pleasantly. "You're sure they do deal on the quiet in all sorts of oddments? Then I'll go along there first thing in the morning. Good-bye, Ernst!"

"I'll come with you a little way," I answer.

Outside she shakes hands. "You mustn't come any farther, I'm being waited for here."

I know it is foolish and sentimental, but I cannot help it—I take off my cap and bow low to her, as if to take a long farewell—not of her, but of all the things that were before. She looks at me searchingly a moment. "You are really quite funny sometimes!" Humming she runs down the path.

The clouds have gone and night is standing clear over the town. For a long time I stand looking at it. Then I go back.

4

The first regimental reunion since we returned from the war is to take place in the main hall at Konersmann's. All the boys have been invited. It should be a great show.

Karl, Albert, Jupp and I arrive an hour too soon. We were so impatient to see all the old faces again.

In the meantime we sit in the lounge outside the main room and wait for the arrival of Willy and the others. We are just tossing for a round of Steinhäger gin, when the door opens and Ferdinand Kosole comes in. We are so taken aback at his appearance that the coin drops from our hands. He's in civvies!

Like most of us, he has till now been wearing his old uniform, but to-day in honour of the occasion he has turned out in civvies, and now there he stands in a blue overcoat with velvet collar, a green hat on his head, and a butterfly collar and tie. It makes an utterly different man of him.

We have hardly recovered from our astonishment when Tjaden appears. He too is in civvies, also for the first time—a striped waistcoat, bright yellow shoes and a walking-stick with a silvered crook. With chin well up he comes strutting down the room. As he encounters Kosole he draws back. Kosole balks likewise. Neither has ever seen the other except in uniform. They look one another up and down for a second, then burst into roars of laughter. Each thinks the other in civilian togs too damned funny for anything.

" Why, Ferdinand, I always thought you were one of the toffs ! " grins Tjaden.

" How do you mean ? " says Kosole ceasing to laugh.

" Why, here ! " Tjaden points to Kosole's overcoat. " Looks to me as if you'd bought it off a rag-and-bone merchant."

" Ass ! " growls Ferdinand fiercely, turning away —but I see that he slowly turns red. I can hardly believe my eyes—he is actually upset ! And when he thinks himself unobserved he surreptitiously examines the ridiculed coat. In uniform he would never have thought of such a thing ; but now he is actually polishing out a couple of stains with the shiny cuff of his sleeve ! Then he looks a long time across at Karl Bröger who has on a swagger new suit. He does not know I have been watching him. After a while he asks me : " What's Karl's father, do you know ? "

" District judge," I answer.

" So—district judge, eh ? " he repeats meditatively. " And Ludwig, what's his ? "

"Income tax inspector."

He is silent a while. Then he says : " Well, I suppose you won't be having anything more to do with me soon——"

" You're potty, Ferdinand," I reply.

He shrugs his shoulders doubtfully. I cannot get over my surprise. It is not merely that he looks different in these damned civilian clothes, but he has actually changed in himself, too. He wouldn't have cared a brass tack about it before—but now he is even taking the thing off and hanging it up in the darkest corner of the place.

" Too hot in here," he says sourly, when he sees me watching him. I nod.

" And your father ? " he asks gloomily after a time.

" Bookbinder," I reply.

" Really ? " He begins to revive. " And Albert's, what's his ? "

" He's dead. But he used to be a locksmith."

" Locksmith ! " he repeats joyfully, as though that were as much as to say the Pope himself. " Locksmith, eh ? Why, that's grand. I'm a fitter myself. We will have been near colleagues then, as you might say, no ? "

" That's so," I say.

The blood of the old army Kosole is mounting again in Kosole the civilian. He takes colour and force again.

" It would have been a pity otherwise," he assures me energetically, and now, just as Tjaden strolls by to make another wry face, without a word and without shifting on his seat Kosole plants one superbly aimed kick. He is his old self again.

The door into the main hall has started banging. The first of the boys are coming. We go in. The empty room with the paper garlands and tables still unset, gives a disagreeable impression. A few groups are standing about in corners. I discover Julius Weddekamp in his faded old military tunic and hastily push aside a few chairs and go to greet him.

"How goes it, Julius?" I say. "Haven't forgotten you owe me a mahogany cross, I hope, have you? You wanted to make me one out of a piano lid, remember? Bear it in mind, old turnip——"

"I might have done with it myself, Ernst," he says gloomily. "You know my wife died?"

"Damn it, Julius, but I'm sorry to hear that," I say. "What was the trouble?"

He shrugs his shoulders. "Knocked herself out with the everlasting standing about in queues outside the shops all the winter. Then a baby came, and that finished her."

"And the baby?" I ask.

"Died too." He hunches his drooping shoulders as if he were freezing. "Yes, and Scheffler's dead too, Ernst—you knew that, I suppose?"

I shake my head. "How did that happen?" Weddekamp lights his pipe. "He got a crack in the head, you know; 1917, wasn't it? Anyway, it healed up all right at the time. Then about six weeks ago he suddenly developed such awful bloody pains that he kept running his head against the wall. It took four of us to get him off to the hospital. Inflammation or something. He pegged out the next day." He takes a second match. "Yes, and now they don't want to give his wife a pension!"

" And Gerhard Pohl ? " I inquire.

" He can't come—Fassbender and Fritsch neither.
Out of work. Not even enough money for the grub.
They would like to have come, too, the old boys."

The room has about half filled in the meantime.
We meet many others of our old pals, but it is strange
—the old spirit is missing. And we have been looking forward to this reunion for weeks, hoping it would
clear up for us all sorts of worries, and uncertainties
and misunderstandings. Perhaps it is because of the
civilian clothes sprinkled about everywhere among
the military togs—or maybe that profession, and
family, and social standing, like so many wedges, have
split us asunder ; but certain it is, the old feeling of
comradeship has gone.

Everything is topsy-turvy. There is Bosse, for
instance, the standing joke of the whole company,
who was always having japes played on him because
he was such a poor fool. Out there he used to be so
filthy dirty and rotten, that more than once we had
to put him under the pump. And now here he is
sitting among us in a flash, worsted suit, with a pearl
tie-pin and spats, quite a well-to-do fellow with a
big line of talk. And beside him is Adolf Bethke,
who towered above him so out there that he was
glad if Bethke would so much as speak to him.
And yet Bethke is now suddenly nothing but a
poor village cobbler with a bit of farm-holding.
And Ludwig Breyer, instead of a lieutenant's uniform
he now wears a shiny, too tight-fitting school-suit
with a boy's knitted cravat tied askew round his
neck; and his former batman is slapping him familiarly
on the back, once more the plumber in a large way

188

of business in water-closet fittings, and owner of fine premises on the main business street. Then there is Valentin—under his ragged, open tunic is an old blue-and-white sweater. He looks like a tramp, but, my God, what a soldier!—and Ledder-hose, the dirty dog, sitting there alongside him, full of importance in a shiny top hat, and a canary-yellow mackintosh, and smoking English cigarettes.—It is all turned bottom up!

Still, that might pass. But even the talk is different, and that derives from the clothes too. Fellows who formerly wouldn't have said booh to a goose are now playing the heavy uncle. The men with good clothes have a patronising air, and those with shabby ones are for the most part silent. A schoolmaster, who was formerly a corporal and a bad one at that, condescends to ask Karl and Ludwig about their examination. If I were Ludwig I'd pour my beer down his neck. Karl, thank Heaven! makes a few unflattering remarks about education and examina-tions and the rest of it, and extols business and trade instead.

The talk here makes me quite ill. I would rather we had never come together again—then at least we might still have preserved a memory. In vain do I try to picture all these fellows in dirty uniforms again, and this Konersmann's Restaurant as a canteen in the rest area. It cannot be done. The things here are stronger—the things that differentiate us from one another are too powerful. The common interest is no longer decisive. It has broken up already, and given place to the interest of the in-dividual. Now and then something still will shine through from that other time when we all wore the same rig, but already it is diminished and dim. These others here are still our comrades, and yet our comrades no longer—that is what is so sad. All else went west in the war, but comradeship we did believe in ; now only to find that what death could not do, life is achieving—it is driving us asunder.

But we are unwilling to believe it. We all sit down at one table together—Ludwig, Albert, Karl, Adolf, Willy, Tjaden, Valentin. A feeling of gloom is over us.

"Anyway, we'll stick together," says Albert glancing toward the big room. We agree and shake hands on it, whilst over yonder the good clothes are already beginning to draw their chairs closer together. We do not mean to be party to this reclassification. We will start with what the others are discarding. "Come on, Adolf," I say to Bethke, "join in too." He lays his great paw on our hands and for the first time in many a day he is smiling again.

We sit there together a while, but Adolf Bethke soon goes. He looks rather bad. I remind myself that I must go and see him one of these days.

A waiter appears and whispers something to Tjaden. He dismisses him with a shake of the head.— "Ladies have no business here." We look up in surprise. Tjaden smiles, flattered. The waiter returns, and behind him, with quick strides, comes a great, strapping wench. Tjaden is taken aback. We grin. But no, he knows how to look after himself. He makes a grand gesture : " My fiancée."

For Tjaden that ends the matter, so Willy undertakes the further introductions. He begins with

Ludwig and ends up with himself. Then he invites the girl to be seated. She does so. Willy sits down beside her and rests his arm along the back of her chair. "Your father is the famous butcher at Neuengraben, I believe?" he says by way of opening the conversation.

The girl nods. Willy draws up closer. That does not worry Tjaden in the slightest. He laps up his beer contentedly. But under Willy's gay and insistent talk the young lady begins to thaw.

"I've so much wanted to meet you gentlemen," she tells us. "Dearie has told me so often about you, but whenever I asked him to bring you out he never would."

"What?" says Willy, annihilating Tjaden with a glance, "bring us out? But of course, we should be awfully pleased, really most extraordinarily pleased to come. The old rascal, he never said a word of it to us!"

Tjaden begins to show signs of uneasiness. Kosole leans forward. "So Dearie has often told you about us, has he? And what has he told you exactly, I wonder?"

"We must be going now, Mariechen," Tjaden breaks in, making to rise. But Kosole pushes him down again into his chair. "Pray, be seated, Dearie. What did he tell you, now, Fräulein?"

Mariechen is utterly confiding. She looks at Willy coyly. "Would you be Herr Homeyer?" Willy bows to the Butchery. "Then it was you that he saved?" she prattles on, while Tjaden fidgets in his chair as if he were seated on an ant-heap. "But you haven't forgotten, surely?"

Willy holds his head. "I was buried afterwards,

you know," he explains. " And that plays the very deuce with a man's memory ! It was most unfortunate. Such a lot of things slipped my memory then."

" Saved ? " asked Kosole eagerly.

" I'm going, Mariechen ; are you coming or aren't you ? " says Tjaden. Kosole holds him fast.

" He is so shy," giggles Mariechen beaming. " And first he had to kill three negroes who wanted to butcher Herr Homeyer with their tomahawks ! One of them with his fist, too——"

" With his fist," repeats Kosole in a hollow voice.

" Yes, and the rest with their own tomahawks ! And then afterwards he carried you back." Mariechen surveys Willy's six feet five and a half inches and nods approbation of her fiancé. " There's no harm in telling for once of what you did, Dearie."

" No, indeed ! " agrees Kosole. " It's a thing that ought to be told, once."

For a moment Willy gazes deliciously into Mariechen's eyes. " Yes, he's a wonderful fellow ! " he assures her. Then he nods across at Tjaden. " Just come outside with me a moment."

Tjaden rises dubiously. But Willy means no harm. A few minutes later the two reappear arm in arm. Willy stoops down to Mariechen : " Well, so that's settled—I'll be calling round to-morrow evening. I have still to thank him for rescuing me from those negroes—— But, you know, I saved your fiancé once, too."

" No! Did you really? " says Mariechen astonished.

" Perhaps he'll tell you about that, too, some day," grins Willy. With a sigh of relief Tjaden now steams out with his lady.

"You see, they're slaughtering to-morrow," says Willy.—But nobody is listening. We have had to control ourselves too long already, and we burst into shrieks of laughter, whinneying like a stableful of starved horses. Kosole almost makes himself sick, he shakes so. It is long before Willy can tell us what a very advantageous contract he has been able to make with Tjaden for a steady supply of horse-sausage. "I've got the old man in the hollow of my hand," he grins.

5

I sat at home all the afternoon and tried to do something, but nothing has come of it. For an hour already I have been roaming aimlessly through the streets. In the course of my patrolling I go past the new restaurant, the Holländische Diele. This is the third gin shop to go up within the last three weeks. These things with their gay placards are springing up like mushrooms everywhere among the houses. The Holländische Diele is the largest and flashiest.

Before the illuminated glass door stands a porter, looking like a cross between a bishop and a colonel of the hussars, an enormous fellow with a gilded baton in his hand. I catch his eye—suddenly his dignity deserts him, and he prods me in the stomach with his club and grins : "Hullo, Ernst, you old scarecrow ! Commong sa va, as the Frenchman says."

It is Corporal Anton Demuth, some time our sergeant-cook. I salute smartly ; in the army we were always being told that salutes should be given to the uniform, not to the wearer. But this trick uniform here is very high class indeed, it calls for a bow at the least.

N

"Hullo, Anton!" I laugh. "But to get down to business, have you got anything to eat?"

"Bet your life," he answers affirmatively. "Franz Elstermann, remember Franz? he's here in this syrup-shop too. He's the cook!"

"And what time did you say I should call?" I ask, for that in itself is sufficient recommendation. Elstermann and Demuth were the prize scroungers of all France.

"Some time after one, to-night," says Anton, giving me a wink. "We've just scored a dozen or so geese off a Food Office Inspector—hush goods, you know. You can bet your life Elstermann will amputate a few of them first. After all, who's to say geese don't have wars where they might lose a leg or so, eh?"

"Nobody," I say. "Get much business here?"

"Packed to the doors every night. Take a look in."

He pulls the curtain a little to one side and through a chink I peer into the room. Soft, warm light over the tables, long trailers of bluish cigar smoke floating through it, carpets glowing, shining porcelain, gleaming silver. Women seated at the tables, surrounded by waiters, and men beside them who do not appear to be sweating in the least, nor are they even embarrassed. With what wonderful self-possession they give their orders!

"Well, my lad, how would you like to have one of them on the switchback, eh?" asks Anton prodding me again in the ribs.

I do not answer; this rich, colourful glimpse of life touches me strangely. There is something almost unreal in it, as if I only dreamed that I stood here on the dark street in the slushing snow and saw through the chink of a door this strange scene. It enchants me—though of course it is nothing, merely a few profiteers disgorging their money. But we lay too long out there in filthy holes under the ground not to feel sometimes a passionate, almost insane craving for luxury and elegance surge up in us— for does not luxury mean to be sheltered, to be cared for?—and that is the one thing we have had no knowledge of.

" Well, lad, what d'you think ? " asks Anton again. " Nice soft little pussies to go to bed with, what ? "

I feel rather foolish, but at the moment I cannot think what to say. All this talk I have been using for years suddenly seems to me crude and repulsive.—Fortunately Anton has now to resume his poise and dignity ; a car is coming. A slim creature steps out and goes in through the door ; she is stooping forward a little ; she holds her fur to her breast with one hand, and her hair shows gleaming under a close-fitting golden toque ; her knees close together, little feet, and a small face. With light, springy ankles she trips by me, wafting a faint, bitter smell, and I am filled with a wild desire to be able to go in with this lovely creature through the revolving doors, in to the tables there, into that pampered, prosperous atmosphere of colour and light, and so to saunter on through a benign, care-free existence, surrounded by waiters and servants, well wrapped in a protective, insulating layer of wealth—rid for ever of all the poverty and filth that for years have been our daily portion.

I suppose I look rather school-boyish, for suddenly Anton looses a peal of laughter from under his beard, and with a sly look and another prod, he says : " Though they go in silks and satins, in bed they're all the same."

" Naturally," I say, and follow up with a smutty joke so that he won't see through me. " Till one o'clock then, Anton ! "

" Why not ? " he responds solemnly, " or Bong-soahr, as the Frenchman says."

I wander on, my hands thrust deep into my pockets. The snow mashes under my shoes. I kick it off angrily. What could I do anyway, even supposing I might dine with a woman like that ? I should only be able to stare at her, that's all. I couldn't even eat without getting into a mess. And how difficult, I think to myself, how difficult to pass a whole day with such a being ! Always on the watch, always on the alert. And then at night—but I wouldn't have even the faintest notion how to begin ! Not that I am altogether ignorant of women, of course, but what I do know I learned from Jupp and from Valentin. With such ladies as these that would clearly never do.

June 1917, was the first time I was with a woman. Our company was back resting in the huts at the time. It was midday and we were fooling about in the meadow with a couple of dogs that had run up to us. With flying ears and glistening coats the beasts would go bounding through the tall, summer grasses, and the sky was blue and the war far away.

Then Jupp came trotting across from the orderly-room. The dogs ran toward him and jumped up on him, but he shook them off and called out :

" An order's just come through. We're to hop over to-night ! "

We knew all that that meant. Day after day the rumble of the drum-fire of the Big Offensive had come rolling back to us over the western horizon ; day after day we had seen the spent regiments returning, and if we asked any man what it was like, he would merely respond with a gesture and continue to stare straight ahead ; day after day truckloads of wounded had been streaming past ; and day after day, to-day for to-morrow, we had been digging long ditches for graves.

We got up. Bethke and Wessling went to their packs for writing-paper ; Willy and Tjaden walked over to the cook-house ; and Franz Wagner and Jupp persuaded me to go with them to the brothel.

" Why, Ernst lad," said Wagner, " you don't mean to say you're never going to know what a woman is ? Who can say but we may all be dead before morning ? Looks to me as if they've a heap of new artillery up there. It would be just too absurd to die virgin."

The Field Brothel was in a small town, distant about an hour's walk. We got permits, though not without waiting a long time—other regiments were also going up the line, so they were many that came there in haste to snatch whatever of life they might still get. In a small office we had to give up our permits and unbutton our flies. Then an A.M.C. corporal examined us to see that we were fit, and we received an injection of a few drops of protargol, while a sergeant-major was explaining that the fee was three marks and that on account of the crush ten minutes was all the time that could be allowed us. Then we queued up on the stairs.

The line moved slowly forward. At the top of the stairs the doors kept banging, and each time a man would come out; then "Next!" would be called.

"How many cows are there?" inquired Franz Wagner of a sapper.

"Three," said he. "But you don't get any choice. It's a lottery—if your luck's out, then you fall for a grandmother."

Stewing there in the heat and sweat and stinking breath of the famished soldiers on the frowsy staircase, I began to feel sick. I would have been glad to get out of it—my curiosity had gone, but I was afraid the others would make fun of me, so I waited.

At last came my turn. The man who had been before me stumbled out and I stepped into the room. It was low and dark, and reeked so of carbolic and sweat that I thought it strange to see the branches of a lime tree just outside the window, and the sun and wind playing in the fresh, green leaves—so withered and used up did everything in the room appear. There was a dish with pink water on a chair and in the corner a sort of camp-bed on which was spread a torn sheet. The woman was fat and had on a short, transparent chemise. She did not look at me at all, but straightway lay down. Only when I still did not come, did she look up impatiently; then a flicker of comprehension showed in her spongey face. She perceived that I was still quite young.

I simply could not; horror seized me and a choking nausea. The woman made a few gestures to rouse me, gross, repulsive gestures; she tried to pull me to her and even smiled as she did so, sweetly and coyly, that I should have compassion on her—what was she, after all, but a poor, army mattress, that must bed twenty and more fellows every day?—but I laid down only the money beside her and went out hastily and down the stairs.

Jupp gave me a wink. " Well, how was it ? "

" So, so," I answered like an old hand, and we turned to go. But no, we must first go before the A.M.C. corporal again and make water under his eyes. Then we received a further injection of protargol.

" So that is love," thought I dumbly, despairingly, as we packed up our things ; " so that is the love my books at home were so full of—of which I had expected so much in the vague dreams of my youth !" I rolled up my greatcoat and packed my ground-sheet, I received my ammunition and we marched out. I was silent and sorrowful, and I thought upon it : how now nothing was left me of those high-flying dreams of life and of love, but a rifle, a fat whore and the dull rumble out there on the sky-line whither we were now slowly marching. Then came darkness, and the trenches and death.— Franz Wagner fell that night, and we lost besides twenty-three men.

Drops of rain fall glittering from the trees ; I turn up my collar. I often long for affection even now, for shy words, for warm, generous emotions ; I would like to escape the crude monotony of these last years. But what if it actually came to pass ?—what if all the gentleness and variety of those other days drew round me again ? if someone actually did love me, some slim, delicate woman, such as the one there with the golden toque and the slim ankles—how would it be ? even though the ecstasy of some blue, silver night should gather about us, endless, self-forgotten, in darkness.—Would not the vision of the fat whore come between us at the last moment? Would not the voices of the drill-sergeants suddenly shout their obscenities? Would not memory, scraps of talk, army jokes, at once riddle and destroy every decent emotion? Even now we are still chaste in ourselves, but our imagination has been debauched without our being aware of it—before we knew anything of love at all we were already being lined up and examined for sexual diseases. The breathless wonder, the impetuousness, the night wind, the darkness, the questionings—all those things that were still with us when, as sixteen-year-old boys, we would race along after Adele and the other girls through the flickering, gas-lit wind—they never came back. Though the time was when the woman was not a whore, yet it did not come back—though I believed it might still be otherwise, and though she embraced me and I trembled with desire, yet it did not come back. Afterwards I was always wretched.

Unconsciously I begin to walk faster, breathe deeper. I will have it again—I must have it again. It shall come again, else what reason is there to live?

I make my way to Ludwig's. There is still a light in his room. I fling pebbles up at his window, and he comes down and opens the door for me.

Up in the room Georg Rahe is standing in front of Ludwig's case of geological specimens, holding a large rock crystal and making it sparkle.

" I'm glad I've seen you after all, Ernst," he smiles. "Just been round at your place. I'm leaving to-morrow."

He is in uniform. "But, Georg," I say haltingly, "you don't mean——"

"Yes," he nods. "That's it. Going to be a soldier again. It's all fixed. I start to-morrow."

"Can you understand that?" I say to Ludwig.

"Yes," he replies, "I think I understand. But it won't help him." He turns to Rahe. "You're disillusioned, Georg, that's your trouble. But just think a moment, after all, isn't it only natural? Up at the Front there our nerves were always strained to the utmost, any minute it might be a matter of life and death. So now, of course, they flap about like sails when the wind has dropped; and for the simple reason that here everything is a matter of small, painful advances——"

"Exactly," agrees Rahe. "This petty pushing and shoving for grub and for place, with an odd ideal or two thrown in to make weight, it just nauseates me; I mean to clear out of it."

"Well, if you must do something of that sort, why not join the Revolution?" I say. "You might even be War Minister."

"Bah! this Revolution!" answers Georg scornfully. "It was made by a bunch of Party Secretaries, with their thumbs in line with the seam of their trousers. They've taken fright again already at the mere thought of their own audacity. Look at the way they are at one another's throats—Social Democrats, Independents, Spartacists, Communists! And in the meantime the other fellows are quietly potting off what few real brains they have among them, and they don't even see it!"

"No, Georg," says Ludwig, "that's not it. We made revolution with too little hate, that's the whole fact of the matter ; we wanted to be just to everybody from the very jump, and with the result that the whole thing has fizzled out. A revolution must first rage like a bush fire ; then afterwards one can start in with the sowing. But we wanted to destroy nothing and yet to start afresh. We hadn't enough strength left to hate, we were so weary and burned up with the war. One can sleep for weariness even through a bombardment, you know that yourself. But even now it may not be too late to achieve by work what was missed in the assault."

"Work ! " answers Georg contemptuously and the rock crystal flashes under the lamp. "We can fight, if you like, but not work."

"Then we must learn again," says Ludwig quietly from the corner of his sofa.

"We're too demoralised for that," objects Georg.

For a while neither speaks. The wind drones outside the windows. Rahe walks with great strides about Ludwig's little room, and it really does seem as if he did not belong here within these walls of books, and quietness and work—his clean-cut, keen features seem to be in place only over a field-grey uniform, as though he belonged to trenches and fighting and war. He props his arms on the table and leans over toward Ludwig. The lamplight falls on his shoulder-straps and behind him glitter the quartzes in the collection of stones.

"What are we doing here, Ludwig ? " he says deliberately. "Look about you. How slack ! how hopeless it all is ! We are a burden to ourselves and to everyone else. Our ideals are bankrupt, our dreams shattered ; and we just run about in this world of earnest, purposeful people and profit-mongers, like so many Don Quixotes loose in a strange land."

Ludwig looks at him a while. "It's my idea that we're sick, Georg. We have the war in our bones still."

Rahe nods. "Yes, and we'll never get it out again!"

"Don't you believe it!" retorts Ludwig, "else it will all have been in vain."

Rahe crashes his fist down on the table. "It was in vain, Ludwig!—that's just what makes me mad! Think what men we were when we marched away in that storm of enthusiasm! It seemed as if a new age had dawned—all the old things, the rotten, the compromising, the partisan, all swept away. We were young then, as men were never young before!"

He takes a lump of crystal from Ludwig's stone collection and holds it like a hand-grenade. His hands are trembling. "I have been in many dugouts, Ludwig," he goes on, "and we were all young men who sat there around one miserable slush lamp, waiting, while the barrage raged overhead like an earthquake. We were none of your inexperienced recruits either; we knew well enough what we were waiting for, and we knew what would come.—But there was more in those faces down in the gloom there than mere calm, more than good humour, more than just readiness to die.—There was the will to another future in those hard, set faces; and it was there when they charged, and still there when they died. We had less to say for ourselves year by year, we shed many things, but that one thing still remained. And now, Ludwig, where is it now? Can't you see how it is perishing in all this pig's-wash of order, duty, women, routine, punctuality and the rest of what they call life here? No, Ludwig, we lived then! And though you tell me a thousand times that you hate war, yet I still say, we lived then. We lived, because we were together, and because something burned in us that was more than this whole muck-heap here!"

He is breathing hard. "It must have been for something, Ludwig! When I first heard there was revolution, for one brief moment I thought: Now the time will be redeemed—now the flood will pour back, tearing down the old things, digging new banks for itself—and by God, I would have been in it! But the flood broke up into a thousand runnels; the revolution became a mere scramble for jobs, for big jobs and little jobs. It has trickled away, it has been dammed up, it has been drained off into business, into family, and party. But that will not do me. I'm going where comradeship is still to be found."

Ludwig stands up. His brow is flaming, his eyes blaze. He looks Rahe in the face. "And why is it, Georg? why is it? Because we were duped, I tell you, duped as even yet we hardly realise; because we were misused, hideously misused!—They told us it was for the Fatherland, and meant the schemes of annexation of a greedy industry.—They told us it was for honour, and meant the quarrels and the will to power of a handful of ambitious diplomats and princes.—They told us it was for the Nation, and meant the need for activity on the part of out-of-work generals!"—He takes Rahe by the shoulders and shakes him. "Can't you see? They stuffed out the word Patriotism with all the twaddle of their fine phrases, with their desire for glory, their will to power,

their false romanticism, their stupidity, their greed of
business, and then paraded it before us as a shining
ideal ! And we thought they were sounding a bugle
summoning us to a new, a more strenuous, a larger
life. Can't you see, man ? But we were making
war against ourselves without knowing it ! Every
shot that struck home, struck one of us !—Can't you
see ?—Then listen and I will bawl it into your ears.
The youth of the world rose up in every land believing
that it was fighting for freedom ! And in every land
they were duped, and misused ; in every land they
have been shot down, they have exterminated each
other ! Don't you see now ?—There is only one fight,
the fight against the lie, the half-truth, compromise,
against the old order. But we let ourselves be taken
in by their phrases ; and instead of fighting against
them, we fought for them. We thought it was for
the Future. It was against the Future. Our future
is dead ; for the youth is dead that carried it. We
are merely the survivors, the ruins. But the other is
alive still—the fat, the full, the well content—that lives
on, fatter and fuller, more contented than ever ! And
why ? Because the unsatisfied, the eager, the storm-
troops have died for it. But think of it ! A generation annihilated ! A generation of hope, of faith,
of will, strength, ability, so hypnotised that they have
shot down one another, though over the whole world
they all had the same purpose ! "

His voice breaks. His eyes are full of passion and
sobs. We are all standing now. "Ludwig," I say
and put my arm about his shoulder.

Rahe takes up his cap and tosses the stone back
into the case. " Good-bye, Ludwig, old comrade ! "

Ludwig stands there facing him. His lips are

pressed together, his cheek bones stand out. " You are going, Georg," he stammers, " but I am staying. I'm not giving in yet ! "

Rahe looks at him a while. " It is hopeless," he says calmly, and adjusts the buckle of his belt.

I go with Georg down the stairs. The leaden dawn is already showing through the door. The stone steps re-echo and we come out into the open as from a dugout. The street is empty and grey. It drags away into the distance. Rahe points along it. " All one long fire-trench, Ernst—" He indicates the houses : " Dugouts, every one—the war still goes on —but a dirty, low-down war—every man against his fellow——"

We shake hands. I cannot speak. Rahe smiles : " What's troubling you, Ernst ? It's not a war at all out East, you know. Cheer up, we're soldiers still. And this isn't the first time we have parted——"

" I think it's the first time we have really parted, Georg," I say hastily.

He stands there a moment longer before me. Then he nods slowly and goes off down the street, spare, calm, without once looking round. And for a space I still hear the clatter of his steps when he has already disappeared.

PART V

I

INSTRUCTIONS have arrived requiring that Returned Men shall be treated with indulgence in the examination. They are to be allowed to submit subjects in which they are specially interested, and in those are to be examined.

Unfortunately the subjects in which we are specially interested do not figure in the syllabus, so we simplify matters after our own fashion. Every man is to submit two questions in each subject and to undertake to be able to answer them. Westerholt has seated himself at the master's desk, and before him are several large, blank sheets of paper with our names. We begin to dictate to him the questions that we wish to be asked.

Willy is uncommonly fastidious. He turns over and over the pages of his history book, and only after long searching up and down does he plump at last for the two questions following: "When was the battle of Zama?" and "When was the reign of Otto the Lazy?"

Westerholt and Albert take the lists of questions and subjects to the several masters. They go first to the Principal, who eyes them with some apprehension; he has not been led to expect any good at our hands. He studies the lists and then lays them aside with a gesture of disgust. "But, gentlemen, the Minister requires that you submit such fields as you may be specially interested in, that is to say, certain definite large sections from each course of study. But what you offer here is no more than bare, simple questions."

" The fields of our interest are no greater," answers Albert.

" But then, don't we make up for it, by knowing them so very *très bon* ? " adds Westerholt.

The Principal hands the lists back. " No, I cannot agree to that. It would merely be to make a farce of the whole examination ! "

" Well, isn't it so, anyway ! " retorts Westerholt, beaming.

The Principal shrugs his shoulders, but eventually accepts the lists.

Willy unfortunately turns up two hours late for the essay, having got drunk with Karl the night before. Hollermann is greatly perturbed, and asks Willy if he thinks he can now finish in time. Willy nods confidently, sits down in his place, takes from the pocket of his cut-away the essay written already for him by Ludwig, spreads it out in front of him and then gratefully lays down his heavy head for a short nap. He is still so befuddled during the Divinity test that he nearly gives up his answers in Nature Study by mistake. He has brought the whole lot along all in one envelope. Albert just prevented it at the last moment.

We profit by the intervals during the oral examinations to have a last game of skat. That is one of the few things we really did learn to some purpose in the army.

Whenever one of the players is summoned for

examination, he either puts down his cards for the moment and resumes the play afterwards, or else gives his hand to someone he can trust to get everything out of it that is in it.

Willy has such incredible luck that he forgets everything else in the excitement of the play. Just as he is beginning to bid on a wonderful hand—a solo grand, without two, and with Schneider—he is called up for examination in Literature. He looks at the cards in despair. "I'd rather fail than not play out this hand!" he declares. But finally he puts his cards into his pocket, making the other two promise over a handshake to wait until he returns, and not to monkey with the hands in the meantime. The consequence is that he has forgotten the answer to one of his questions in Literature. "Literature is the crucial subject, you know," says Hollermann, full of concern—"if you get below three, you fail."

Willy brightens up. "What will you bet I don't make it?" answers Willy, his head still full of the solo grand in his pocket, and persuaded that a Returned Man could not possibly fail. The formmaster shakes his head. He is used to taking a lot from Willy. He waits patiently. Then all at once Willy pulls it off, and comes back in hot haste to take Reinersmann's and Westerholt's scalps. "Ninety-one!" says he triumphantly, and collects the money.

We all pass, of course. The Principal, taking heart again a little now that he is about to get rid of the worst of the blackguards, cannot deny himself this opportunity of addressing to us yet a few golden words. He would like to make this leaving school a solemn sacrament, and begins to explain to us that having been so strengthened by our arduous experience, we are now to pass out into life with high hope and good will. "'Pass out' is not good," interrupts Willy. "We've damned near passed out too often already in the other direction." The Principal draws in his horns. He sees that we are not amenable to soft soap. Even now reconciliation is not possible with such unprofitable, ungrateful material.

We go our ways. The next draft take their examination in three months' time. Ludwig has to wait till then, though it was he who wrote the answers for at least four of our fellows. But it is the primary law of this world where the old rule the young, that one must serve one's time. It is no question of ability. Else what would become of the old dodderers who cling to their power?

A few days after the examination we are sent out on probation to teach in the neighbouring villages. I am glad. I am fed up with this aimless loafing around. It has produced only brooding, and melancholy, and senseless noisy riot. Now I will work.

I pack my trunk and set off with Willy. We have the good luck to be neighbours, our villages being barely an hour apart.

I get lodgings in an old farmhouse. There are oak trees just outside the window and the mild bleating of sheep comes in from the stalls. The farmer's wife at once settles me into a big armchair and begins to lay the table. She has a fixed idea that all townsmen are half starved, and indeed, she is not so far wrong. With suppressed emotion I watch things almost forgotten make their appearance on the table—an enormous ham, sausages as long as your arm, snow-white wheaten bread and those buck-wheat cakes with big lumps of ham in the middle, so beloved by Tjaden. There is a supply enough to feed a whole company.

I begin to hoe in. The farmer's wife stands by smiling broadly, hands on hips, obviously delighted. At the end of an hour I have to stop with a sigh, though Mother Schomaker still urges me on.

At that moment Willy comes in to visit me. " Now you can have your wish," I say to my hostess. " Now you will see something ! I'm not a patch on him."

Willy does as a soldier should do. He wastes no time in ceremony, but gets on with the job. At the invitation of Mother Schomaker he begins with the buck-wheat cakes. By the time he has reached the cheese, the farmer's wife is leaning back against the cupboard and looking at Willy with admiration and astonishment, as if he were the eighth wonder of the world. Highly flattered she produces yet another great dish of pudding, and Willy puts that away too. " Well," says he taking a breather, but retaining his spoon when she clears away the dish, " that has given me a real appetite. What about a good square meal now ? "

With this remark he wins Mother Schomaker's heart for ever.

Embarrassed and unsure of myself I perch at the Teacher's desk. Before me forty children are seated.

These are the youngest. There they sit all in perfect alignment, their fat little fists folded over their boxes of slate-pencils and pens, their slates and note-books before them. The school has only three classes, so that in each there are children of varying ages. The smallest are seven, the oldest ten years of age.

The wooden shoes are scraping on the floor. There is a peat fire crackling in the stove. Some of the children with their woollen scarves and hairy, cow-hide satchels, have had to walk two hours to school. Their things have become wet and are now beginning to steam in the dry air of the room.

The smallest ones with their round apple cheeks stare up at me. A couple of girls are giggling secretly. One fair-headed child is absorbed in picking his nose. Another, under cover of the back of the boy in front of him, is stuffing down a thick slice of bread and butter. But every one of them watches my least movement with closest attentiveness.

I shift uncomfortably on my stool. It is only a week since I too was sitting on a form even as they, watching Hollermann's florid, hackneyed gestures while he talked about the poets of the Wars of Liberation. Now I am a Hollermann myself. At least to the youngsters down there.

" Children, now we shall try to write a capital letter L," I say, and go to the blackboard. " Ten lines of L's, then five lines of Lina, and five lines of Larch."

I write out the words slowly with chalk. A shuffling and rustling begins behind me. I expect to find that they are laughing at me and turn round. But it is only the notebooks being opened and the slates put in readiness. The forty heads are bent obediently over their task.—I am almost surprised.

The slate-pencils are squeaking, the pens scratching. I pass to and fro between the forms.

On the wall hangs a crucifix, a stuffed barn-owl and a map of Germany. Outside the windows the clouds drive steadily by, swift and low.

The map of Germany is coloured in brown and green. I stop before it. The frontiers are hatched in red, and make a curious zig-zag from top to bottom. Cologne—Aachen, there are the thin black lines marking the railways—Herbesthal, Liége, Brussels, Lille—I stand on tiptoe—Roubaix—Arras —Ostend—where is Mount Kemmel, then? It isn't marked at all—but there is Langemarck, Ypres, Bixschoote, Staden—how small they are on the map! tiny points only, secluded, tiny points—and yet how the heavens thundered and the earth raged there on the 31st July when the Big Offensive began, and before nightfall we had lost every officer——

I turn away and survey the fair and dark heads bending zealously over the words, Lina and Larch. Strange—for them those tiny points on the map will be no more than just so much stuff to be learnt—a few new place names, and a number of dates to be learned by rote in the history lesson—like the Seven Years' War or some battle against the Romans.

A little Tom Thumb in the second row jumps up and waves his notebook in the air. He has done his twenty lines. I go over and point out that he has made the bottom stroke of the L a trifle too long. He looks up at me so radiantly with his liquid blue eyes that I must drop my gaze a moment. I go hastily to the blackboard to write two more words with another capital letter. *Karl and*—I pause for a second ; but I can do no other, an invisible hand guides the chalk—*Mount Kemmel.*

" ' Karl,' what is that ? " I ask.

Every hand goes up. " A man," shouts the little Tom Thumb of before.

" And Mount Kemmel ? " I ask after a short pause, almost choking.

Silence. At last a little girl puts up her hand. " Out of the Bible," she says, hesitatingly.

I look at her a while. " No," I then say, " that is not right. You mean the Mount of Olives, or Lebanon, perhaps, do you ? "

The girl nods, crestfallen. I stroke her hair. " Then we shall write that this time. Lebanon is a very pretty word."

Thoughtfully I resume my patrolling to and fro between the benches. Now and again I catch a searching glance above the edge of a copy-book. I stand still near the stove and look at the young faces. Most of them are good-natured and ordinary, some are sly, others stupid—but in a few there is a flicker of something brighter. For these life will not be so obvious, and all things will not go so smoothly.

Suddenly a great sense of despondency comes over me.—To-morrow we shall take the prepositions, I think to myself—and next week we shall have a dictation.—In a year's time you will have by heart fifty questions from the Catechism—in four years you will start the larger multiplication tables.—And so you will grow up, and Time will take you in his pincers—one dumbly, another savagely, or gently or shatteringly.—Each will have his own destiny, and thus or thus it will overtake you. What help shall I be to you then with my conjugations and enumeration of all the rivers of Germany? Forty of you—forty different lives are standing behind you and waiting. How gladly would I help you, if I could.—But who can really help another here? Have I even been able to help Adolf Bethke?

The bell rings. The first lesson is over.

Next day we don our swallow-tailed coats. Mine was only just ready in time—and go to call on the parson. This is matter of breviary.

We are quite well received, though with a certain reserve—our insubordination at college having won for us a rather doubtful reputation in respectable circles. In the evening we propose to visit the Mayor, that also being part of our duties. We encounter him however in the village pub, which does service also as post office.

He is a shrewd-looking old farmer with a wrinkled face, who at once invites us to a round of double schnapps. We accept. Then two or three more farmers come in, wink at one another, greet us, and also invite us to a glass.—They are winking and mouthing at each other behind their hands, the poor fools. We realise at once what they would be at— they mean to try and get us tight, by way of having a little joke among themselves. They have worked it often before, so it would seem, for with a knowing smirk they now begin to tell us of certain other young teachers who have been here. There are three reasons why they think they should soon get the better of us : First, because, so they imagine, no townsman could possibly carry so much liquor as they ; second, because schoolmasters are educated and therefore must *a priori* be weaker than they ; and third, because lads so young as ourselves cannot really have had any practice. And that may well have been so with the other probationers who have been here, but in our case they are reckoning without one thing, namely, that we have been soldiers for a few years, and so understand very well how to drink schnapps by the mess-tin-full. We accept the challenge. The farmers merely want to make us look a little bit foolish—but we, on the other hand, are undertaking to uphold a threefold honour, which, of course, multiplies our strength.

The Mayor, the Village Clerk and a couple more tough-looking farmers sit down over against us. These are apparently their most confirmed topers. With a faintly sly farmers' grin they touch glasses with us. Willy is already acting as if he were a bit merry. The grin broadens.

Willy and I stand a round of beer-with-schnapps. That draws a broadside of seven more rounds from the others. They count on that to see us under. A little astonished, they watch us empty our glasses. A certain mild approbation is discernible in the way that they eye us. Willy imperturbably orders a fresh round. "But no beer this time, mind you ; only double schnapps ! " he calls to the barman.

" 'Struth ! neat schnapps ? " says the Mayor.

"Why, sure," says Willy calmly, "else we'll be sitting here till early morning.—Beer only makes a man sober."

The astonishment in the eyes of the Mayor is waxing visibly. One of the farmers admits in an unsteady voice that we certainly can swill pretty well. Two others rise up silently and go off. Already one or two of our antagonists are trying to empty out their glasses furtively under the table. But Willy watches that none gets away with it. "Hands above the table!" he insists, forcing the glasses to their lips. The smile has vanished. We are gaining ground.

Within an hour most of them are lying about the room with cheese-like faces, or else have staggered out humiliated. The group about the table has dwindled to the Mayor and the Village Clerk. Now begins a duel between these two and ourselves. Already we are seeing double, but the others have been lisping for some time now, and that renews our heart.

After another half-hour, when we are all as red as turkeys, Willy delivers the *coup de grâce*.

"Four beer-mugs of cognac!" he booms across the counter. The Mayor starts back in his chair. The glasses come. Willy pushes two into their hands. "Cheero!"

They stare at us. "Now, all in one go!" cries Willy, his face glowing. The Village Clerk tries to back out, but Willy is inflexible. "In four gulps!" pleads the Mayor, much humbled. "In one gulp!" insists Willy, getting up and touching glasses with the Clerk. I stand up likewise. "Well! Cheero! To your very good healths! Here goes!" we shout at our two befuddled opponents.

They look at us like a couple of calves about to be slaughtered, and take a gulp. "No, on with it! Or do you want to go down?" yells Willy. "Stand up to it!" They stagger to their feet and drink. In various ways they try to take a breather, but we jeer at them and show our empty glasses. "Your

very best health!" "No, all of it!" "Mop it
up!" They gulp it down. Then slowly, but surely,
they sink to the floor. We have won.—At slow
drinking they might perhaps have seen us out; but
we have had special training in the express method,
and to make them take it at our pace was our salvation.

Swaying and tottering we survey the field with
pride. Beside ourselves not a man is left standing.
The postman, who at the same time is the bar-
tender, is resting his head on the counter and wailing
intermittently for a wife who died in child-bed while
he was away at the war. "Martha, Martha," he
sobs in a weird, high-pitched voice. "Don't mind
him," says the barmaid, "he always does that at
these times." The lamentation offends our ears;
and anyway, it is time to be going.

Willy picks up the Mayor, and I take the lighter,
more wizened Village Clerk, and so we trundle them
home. That is the final touch to our triumph. We
deposit the Clerk outside his own door and knock
until a light appears. But someone is awaiting the
Mayor. His wife is already standing in the door.

"Herr Jesus!" she cries. "The new school
teachers! So young, and such topers! A nice
beginning, I must say!"

Willy tries to explain that it was an affair of honour,
but gets sadly mixed.

"Where would you like us to put him?" I ask at
last.

"Let the old pig lie!" she snaps. We dump him
down on a sofa. Then Willy, with a smile like a
child, asks if we might have some coffee. The
woman looks at him as if he were a Hottentot.

" But we brought your husband home for you ! " explains Willy beaming. Not even this hard-baked old body can withstand such sublimely unwitting impudence. Shaking her head solemnly, she pours out a couple of large cups of coffee, meantime giving us a good scolding. We say " Yes " to everything. It is always best at such times.

From this day on we are regarded as men of standing in the village and everywhere are saluted with respect.

2

Uniformly, monotonously the days follow each other—in the morning four hours' teaching, in the afternoon two. But between, all the hours of sitting about, running around, alone with oneself and one's thoughts.

Sundays are worst of all. When one does not want merely to sit in the pub, it is simply unbearable. The headmaster, the only other male teacher besides myself, has been here thirty years, and has made use of his time to become an expert breeder of pigs. He has won many prizes. But beyond that there is nothing one can talk to him about. When I look at him I want to clear out at once ; so dreadful is the thought that some day I shall be like him. There is one woman teacher as well, a worthy, middle-aged creature, but she would have a fit if one were to say " Damn and blast ! " Also not exactly inspiriting.

Willy has settled in much better. He goes as an official personage to all weddings and christenings. When the horses get colic or the cows won't calve, he helps the farmers with his advice and support. And in the evenings he will sit with them in the taverns and fleece them at skat.

But I have no wish now to lounge in the pubs, I prefer to stay in my room. But the hours are long, and strange thoughts often creep out of the corners—pale, wasted hands, beckoning, threatening ; ghostly shadows of things past, but strangely changed ; memories that rise up again, grey, sightless faces, cries and accusations——

One dismal Sunday morning I get up early, put on my things and go to the station to visit Adolf Bethke. This is a good idea—for so I shall sit again with a human being really dear to me, and by the time I get back the dreary Sunday will be over.

I arrive there in the afternoon. The gate creaks, and the dog in his kennel begins to bark. I walk quickly down the path between the fruit trees. Adolf is at home. His wife is there too, but as I enter and shake hands with Adolf she leaves the room. I sit down. We talk, and after a while Adolf says :

" You're surprised, I suppose, Ernst, eh ? "

" How do you mean, Adolf ? "

" Finding her back again."

" No—seems to me that's your affair, Adolf."

He pushes a dish of fruit toward me. " Have an apple ? " I take one and offer him a cigar. He bites off the end, and goes on : " Well, it was this way, Ernst—I sat and sat here, and pretty soon I began to go crazy. When you're alone as I was alone, a house is an awful place. You go around the room. There is one of her blouses still hanging—those are her sewing things—that's the chair she used to sit in and sew.—And then at night, the other bed, so white

220

and deserted beside you ; you look across there every few minutes, you toss and turn over and over, you can't get to sleep—all kinds of things begin to go through your head, Ernst——"

" I can well believe it, Adolf——"

" And then at last you clear out and get tight and do something silly——"

I nod. The clock is ticking. The stove crackles. His wife comes in quietly, puts bread and butter on the table, and goes away again. Bethke smooths his hand over the table-cloth.

" Yes, Ernst. And that's how it was here for her, too. She had to sit about here just like that, all those years. She would lie there, in fear and uncertainty, she brooded and listened—then at last it came. She didn't want it at first, no doubt, but then when once it was there—well, she didn't know how to help herself any more, and so one thing led on to another."

His wife enters bringing coffee. I would like to say Good-day to her, but she does not look at me.

" Won't you bring a cup for yourself, too ? " asks Adolf.

" There is something I must do in the kitchen," she says. She has a soft, deep voice.

" I sat here," resumes Adolf, " and said to myself : ' Well, you've fired her out. You've vindicated your honour.' Then I would think : ' And what comfort does your honour bring you ?—You know it's only a tag. You're alone ; and honour or no honour, it doesn't make that any better.'—So then I told her she could come back.—What the hell does it all matter, anyway ? A man is tired and will only live a few years. If he'd never known, things would have gone

221

on as before. And who can say what would happen if one always knew everything ? "

Adolf plays nervously with his fingers on the arm of his chair. " Have some coffee, Ernst ; and there's butter too."

I fill the cups and we drink.

" You see, Ernst," he says gently, " it's so much easier for you.—You've your books and your education and all the rest of it. But I—I have nothing else, only my wife——"

I say nothing to that, I could not explain it to him. He is no longer the man he was at the Front—nor am I.

" And what does she say about it ? " I ask after a pause.

Adolf lets his hands fall. " She says very little, and one can't get much out of her either—she just sits there and looks at you. At most she only cries. She hardly ever speaks."

He pushes his cup aside. " Once she said it was just to have somebody here. And then again, she says she did not realise—she didn't know she was doing me any harm by it ; it was as if I were there.—But one can't believe that.—Surely it must be possible to discriminate in things of that sort.—She's quite all right otherwise."

I think a while. " Perhaps she means she wasn't quite sure what she was doing at the time—as if she dreamed it, you know. One does dream queer things sometimes, Adolf."

"Maybe," he replies, " but I don't understand it.— It certainly did not go on for long."

" And she doesn't want to have anything more to do with the other fellow ? " I ask.

" She belongs here, that's what she says."

I think it over awhile. What else should one ask?

" And are things any better with you now, Adolf? "

He looks at me. " Not much, Ernst—but then that's not to be wondered at—not as yet. That will all come in time, don't you think so, too? "

He doesn't look as if he quite believes it himself.

" Sure, it'll all come right again some day," I say, and put a few more cigars on the table. We continue to talk a while still, then I go. In the passage I encounter his wife, who makes to pass by me hastily. " Good-bye, Frau Bethke," I say offering to shake hands. " Good-bye," she answers, turning her face away as she gives me her hand.

Adolf comes with me to the station. The wind is blustering. I steal sidelong glances at him as we walk, and remember how he would smile wistfully to himself whenever we would speak of peace out in the trenches there. Now what has come of it all?

The train starts. " Adolf," I say quickly from the window, " I understand you all right—you don't know how well I do understand."

He is going back alone over the fields to his house.

The bell sounds for the ten o'clock play interval. I have just given an hour's lesson to the upper form. The fourteen-year-olds are now charging past me out into the open. I watch them from the window. Within a few seconds they have altered completely ; they have stripped off the discipline of the schoolroom and put on again the freshness and untamedness of their youth.

Seated here on their forms in front of me they are not true to themselves ; there is something either of sneaks and suckers about them, or of shammers and rebels. Seven years of teaching it has needed to bring them to this. Unspoiled by education, frank and unsuspecting as young animals, they came up to school from their meadows, their games and their dreams. The simple law of life was alone valid for them ; the most vital, the most forceful among them was leader, the rest followed him. But little by little with the weekly portions of tuition another, artificial set of values was foisted upon them—he who knew his lesson best was termed excellent and ranked foremost, and the rest must emulate him. Little wonder indeed, if the more vital of them resist it ! But they have to knuckle under, for the ideal of the school is the good scholar. But what an ideal ! What ever came of the good scholars in the world ? In the hot-house of the school they do enjoy a short semblance of life, but only the more surely to sink back afterwards into mediocrity and insignificance. The world has been bettered only by the bad scholars.

I watch them at their games. With vigorous, supple movements they are led on by the curly-headed Dammholt, ruling the whole playground with his energy. His eyes are flashing with courage and eagerness for the assault, all his muscles, his sinews tense, his glance keen, and the rest follow him unhesitatingly. Yet in ten minutes' time, when he is sitting here on the form again, from this same boy will emerge an obdurate, pig-headed little devil who never can do his tasks, and who will surely be left behind again at the next Easter promotions. He will put on a pious face when I look at him, and as soon as my back is turned he will be making grimaces. He will lie like a knave when I ask him if he did his own homework ; and if he gets half a chance he will spit on my breeches or put a drawing-pin on my chair. But the Top Boy, who now cuts such a sorry figure out there on the playground, will swell visibly here in the classroom. Full of conceit and knowledgeableness he will shoot up his hand at every question, while Dammholt sits there and knows nothing, hopeless and furious, awaiting his plucking. The Top Boy knows everything, and even knows that. Yet Dammholt, whom I really should punish, is a thousand times more to my liking than this pale-faced, model boy.

I shrug my shoulders. Haven't I seen something like it before ? At that regimental reunion at Konersmann's ? There also did not the man suddenly count for nothing and his occupation for everything, though before, out at the Front, it had been the other way ? I shake my head. What a world to come back to !

Dammholt's voice goes yelling through the playground. I wonder to myself whether a more comradely attitude on the part of the teacher towards the pupil might not help matters. It might possibly improve the relationship a little and get over a few of the difficulties—but at bottom it would merely be an illusion. Youth is sharp-sighted and incorruptible. It hangs together, and presents an impenetrable front against the grown-ups. ·It is not sentimental ; one may approach to it, but one cannot enter in to it. Who has once been evicted from that paradise can never get back. There is a law of the years. Dammholt with his sharp eyes would cold-bloodedly turn any such cameraderie to his own advantage. He might show even a certain affection, yet that would not prevent him looking to his own interest. Educationalists who think they can understand the young are enthusiasts. Youth does not want to be understood ; it wants only to be let alone. It preserves itself immune against the insidious bacillus of being understood. The grown-up who would approach it too importunately, is as ridiculous in its eyes as if he had put on children's clothes. We may feel with youth, but youth does not feel with us. That is its salvation.

The bell rings. The break is over. Reluctantly Dammholt falls into line before the door.

I stroll out through the village on my way to the moors. Wolf is running ahead of me. A bulldog suddenly rushes out from a neighbouring farm-yard and goes for him. Wolf has not seen it, so that in the first onset the dog manages to get him down. The next instant all is lost in a wild mêlée of dust, threshing bodies and fearsome growls.

The farmer, armed with a cudgel, comes running out of the house. " For God's sake, teacher," he shouts out of the distance, " call your dog off ! Pluto will tear him to pieces."

I take no notice. " Pluto ! Pluto ! You butcher, damn you ! come here ! " he yells excitedly and dashes up all out of breath to beat them apart. But the whirlwind now sweeps off with wild yelpings for another hundred yards, and there the coil begins again.

" He's lost," gasps the farmer lowering his cudgel. " But I tell you right now, I don't pay a farthing. You ought to have called him off ! "

" Who is lost ? " I ask.

" Your dog," returns the farmer respectfully. " That rapscallion of a bulldog has already made cold meat of a dozen of them."

" Well, I don't think we need worry about Wolf," I say. " That's no ordinary sheep dog, I tell you, old timer. He's a war-dog, an old soldier, you know ! "

The dust clears. The dogs have shifted to a grassy patch. I see the bulldog trying to drag Wolf down, so as to get its teeth into the nape of his neck. If he succeeds Wolf is certainly lost, for then it will be a simple matter for the bulldog to break his neck. But now like an eel the sheep dog glides swiftly over the ground, clears the fangs by half an inch, whips round and immediately attacks again. The bulldog is growling and yelping—but Wolf fights without a sound.

" Damn ! " exclaims the farmer.

The bulldog shakes itself, makes a spring, but snaps the empty air—it turns again furiously, springs again, and again shoots by, wide of the mark—one might almost think it was alone, so little is the sheep dog visible. He flies like a cat close over the ground— he learned that as a messenger dog—he slips between the bulldog's legs and goes for it from below. He encircles it, spins round ; then suddenly has his teeth into its belly and holds fast.

The bulldog howls like mad and throws itself on the ground to get him that way. But quick as lightning, with a sudden jerk Wolf lets go and takes his chance to go for its throat. Now for the first time I hear him growl, muffled and dangerous. Now he has his opponent, and holds fast, indifferent to the way the bulldog struggles and rolls about on the ground.

" For God's sake, teacher," shouts the farmer, " call your dog off! He will tear Pluto to pieces ! "

" I might call till the cows came home, but he wouldn't listen now," I tell him. " And a good thing too ! It's high time your bloody Pluto was shown something."

The bulldog yelps and howls. The farmer raises his cudgel to go to his help. I wrench the thing from him, seize him by the front of his jacket, and shout angrily : " What the hell ! Your damned mongrel started it ! " It would not need much and I should be going for the farmer myself.

But from where I stand I see that Wolf has suddenly let go the bulldog and is rushing toward us, imagining that I am being attacked. So I am luckily able to intercept him, else the farmer would soon be needing a new coat, to say the least of it.

Pluto in the meantime has made off. I pat Wolf on the neck and soothe him down. " He's a devil, no mistake ! " stammers the farmer, quite crestfallen.

" Too right he is," I say with pride, " that's the old soldier in him. It doesn't do to make trouble with that breed."

We go on our way. Beyond the village are a few meadows, then begins the moor with its junipers and ancient burial mounds. Near the birch wood a flock of sheep is grazing, and their woolly backs glow golden under the light of the descending sun.

Suddenly I see Wolf make off at full tilt toward the flock. Imagining that the fight with the bulldog has made him wild, I dash after him to prevent a massacre among the sheep. " Hey ! Look out for the dog ! " I shout to the shepherd.

He laughs. "He's only a sheep dog, he won't do anything!"

"Won't he though!" I shout back. "You don't know him. He's a war-dog!"

"What's it matter?" says the shepherd. "War-dog or no war-dog, he's all right."

"There, see!—just look at him! Good! good dog! go for 'em. Fetch 'em in!"

I can hardly believe my eyes. Wolf—Wolf, who has never seen a sheep in his life before, is now driving the flock as if he had never done anything else! With long bounds he sweeps off barking after two straggling lambs and drives them back. Every time they want to stand still or to go off at a tangent, he bars their way and snaps at their heels so that they run on again straight ahead.

"Tip top!" says the shepherd, "he's only nipping them, couldn't be better!"

The dog seems transfigured. His eyes sparkle, his tattered ear flaps as he circles watchfully round the flock, and I can see he is immensely excited.

"I'll buy him from you right now," says the shepherd. "My own can't do it better than that. Just look now, how he is heading them home to the village! He hasn't a thing to learn."

I am quite beside myself. "Wolf," I cry, "Wolf," and could shout for joy to see him. He grew up out there among the shells and yet now, without anyone ever having shown him a thing, he knows what his job is!

"I'll give you five pounds down for him, and a sheep ready killed into the bargain," says the shepherd.

I shake my head. "You couldn't have him for a million, man," I retort.

Now it is the shepherd who is shaking his head.

The harsh spikes of the heather tickle my face. I bend them aside and rest my head on my arm. The dog is breathing quietly beside me and out of the distance sounds faintly the tinkle of sheep bells. Otherwise all is still.

Clouds float slowly over the evening sky. The sun goes down. The dark green of the juniper bushes turns to a deep brown and I perceive the night wind rise up lightly out of the distant woods. Within the hour it will be playing here among the birches. Soldiers are as familiar with the country as farmers and foresters ; they have not lived in rooms. They know the times of the wind and the yellow-brown, cinnamon haze of the gathering evening ; they know the shadows that ride over the ground when clouds hide the sun, and the ways of the moon.

In Flanders once after a fierce bombardment, it was long before help could come up for one of our men who had been wounded. We put all our field-dressings on him and bandaged him as best we could, but it was no use; he still bled on, just bled away to death. And behind him all the while stood an immense cloud in the evening sky—a solitary cloud—but it was a great mountain of white, golden and red splendour. Unsubstantial and lofty it towered up over the shattered brown of the landscape. It was quite still and it glowed, and the dying man was quite still and he bled, as if the two belonged together ; and yet to me it was incomprehensible that the cloud stood there so lovely and unconcerned in the sky while a man died.

The last light of the sun has tinged the heather

to a dusky red. Plovers rise complaining on unstable wing. The cry of a bittern sounds up from the lake. I still gaze out over the wide, purple-brown plain. There was a place near Houthoulst where so many poppies grew in the fields that it was entirely red with them. We called it the Fields of Blood, because whenever there was a thunderstorm it would take on the pale colour of fresh, newly spilled blood. It was there Köhler went mad one clear night as we marched by, utterly wasted and weary. In the uncertain light of the moon he thought he saw whole lakes of blood and wanted to plunge in——

I shiver and look up.—What does this mean? Why do these memories come so often now? And so strangely, and so differently from out there at the Front? Am I too much alone?

Wolf stirs and barks quite loudly, though gently, in his sleep. Is he dreaming of his flock, I wonder? I look at him a long time. Then I wake him and we go back.

It is Saturday. I go over to Willy and ask him if he will come into town with me over Sunday. But he dismisses the idea altogether. "We're having stuffed goose to-morrow," says he. "I can't possibly leave that in the lurch. What do you want to go away for?"

"I can't stick Sundays here," I say.

"I don't understand that," he objects, "not considering the grub!"

So I set off alone. In the evening, vaguely hoping for something, I go out to Waldman's. Here is immense activity. I stand about and look on for a while. A mob of young fellows who missed the war by a hair, is swilling about and about on the dance-floor. These are sure of themselves, they know what they want. Their world has had a clear beginning, it has a definite goal—success. And though younger than we, they are much more accomplished.

Among the dancers I discover the dainty little seamstress with whom I won the prize for the one-step. I ask her to dance and after that we remain together. I had my pay only a few days ago, and on the strength of it I now order a couple of bottles of a sweet, red wine. We drink it slowly, but the more I drink the more I sink into a strange moodiness.—What was it Albert said about having somebody all to oneself?—I listen pensively to the chatter of the girl as she twitters like a swallow of the other seamstresses, about the pay for making underclothing, about new dances and a thousand other nothings. If only the pay would go up by a couple of pence a piece, she would be able to lunch in a restaurant, and then she would be happy. I envy her her simple existence and ask her more and more questions. I should like to ask everyone who is here so laughing and gay, how he lives. Perhaps among them is one who could tell me something that would help me.

Afterwards I go home with the Swallow. She lives in a grey block of tenements, high up under the roof. We stand a while at the door. I feel the warmth of her hand in mine. Her face glimmers uncertain in the darkness. A human face, a hand, wherein is warmth and life. "Let me go with you!" I say hastily. "Let me come in——"

Cautiously we steal up the creaking stairs. I strike a match but she blows it out immediately, and taking me by the hand, leads me after her.

A little narrow room. A table, a brown sofa, a

bed, a few pictures on the wall ; in the corner a sewing-machine, a lay-figure of bamboo, and a basket of white linen to be sewn.

The little girl promptly produces a primus and brews tea of apple-peelings and tea-leaves that have been ten times boiled and dried out again. Two cups, a laughing, slightly mischievous face, a disturbing little blue dress, the friendly poverty of lodgings, and a little Swallow, its youth its only possession—I sit down on the sofa. Is this how love begins ? So light and playfully ? Is that all it needs, just to jump over oneself and away ?——

The little Swallow is fond. It belongs, of course, to her life that someone should come here, take her in his arms, and then go away again. Then the sewing-machine drones, another comes, the Swallow laughs, the Swallow weeps, and sews away for ever.— She casts a gay coverlet over the sewing-machine, thereby transforming it from a nickel and steel creature of toil into a hillock of red and blue silk flowers. She does not want to be reminded now of the day. In her light, soft dress she nestles down in my arms, she chatters, she whispers and murmurs and sings. So slender and pale—half-starved she is, too —and so light that one can easily carry her to the bed, the iron camp-bed. Such a sweet air of surrender as she clings about one's neck ! She sighs and she smiles—a child with closed eyes, sighs and trembles and stammers a little bit. She breathes deep and she utters small cries. I look at her. I look again and again. I too would be so. Silently I ask : Is this it ? Is this it ?—And the Swallow names me with all kinds of fair names, and is embarrassed and tender and nestles close to me. And as I leave her I ask :

" Are you happy, little Swallow ? " Then she kisses me many times and makes faces and waves and nods and nods——

But I go down the stairs and am full of wonder. She is happy !—How easily ! I cannot understand. For is she not still another being, a life unto herself, to whom I can never come ? Would she not still be so, though I came with all the fires of love ? Ach, love—it is a torch falling into an abyss, revealing nothing but only how deep it is !

I set off down the street to the station.—No, this is not it ; this is not it either. One is only more alone here than ever——

3

The lamp casts a circle of light upon the table. Before me is a pile of blue exercise books, and alongside a bottle of red ink. I look through the note-books, mark the mistakes, lay the blotting-papers inside and clap them to.

I stand up. Is this life, then ? This dreary uniformity of days and lessons ? But how empty it leaves all the background ! There is left still much too much time to think. I hoped the routine would quiet me, but it only makes me more restless.—How long the evenings are here !

I go across to the barn. The cows snuff and stamp in the gloom. Beside them on low stools squat the milkmaids, each in a little room to herself, the walls formed by the black and white bodies of the animals. Small lanterns are flickering over them in the warm air of the stall, the milk spurts in thin streams into the buckets and the breasts of the girls joggle beneath their blue cotton blouses. They lift their heads and smile and breathe and show sound, white teeth. Their eyes shine in the darkness, and there is a smell of cattle and hay.

I stand a while at the door, then go back to my room. The blue note-books still lie under the lamp. Will they always lie so? And I? Shall I always sit there, till little by little I grow old and at last die? I decide to go to bed.

The red moon climbs slowly up over the roof of the barn and casts an image of the window on the floor, a diamond and a cross within it, that becomes gradually more and more askew the higher the moon rises. In an hour it has crept on to my bed, and the shadowed cross is moving over my breast.

I lie in the big, peasant bed with its cover of red and blue squares, and cannot sleep. Sometimes my eyes close, and I sink down whizzing through limitless space—but at the last moment a sudden, bounding fear jolts me back into wakefulness, and again I am listening to the church clock as it strikes the hours. I listen and wait and toss to and fro.

At last I get up and dress again. I climb through the window, lift out the dog and go off to the moor. The moon is shining, the wind blows gently and the plain stretches away. The railway embankment cuts darkly across it.

I sit down under a juniper bush. After a time I see the chain of signal-lamps light up along the track. The night train is coming. The rails begin to rumble softly, metallic. The headlight of the locomotive leaps up over the skyline, driving a billow of light before it toward me. The train roars past with bright windows ; for one moment, scarce a breath, the compartments with their trunks and their fates are right close to me ; they sweep onward ; the rails gleam again with wet light and out of the distance now stares only the red rear-lamp of the train, like a glowing evil eye.

I watch the moon turn clear, then yellow. I walk through the blue twilight of the birch woods ; rain-drops spill down from the branches into my neck ; I stumble over roots and on stones, and when I return the leaden dawn has come. The lamp is still burning —desperately I glance round the room—no, I cannot stick this ! I should need to be twenty years older to be so resigned——

Weary and spent I begin to undress. It is too much trouble. As I go off to sleep my hands are still pressed together—I will not give up—I will not give up yet——

Then again I sink down through limitless space——

——and cautiously worm my way out. Slowly, one inch, and then another. The sun is burning on the golden slopes, the broom is in flower, the air hot and still ; observation balloons and white wind-clouds hang on the horizon. The red petals of a poppy flower rock to and fro before my steel helmet.

A very faint, hardly audible scratching comes across to me from beyond the brambles ahead. It is silent again. I wait on. A beetle with greenish-gold wings crawls up a camomile stalk in front of me. His feelers are groping over the jagged leaves. Again a light rustling in the noonday silence. The rim of a helmet shows over the bushes. A forehead, clear eyes, a firm mouth—searchingly the eyes move over the landscape and return again to a pad of white paper and some crayons. Quite unsuspecting of danger, the man is making a pastel of the farm yonder and the dark copper-beeches in the quivering air——

I drag the hand-grenade toward me. It takes a long time. At last it is lying beside me. With my left hand I pull the button and count under my breath ; then send the bomb flying in a low curve to the blackberry bushes and slip back swiftly into my hollow. I press my body close down on the earth, bury my face in the grass and open my mouth.

The crash of the explosion tears the air, splinters twanging—a cry goes up, long drawn, frantic with horror. I hold the second bomb in my hand and peer out from my cover. The Englishman is lying clear in the open field ; his two legs are blown off at the knee, the blood is pouring out ; the bands of his puttees far unrolled trail out behind him like loose ribbons ; he is lying on his belly, with his arms he paddles the grass ; his mouth is wide open, shrieking.

He heaves himself round and sees me. Then he props himself on his arms and rears his trunk like a seal, he shrieks at me and bleeds, bleeds. The red face grows pale and sinks in, the gaze snaps, and eyes and mouth are at last no more than black caverns in a swiftly decaying countenance, that slowly inclines to the earth, sags and sinks into the dandelions. Finished.

I worm myself off and begin to work my way back to our trenches. But I look round once more. The dead man has suddenly come to life again ! he straightens up as if he meant to run after me ! I pull the string of the second hand-grenade and hurl it toward him. It falls a yard short, rolls on, and lies still. I count, count—why doesn't it explode ? The dead man is standing upright ; he is showing his teeth ! I throw the next hand-grenade—it, too, misses fire. He has made a few steps already—he is running on his stumps, grinning, his arms stretched out toward me—I hurl my last hand-grenade. It goes flying to his chest, he wards it off. I jump up to run, but my knees refuse to work, they are soft as butter. Endlessly, painfully I drag them forward ; I stick fast to the ground ; I wrench, I hurl myself forward. Already I hear the panting of my pursuer. I drag my failing legs with my hands. But from behind me two hands close round my neck, they bear me backwards, to the ground. The dead man is kneeling on my chest ; he hauls in the puttees trailing out behind him over the grass ; he twists them round my neck. I bend my head away, I brace all my muscles, I fling myself to the right to escape the noose—ah ! a jerk, a strangling pain in the throat. The dead man is dragging me toward the precipitous edge of the chalk-pit. He is rolling me down into it, I lose balance, struggle to catch hold—I am slipping, I fall, cry out, fall endlessly, cry, hit something, cry——

Darkness comes away in great clods under my clutching hands. With a crash something falls down beside me. I strike upon stones, on sharp corners, iron ; I shriek uncontrollably, swift wild yelling, I cannot stop. Shoutings, clutchings at my arms. I beat them off ; somebody trips over me. I snatch a rifle, grope for cover ; I wrench the weapon to my shoulder, pull the trigger, still yelling. Then suddenly, like a knife, it pierces the uproar. " Birkholz "—again—" Birkholz "—I jump up. That's help coming ! I must cut my way through ! I wrench free, I run. A blow on my knee, and I fall into a soft hollow, into light, shrill, stabbing light—" Birkholz "—" Birkholz "—now nothing but my own cry like a spear in space. Suddenly it breaks.

The farmer and his wife are standing before me. I am lying half on the bed and half on the floor. The farmer beside me is picking himself up. I am desperately clutching a walking-stick in my hand, as if it were a rifle. I must be bleeding somewhere—then I see it is only the dog licking my hand.

" Teacher ! " says the farmer's wife trembling. " Teacher ! whatever is the matter ? "

I understand nothing. " How have I got here ? " I ask in a gruff voice.

" But teacher—wake up—you've been dreaming."

" Dreaming," I say. " You think I could have dreamed that ! " Suddenly I burst out laughing, laughing, shrill, it racks me, shrieks of laughter, that it pains me, laughter——

Then the laughter in me suddenly dies. " It was the English captain," I whisper. " The one—— "

The farmer is busily rubbing his bruised arm. " You were dreaming, teacher, and fell out of bed," he is saying. " You wouldn't listen to anything, and you nearly murdered me—— "

I do not understand him. I am utterly spent and forlorn. Then I see the stick in my hand. I put it away and sit down on the bed. The dog pushes in between my knees.

But I do not lie down again. I wrap myself in a blanket and sit at the table. The light I leave burning.

And so I sit a long while, motionless and with absent gaze, as only soldiers can sit when they are alone. After a time I begin to be disturbed and have a feeling as if someone else were in the room. Slowly, how slowly! without effort, I feel sight and perception returning to my eyes. I raise my eyelids a trifle and see that I am sitting directly opposite the mirror that hangs over the little wash-stand. From its slightly wavy surface there looks out at me a face with dark shadows and black eye-hollows. My face——

I get up and take down the mirror and put it away in a corner, glass to the wall.

Morning comes. I go to my class. There sit the little ones with folded arms. In their eyes is still all the shy astonishment of the childish years. They look up at me so trustingly, so believingly—and suddenly I get a spasm over the heart.

Here I stand before you, one of the hundreds of thousands of bankrupt men in whom the war destroyed every belief and almost every strength. Here I stand before you, and see how much more alive, how much more rooted in life you are than I. Here I stand and must now be your teacher and guide. What should I teach you? Should I tell you that in twenty years you will be dried-up and crippled, maimed in your freest impulses, all pressed mercilessly into the self-same mould? Should I tell you that all learning, all culture, all science is nothing but hideous mockery, so long as mankind makes war in the name of God and humanity with gas, iron, explosive and fire? What should I teach you then, you little creatures who alone have remained unspotted by the terrible years?

What am I able to teach you? Should I tell you how to pull the string of a hand-grenade, how best to throw it at a human being? Should I show you how to stab a man with a bayonet, how to fell him with a club, how to slaughter him with a spade? Should I demonstrate how best to aim a rifle at such an incomprehensible miracle as a breathing breast, a living heart? Should I explain to you what tetanus is, what a broken spine is, and what a shattered skull? Should I describe to you how brains look when they spatter about, what crushed bones are like, and intestines when they pour out? Should I mimic how a man with a stomach-wound will groan, how one with a lungwound gurgles and one with a head-wound whistles? More I do not know. More I have not learned.

Should I take you to the green-and-grey map there, move my finger across it and tell you that here love was murdered? Should I explain to you that the books you hold in your hands are but nets with which men design to snare your simple souls, to entangle you in the undergrowth of fine phrases, and in the barbed wire of falsified ideas?

I stand here before you, a polluted, a guilty man and can only implore you ever to remain as you are, never to suffer the bright light of your childhood to be misused as a blow-flame of hate. About your brows still blows the breath of innocence. How then should I presume to teach you? Behind me, still pursuing, are the bloody years. How then can I venture among you? Must I not first become a man again myself?

I feel a cramp begin to spread through me, as if I were turning to stone, as if I were crumbling away. I lower myself slowly into the chair, and now know that I cannot stay here any longer. I try to take hold of something but cannot. Then, after a time that has seemed to me endless, the catalepsy relaxes. I stand up. "Children," I say with difficulty, "you may go now. There will be no school to-day."

The little ones look at me to make sure I am not joking. I nod once again. "Yes, that is right—go and play to-day—the whole day—go and play in the woods—or with your dogs and your cats—you need not come back till to-morrow——"

With a clatter they toss their pencil-boxes into their satchels, and twittering and breathless they scurry off.

I pack up my things and go over to the neighbouring village to take leave of Willy. He is leaning out of the window in his shirt-sleeves, practising on the fiddle *In the merry month of May all things are renewed.* A huge supper is spread out on the table.

"My third to-day," he says gaily. "You know, I find I can eat now like a camel, from pure foresight."

I tell him that I mean to quit this evening. Willy is not a man to ask questions. "Well, Ernst," he says thoughtfully, " it certainly is slow here, I admit— but so long as they keep feeding me like this," he points to the table, " not ten horses will drag me out of this Pestalozzi horse-box."

Thereupon he hauls out from under the sofa a large case of bottled beer. "High frequency," he beams, and holds the label up to the lamp.

I look at him a long while. "Ah, Willy, I wish I were like you ! "

" I can believe it," he grins and a cork pops.

As I go to the station, a couple of little girls with smeary mouths and flying hair-ribbons come running out from the neighbouring house. They have just been burying a dead mole in the garden, so they tell me, and have said a prayer for him. Then they curtsy and shake hands with me. " Good-bye, Herr Teacher."

PART VI

I

"ERNST, I must speak with you a moment," says my father.

I can guess what is coming. For days he has been going about with an anxious air dropping hints. But I have always escaped him until now, for I am not often at home.

We go to my room. He sits down on the sofa and looks uncomfortable. "We are worried about your future, Ernst." I produce a box of cigars from the bookcase and offer them to him. His face brightens a little, they are good cigars. I had them from Karl, and Karl smokes no beech-leaf.

"Have you really given up your position as a teacher?" he asks. I nod.

"And why did you do that, may I ask?"

I shrug my shoulders. How should I even begin to explain it to him? We are two utterly different men and have got along well together thus far, only because we have not understood one another at all.

"And what do you propose doing now?" he goes on.

"Oh, anything," I say. "It's all one to me."

He looks at me shocked, and begins to talk about a good and respected calling, about getting on and making a place in life for myself. I listen to him sympathetically but am bored. How strange that this man on the sofa here should be the father who formerly regulated my life! Yet he was not able to look after me in the years out there; he could not even have helped me in the barracks—any N.C.O. there carried more weight than he. I had to get through as best as I could by myself, and it was a matter of entire indifference whether he existed or not.

When he has finished I pour him out a glass of cognac. "Now listen, father," I say, and sit down over against him, "you may be right in what you say. But you see, I have learned how to live in a hole in the ground on a crust of bread and a little drop of thin soup. And so long as there was no shelling I was quite content. An old hut seemed to me to be positive luxury, and a straw mattress in the rest area was paradise. So you see, the mere fact that I am still alive and that there is no shelling, is enough for me for the moment. What little I need to eat and drink I can rake together all right; for the rest there is my whole life before me."

"Yes," he objects, "but that is no life, a bare hand to mouth existence like that——"

"Every man to his taste," I say. "To me it would seem no life to be able to say at the finish that I had entered every day for thirty years the same schoolroom or the same office."

Rather astonished he replies: "It's twenty years now that I have been going to the carton factory, yet I have always contrived to be my own master."

"I don't want to contrive to be anything, father, all I want is to live."

"And I have lived, and uprightly and respectably, too," he says with an accession of pride. "It wasn't for nothing I was elected to the Chamber of Commerce."

"Then be thankful that you have had it so easy," I retort.

"But you must do something, you know," he complains.

"I can get a job for the present with one of my army pals ; as a matter of fact he has already offered me one," I say. "That will bring in all I need."

He shakes his head. "And for that you would give up a good civil-service job ! "

"I have often had to give up things before now, father."

He puffs away at his cigar distressfully. "And even assured of a pension, too ! "

"Ach," I say laughing, "where's the soldier will live to see sixty ? There are things in our bones that will only show themselves later. We'll all have packed up before then, don't you worry." With the best will in the world I cannot believe I shall reach sixty. I have seen too many men die at twenty.

I smoke away thoughtfully and look at my father. I still see that this is my father, but I can see too that he is just a kindly, somewhat older man, rather cautious and pedantic, whose views have no longer any meaning for me. I can quite well picture what he would have been at the Front—somebody would always have had to be looking after him one way or another, and he would certainly never have become an N.C.O.

I go to see Ludwig. He is sitting amid a pile of pamphlets and books. I should like to talk with him about many things that are troubling me ; I have a feeling that he might perhaps be able to show me the road. But he himself is disturbed and agitated to-day. We talk a while aimlessly of this and of that, then at last he says : "I must go to the doctor now——"

"The dysentery still ? " I ask.

" No—something else."

" Why, what's the matter now, Ludwig? " I ask in surprise.

He is silent a while. His lips quiver. Then he says :
" I don't know."

" Like me to come with you ? I haven't anything particular to do——"

He hunts for his cap. " Yes, do come."

As we walk he takes occasional stealthy, sidelong looks at me. We turn down Linden Street and go in at a house that has a small cheerless front garden with a few miserable shrubs in it. I read the white enamel plate on the door : *Dr. Friedrich Schultz, Specialist in Skin, Urinary and Sexual Diseases*. I stand still. " What's up, then, Ludwig ? "

He turns a pale face toward me. " Nothing much, Ernst. I had a sort of a boil out there once, and it's come back again now."

" Oh, why if that's all it is, Ludwig," I say relieved, " you should have seen some of the carbuncles I've had ! As big as a baby's head, some of them. Comes from all this substitute food muck we've had."

We ring the bell. A sister in a white overall opens to us. We are both terribly embarrassed and with faces like beetroots go into the waiting-room. There, God be thanked ! we are alone. On the table is a litter of numbers of the magazine, *Die Woche*. We turn the pages. They are rather ancient. They have only just reached the Peace of Brest-Litowsk, here.

The doctor comes in, spectacles flashing. The door into the consulting-room stands half open behind him, and one can see a chair there made of nickel piping and leather, dreadfully practical and painful looking.

It's queer that so many doctors should have a

preference for treating their patients as if they were children ! With dentists of course it is part of the regular training ; it would appear to be so with this sort here, too.

"Well, Mr. Breyer," says the bespectacled cobra playfully, "so we are to become a little better acquainted shortly ! "

Ludwig stands there like a ghost and swallows hard. "Is it——"

The doctor nods encouragingly. "Yes, the blood test is back. Positive. Now we must really begin to talk to the old rascal severely."

"Positive," stammers Ludwig, "then that means ——"

"Yes," answers the doctor, "we must make a little cure."

"Then that means, I've got syphilis ? "

"Yes."

A blow-fly buzzes through the room and bumps against the window. Time has stopped. The soggy air sticks fast between the walls. The world has changed. An awful fear has turned to an awful certainty.

"Can there not be a mistake ? " asks Ludwig. "Couldn't they make a second blood test ? "

The doctor shakes his head. "It is better we should start the cure soon. The stage is secondary."

Ludwig gulps. "Is it curable ? "

The doctor becomes animated. His face is almost jovial with reassurance.

"Absolutely ! These little tubes here, all we do is to inject them for a period of, let us say, six months to begin with. Then we shall see. Perhaps hardly anything more will be necessary. Oh yes, syphilis is quite curable these days."

Syphilis—revolting word !—sounds as if it were a thin black snake.

" Did you get it out at the Front ? " asks the doctor. Ludwig nods.

" Why didn't you have it treated at once ? "

" I didn't know what it was. No one ever told us about these things before. And it only showed itself a long time after, and seemed harmless enough. Then it went away again of itself."

The doctor shakes his head. " Yes, that is the reverse side of the medal," he says glibly.

I would like to bash him one over the head with a chair. A lot he knows what it means to get three days' leave to Brussels, to come by the night train straight from shell-holes and slush and filth and blood into a city with streets, lamps, lights, shops and women ; where there are fine hotel-rooms and white bath-tubs, and a man can soak himself and scour off all the dirt ; where is soft music, and terraces and cool, rich wine ! A lot he knows of the enchantment that is in the blue, misty twilight of such a little moment between horror and horror—a rift in the clouds it is, a wild outcry of life in the brief interval between death and death ! Who knows but that in a few days he may be hanging on the barbed-wire, with torn limbs, bellowing, thirsting, perishing ? Yet one more swig of this heavy wine, yet one more breath, one glimpse more into this insubstantial world of moving colour, dreams, women, inflaming whispers, words, under whose spell the blood turns to a black fountain ; under whose touch the years of filth and madness and hopelessness resolve and change to sweet, singing eddies of memory and hope. To-morrow death will rush in again with his guns, hand-grenades, flame-throwers, blood and annihilation—but to-day, this soft skin, fragrant and calling as life itself. What intoxicating shadows upon the shoulders, what soft arms! It crackles and flashes and bursts and pours down, the sky burns. Who will think then that in such whispering charm, in such fragrance, such skin, that other thing, syphilis, may be in ambush, watching, hidden, crouching, waiting? Who knows, and who wants to know, who thinks then of anything but of to-day? to-morrow? why to-morrow it may all be over. Bloody war! that taught us to recognise only the moment and to have it.

" And now? " asks Ludwig.

" Let us begin as soon as we can."

" At once then," says Ludwig quietly. He goes with the doctor to the consulting-room.

I remain in the waiting-room, where I occupy myself tearing up a few numbers of *Die Woche*, in which is figured nothing but parades, and victories and pithy sayings of war-intoxicated clergymen.

Ludwig comes back. " Go and see another doctor, Ludwig," I whisper to him. " I'm sure this fellow doesn't know his job. He hasn't any brain." Ludwig makes a tired gesture and we go down the stairs in silence. At the bottom, with averted face he says suddenly : " Well, good-bye——"

I look up. He is leaning against the railing and his fists are clenched in his pockets.

" What's wrong? " I ask, rather startled.

" I am going now," he answers.

" Well, give us your paw, can't you? " I say mystified. With trembling lips he protests : " But you mustn't touch me now, now I've——"

Shy and slim there he stands by the railing—just as he would lean against the parados, with sad face and owered eyes. "Ach, Ludwig! Ludwig! what rot will you say next? Not touch you! you old fathead, you silly ass! touch you? there, I touch you, a hundred times I touch you"—it has so hurt me, blast it! now I am blubbing, damned fool! and I put my arm about his shoulder and press him to me, and I feel how he is trembling—"Ach, Ludwig, that's all bunk, and anyway, I may have it myself, for all I know. You just keep calm now, and that goggle-eyed old snake up there will soon put you right again." But he trembles and trembles, and I hold him fast.

2

Demonstrations in the streets have been called for this afternoon. Prices have been soaring everywhere for months past, and the poverty is greater even than it was during the war. Wages are insufficient to buy the bare necessities of life, and even though one may have the money it is often impossible to buy anything with it. But ever more and more gin-palaces and dance-halls go up, and ever more and more blatant is the profiteering and swindling.

Scattered groups of workers out on strike trail through the streets. Now and again there is a disturbance. A rumour is going about that troops have been concentrated at the barracks. But there is no sign of it as yet.

Here and there one hears cries, and counter cries. Somebody is haranguing at a street corner. Then suddenly everywhere is silence.

A procession of men in the faded uniforms of the front-line trenches is moving slowly toward us.

It is formed up by sections, marching in fours. Big white placards are carried in front: *Where is the Fatherland's gratitude? The War Cripples are starving.*

The men with one arm are carrying the placards, and they look round continually to see if the procession is still coming along properly behind them, for they are the fastest.

These are followed by men with sheep dogs on short, leather leads. The animals have the red cross of the blind at their collars. Watchfully they walk along beside their masters. If the procession halts they sit down, and then the blind men stop. Sometimes dogs off the street will rush in among the column, barking and wagging their tails, wanting to romp and play with them. But these merely turn their heads and take no notice of all the sniffing and yapping. Yet their ears are erect, pricked and alert, and their eyes are alive; but they walk as if they no longer wished to run and to jump, as if they understood for what they are there. They have separated themselves from their fellows, as Sisters of Mercy separate themselves from jolly shop girls. Nor do the other dogs persist long: after a few minutes they give up, and make off in such haste that it looks almost as if they were flying from something. Only a powerful mastiff stands still, and with front legs widely straddling, barks slowly, deep and hollow, till the procession is past.

It is strange how a face without eyes alters—how in the upper half it becomes extinct, smooth and dead, and how odd the mouth is in comparison, when it speaks: only the lower half of the face lives. All these have been shot blind; and so they behave differently from men born blind. They are more violent, and at the same time more cautious, in their gestures that have not yet gained the sureness of many years of darkness. The memory of colours, of sky, earth and twilight still lives with them. They move still as if they had eyes, involuntarily they lift and turn their heads to see who it is that speaks to them. Some have black patches or bandages over their eyes, but most go without them, as if by that means they would stand nearer to colours and the light. Their eyelids are withered and closed—only the narrow strip of the lower lid still protrudes a little, blotched, wet and red like a dim, cheerless dawn. Many of them are healthy, powerful fellows with strong limbs that would like well to move freely and have play. The pale sunset of the March sky gleams behind their bowed heads. In shop windows the first lamps are being lighted. But they hardly feel the mild, sweet air of evening on their brow. In their heavy boots they move slowly through the everlasting darkness that stretches about them like a cloud ; and troubled and persistent, their thoughts clamber up and down the meagre scale of figures that would mean bread and comfort and life to them, and yet cannot be. Hunger and penury stir idly in the darkened rooms of their mind. Helpless and full of dull fear they sense their nearness ; yet they cannot see them nor do aught against them but to walk slowly in their numbers through the streets, lifting up their dead faces from the darkness toward the light, in dumb appeal to others, who can still see, that they should see.

Behind the blind come the men with one eye, the tattered faces of men with head-wounds, wry, bulbous mouths, faces without noses and without lower jaws, entire faces one great red scar with a couple of holes in it where formerly were a mouth and a nose. But above this desolation quiet, questioning, sad human eyes.

On these follow the long lines of men with legs amputated. Some already have artificial limbs that spring forward obliquely as they walk and strike clanking on the pavement, as if the whole man were artificial, made up of iron and hinges. Others have their trouser-legs looped up and made fast with safety-pins. These go on crutches or sticks with black rubber pads.

Then come the shakers, the shell-shocked. Their hands, their heads, their clothes, their bodies quake, as though they still shuddered with horror. They no longer have control of themselves, the will has been extinguished, the muscles and nerves have revolted against the brain, the eyes become void and impotent.

One-eyed and one-armed men are pushing along wicker carriages with oilcloth covers, wherein are other men, so badly wounded that they can now only live in wheeled-chairs. Among them come a few men trailing a flat hand-cart, such as carpenters use to transport bedsteads or coffins. On it there sits a torso. The legs are gone from the hips. It is the upper half of a powerful man, nothing more. He has broad, stalwart shoulders, and a big, brave face with a heavy moustache. On his head he wears a peaked cap. It may be that he was formerly a furniture remover. Beside him is a placard with wobbly lettering that he has, no doubt, painted himself: *I should like to walk too, mate.* With solemn face he sits there ; now and then, supporting himself on his arms, he will swing a little farther up the wagon so as to change his seat.

A young, pale fellow without arms, and legs amputated at the knees, follows after him. The knees stand in thick, leather wrappings like great hooves. It looks so odd that one involuntarily glances under the wagon, as if the legs must surely carry on there beneath it. In his arm-stumps he carries a placard : *Many thousands of us are still lying in the hospitals.*

The procession drags slowly along the streets. Wherever it passes all is still. Once, at the corner of Hook Street, it has to wait a long time. A new dance palace is being erected there, and the street is blocked with heaps of sand, cement-mixers and girders. Between the struts over the entrance is the name in illuminated letters : *Astoria Dance-Palace and Wine Saloon.* The trolley with the torso stands directly beneath it, waiting until some iron girders have been shifted. The dull glow of the lighted sign floods over him, colouring the silent face to an awful red, as if it were swelling with some terrible fury and must suddenly burst into a hideous cry.

But then the column moves on, and again it is just the face of the furniture remover, pallid from the hospital in the pale evening, and smiling gratefully as a comrade puts a cigarette between his lips. Quietly the groups pass on through the streets, without cries, without indignation, resigned—a complaint, not an accusation. They know that those who can shoot no more need not expect over-much help. They will go on to the Town Hall and stand there a while ; some secretary or other will say something to them, then they will break up and return singly to their rooms, their narrow dwellings, their pale children and their awful misery, without much hope, prisoners of the destiny that others made for them.

The later it gets the more disturbed the city becomes. I go with Albert through the streets. Men are standing in groups at every corner. Rumours are flying. It is said that the military have already fired on a procession of demonstrating workers.

From the neighbourhood of St. Mary's Church comes suddenly the sound of rifle shots, at first singly, then a whole volley. Albert and I look at each other; without a word we set off in the direction of the shots.

Ever more and more people come running toward us. "Bring rifles! the bastards are shooting!" they shout. We quicken our pace. We wind in and out of the groups, we shove our way through, we are running already—a grim, perilous excitement impels us forward. We are gasping. The racket of rifle-fire increases. "Ludwig!" I shout.

He is running beside us. His lips are pressed tight, the jaw bones stand out, his eyes are cold and tense—once more he has the face of the trenches. Albert too. I also. We run toward the rifle shots, as if it were some mysterious, imperative summons.

The crowd, still shouting, gives way before us. We plough our way through. Women hold their aprons over their faces and go stumbling away. A roar of fury goes up. A wounded man is being carried off.

We reach the Market Square. There the Reichwehr has taken up a position in front of the Town Hall. The steel helmets gleam palely. On the steps is a machine-gun ready for action. The square is empty; only the streets that lead into it are jammed with people. It would be madness to go farther—the machine-gun is covering the square.

But one man is going out, all alone! Behind him the seething crowd surges on down the conduits of the streets; it boils out about the houses and gathers together in black clots.

But the man is far in advance. In the middle of the square he steps out from the shadow thrown by the church and stands in the moonlight—" Back ! " calls a clear, sharp voice.

The man is lifting his hands. So bright is the moonlight that when he starts to speak his teeth show white and gleaming in the dark hole of his mouth. " Comrades——" All is silence.

His voice is alone between the church, the great block of the Town Hall and the shadow. It is alone on the square, a fluttering dove. " Comrades, put up your weapons ! Would you shoot at your brothers ? Put up your weapons and come over to us."

Never was the moon so bright. The uniforms on the Town Hall steps are like chalk. The windows glisten. The moonlit half of the church tower is a mirror of green silk. With gleaming helmets and visors the stone knights by the doorway spring forward from the wall of shadow.

" Back ! or we fire ! " comes the command coldly. I look round at Ludwig and Albert. It was our company commander ! That was Heel's voice. A choking tension grips me, as if I must now look on at an execution. Heel will fire—I know.

The dark mass of people moves within the shadow of the houses, it sways and murmurs. An eternity goes by. Two soldiers with rifles detach themselves from the steps and make toward the solitary man in the midst of the square. It seems endlessly long before they reach him—as though they marked time in some grey morass, glittering, tinselled rag puppets with loaded, lowered rifles. The man awaits them quietly. " Comrades——" he says again as they come up.

They grab him by the arms and drag him forward.

The man does not defend himself. They run him along so fast that he stumbles. Cries break out behind us. The mob is beginning to move, an entire street moving slowly, irregularly forward. The clear voice commands : " Quick ! back with him ! I fire ! "

A warning volley crackles out upon the air. Suddenly the man wrenches himself free. But no, he is not saving himself ! he is running toward the machine-gun ! " Don't shoot, Comrades ! "

Still nothing has happened. But when the mob sees the unarmed man run forward, it advances too. In a thin stream it trickles along the side of the church. The next instant a command resounds over the square. Thundering the tick-tack of the machine-gun shatters into a thousand echoes from the houses, and the bullets, whistling and splintering, strike on the pavement.

Quick as lightning we have flung ourselves behind a jutting corner of the houses. In the first moment a paralysing, cur-like fear seizes me, quite different from any that ever I felt at the Front. Then it changes into rage. I have seen the solitary figure, how he spun round and fell forward. Cautiously I peer round the corner. He is trying to rise again, but he cannot. He only props on his arms, lifts up his pale face and groans. Slowly the arms bend, the head sinks, and, as though exceeding weary, his body sags down upon the pavement—— Then the lump loosens in my throat—— " No ! " I cry, " No ! " The cry goes up shrill between the walls of the houses.

I feel myself pushed aside. Ludwig Breyer stands up and goes out over the square toward the dark lump of death.

" Ludwig ! " I shout.

But he still goes on—on—I stare after him in horror.

" Back ! " comes the command once again from the Town Hall steps.

For a moment Ludwig stands still. " Fire away, Lieutenant Heel ! " he calls back to the Town Hall. Then he goes forward and stoops down to the thing lying there on the ground.

We see an officer come down the steps. Without knowing quite how, we are suddenly all standing there beside Ludwig, awaiting the coming figure that for a weapon is carrying only a walking-stick. He does not hesitate an instant, though there are now three of us, and we could drag him off if we wanted to—his soldiers would not dare to shoot for fear of hitting him.

Ludwig straightens up. " I congratulate you, Lieutenant Heel. The man is dead."

A stream of blood is running from under the dead man's tunic and trickling into the cracks between the cobble-stones. Near his right hand that has thrust forward, thin and yellow, out of the sleeve, it is gathering to a pool of blood that reflects black in the moonlight.

" Breyer," says Heel.

" Do you know who it is ? " asks Ludwig.

Heel looks at him and shakes his head.

" Max Weil."

" I wanted to let him get away," says Heel after a time, almost pensively.

" He is dead," answers Ludwig.

Heel shrugs his shoulders.

" He was our comrade," Ludwig goes on.

Heel does not answer.

Ludwig looks at him coldly. " A nice piece of work ! "

Then Heel stirs. " That does not enter into it," he says calmly. " Only the purpose—law and order."

" Purpose——" replies Ludwig contemptuously. " Since when do you offer excuse for yourself? Purpose! Occupation—that is all that you ask. Withdraw your men, so that there shall be no more shooting!"

Heel makes a gesture of impatience. " My men stay where they are! If they withdrew they would be attacked to-morrow by a mob ten times as big—— You know that yourself. In five minutes I occupy all the road heads. I give you till then to take off this dead man."

" Set to it," says Ludwig to us. Then he turns to Heel once again. " If you withdraw now, no one will attack you. If you stay more will be killed. And through you! Do you realise that?"

" I realise it," answers Heel coldly.

For a second longer we stand face to face. Heel looks at the row of us. It is a strange moment. Then something snaps.

We take up the limp body of Max Weil and bear him away. The streets are again filled with people. A wide passage opens before us as we come. Cries go up. "Noske bloodhounds!" "Police thugs!" "Murderers!" From Max Weil's back the blood drips.

We take him to the nearest house. It is the restaurant, the Holländische Diele. A couple of ambulance men are already there binding up two people who lie on the dance floor. A woman with a blood-stained apron is groaning and keeps asking to go home. With difficulty they detain her till a stretcher is brought and a doctor arrives. She has a wound in the stomach. Beside her lies a man still wearing his old army tunic. Both his knees have been shot through. His wife is kneeling beside him moaning : " He didn't do anything ! He was only walking by. I was just bringing him his supper——" She points to a grey enamel billy-can. "Just his supper——"

The women dancers are huddled together in a corner. The manager is running to and fro excitedly, asking if the wounded cannot be taken elsewhere.—His business will be ruined, if it gets about. No guest will want to dance there again.—Anton Demuth in his gilded porter's uniform has fetched a bottle of brandy and is holding it to the wounded man's lips. The manager looks on in horror and makes signs to him, but Anton takes no notice. "Do you think I'll lose my legs?" the wounded man asks. "I'm a chauffeur."

The stretchers come. Again shots are heard outside. We spring up. Hoots, screams, and a clatter of broken glass. We run out. "Rip up the pavement," shouts someone, driving a pick into the cobbles. Mattresses are being thrown down from the houses, chairs, a perambulator. Shots flash out from the square, and now are answered from the roofs.

"Lights out !" A man springs forward and throws a brick. Immediately it is dark. "Kosole !" shouts Albert. It is he. Valentin is beside him. Like a whirlpool the shots have drawn everyone in. "Into 'em Ernst ! Ludwig ! Albert ! " roars Kosole. "The swine are shooting at women ! "

We crouch in the doors of the houses, bullets lashing, men shouting ; we are submerged, swept away, devastated, raging with hate ; blood is spurting on the pavement, we are soldiers once more—it has us again, crashing and raging war roars above us, between us, within us—it is finished, comradeship riddled by machine-guns, soldiers shooting at soldiers, comrades at comrades, ended, it is finished——

3

Adolf Bethke has sold his house and come to live in the town.

After he took his wife back to live with him again all went well for a while. He did his work, she did hers, and it looked as if things would be all right again.

Then the village began to whisper. When his wife would go down the street in the evening voices would call after her ; young men meeting her would laugh impudently to her face ; women gathered up their skirts with pointed gestures. His wife never mentioned these things to Adolf. But she wilted under it and grew daily paler.

With Adolf it was the same. If he went to a pub, the conversation would immediately stop ; if he visited anyone, he would be received with an embarrassed silence. Veiled hints and oblique questions were gradually ventured. Over the cups coarse innuendoes would be spoken, and after him would sound mocking laughter. He did not know quite what to do about it. —Why, thought he, should he be accountable to the whole village for what was no man's affair but his own ?—A thing that not even the parson appreciated, but eyed him disapprovingly through his gold spectacles whenever he passed him. It tormented him ; but neither did Adolf speak of it to his wife.

And so they lived for some time, till one Sunday evening the pack of tormentors, grown venturesome, presumed to call after his wife in Adolf's presence. Adolf flared up. But she put her hand on his arm. " Don't mind them, they do it so often that now I don't hear any more."

" Often, do they ? " Now at last he understood why she had become so silent.—In a fury he made a rush to catch one of the fellows that had called out, but he vanished behind his companions who presented a barricade with their backs.

They went home and in silence turned in to bed. Adolf stared into the darkness. Then he heard a hushed, subdued sound, his wife was weeping under the bedclothes.—Probably she had often lain so, while he slept. " Don't worry, Marie," he said gently, " though they should all talk." But she cried on.

He felt helpless and alone. Darkness stood hostile at the window, and the trees outside whispered like gossiping crones. Gently he laid his hand on his wife's shoulder. She looked at him, her eyes filled with tears. " Let me go away, Adolf; then they will stop."

She got up. The candle was still burning and her shadow staggered large through the room, it slid across the walls ; and by contrast she was small and frail in the feeble light. She sat down on the edge of the bed and reached for her clothes. Weird and gigantic the shadow reached out also, like a noiseless fate that had stolen in through the window out of the watchful darkness, and now grotesque, distorted, and tittering, was mocking her every movement.—Soon he would fall on his prey and drag her off into the outer, droning darkness.

Adolf jumped up and plucked the white muslin curtains across the windows, as if thereby to shut off the low room against the night that stared in through the black, rectangular panes with its lusting owl's eyes.

The woman had already drawn on her stockings, and now reached for her bodice. Then Adolf stood beside her. " But, Marie——" She looked up, and her hands dropped. The bodice fell to the floor. Adolf saw in her eyes the misery, the misery of dumb creation, the misery of a stricken animal, the forlorn, comfortless misery of those who cannot defend themselves. He put his arm about her shoulders. How soft and warm she was! How could anyone throw stones at her?—Did they not both mean well? Why then, should men torment and hound them so mercilessly?—He drew her to him and she yielded herself, her arm was about his neck and her head was on his breast. And so they both stood in their night-shirts, shivering, each sensible of the nearness of the other, each desiring to take comfort in the warmth of the other. They squatted together on the edge of the bed and said little; and when the shadows on the wall before them again began to dance because the wick of the candle had fallen over and the flame was about to go out, Adolf with a gentle motion of his great hand drew his wife into bed with him, as much as to say: Let us stay together; Let us try again—and he said: "We will go away from here, Marie." That was the only escape.

"Yes, let us go away, Adolf!" She flung herself upon him, and for the first time she now wept aloud. He held her close and kept repeating: "We'll look for a buyer to-morrow—to-morrow morning, first thing——" And in a storm of resolution, of hope, anger and misery he took her. So despair gave place to passion, until at last it was silenced; and the weeping grew feebler and feebler, until it succumbed at last like a child's, to exhaustion and quiet breathing.

The candle was extinguished, the shadows were gone, and the woman slept, but Adolf still lay awake brooding. During the night the woman awoke, and feeling that she was still wearing the stockings she had pulled on when she meant to go away, she took them off and smoothed them lightly before placing them on the chair beside the bed.

Two days later Adolf Bethke sold his house and his workshop. Soon after he found rooms in the town, and the furniture was moved in. The dog had to be left behind. But hardest of all was to say farewell to his garden, which was then just in flower. It was not easy to go away so, and Adolf did not know what might come of it. But his wife was ready and resigned.

The apartment in the town is damp and dark, the stairway dirty and beset with an odour of washing, and the atmosphere heavy with neighbourly hate and stuffy rooms. There is little work, but only the more time to brood. The two are not happy. It is as if all they had fled from had followed them here.

Adolf squats in the kitchen and cannot understand why things do not get better. At night after the paper has been read and the food cleared from the table they sit down opposite each other, then the vacancy of gloom settles down over the place, until Adolf is dazed with listening and brooding. His wife makes herself something to do, she polishes the stove perhaps, and when he says : " Come, Marie," then she puts away her cloths and her emery-paper and comes. And when, pitifully alone, he draws her down to him and whispers : " We'll do it yet," then she nods. But she continues silent ; she is not gay as he would like. He does not realise that it is as much his fault as hers —that they have grown away from one another during the four years they have been separated, and that now they are only a burden to each other.—" Say something, can't you ? " he reproaches her. She looks scared, and, complying, she says something—" What can she talk about ? when does anything ever happen here in this house, in her kitchen ? "—But when things so stand between two people that they must talk, already it is beyond their power ever to say enough to mend them. Talk is good only when happiness is behind it—then it runs easy and light ; but where man is unhappy, what help is there then in such fickle, ambiguous things as words ? They can only make matters worse.

Adolf follows his wife's movements with his eyes, and behind them he sees another, a younger, light-hearted woman, the wife of his memory whom he cannot forget. Then suspicion flares up, and in exasperation he says : " Still thinking of him, are you ? " And as she looks at him in surprise, he knows the injustice of what he has said ; yet for that very reason he plunges in still deeper : " You must be ! You weren't like this before! What did you come back for, then ? You could have stayed with him, you know."

Every word does violence to himself—but who is silent for that ? He talks on until his wife retreats to the corner and stands up on the curb of the sink out of reach of the light ; and again she is crying like a child who is lost.—Ach, but we are all children, foolish, lost children, and ever the night stands round our house !

He can bear it no longer ; he goes out and wanders aimlessly through the streets. He stands before shop windows but without seeing. He goes wherever there is light. Electric trams ringing, motor-cars hooting by ; people bump into him, and within the yellow circle of the lamp-posts stand the whores. They rock their fat behinds, they laugh and prod one another. —" Are you happy ? " he asks, and goes with them, glad to see and to hear something fresh. But afterwards he mopes round again. He will not go home, and yet he would like to go. He makes the round of the pubs and drinks himself tight.

So I find him, and listen to him and look at him as he sits there, blear-eyed, belching his words, and drinking still—Adolf Bethke, the wariest, best soldier! the most faithful comrade, that has helped so many and saved so many! who was shelter and comfort, and mother and brother to me so often out there, when the parachute-stars hovered and the nerves were broken by long attack and threatening death. We slept side by side in the wet dugouts; and when I was sick, he would cover me. He could do everything, he was never at a loss.—And now here he is, caught in the barbed-wire, tearing his hands and his face, and already his eyes have become bleared. " Ah, Ernst," he says cheerlessly, " if only we had stayed out there !—at least we were together there——" I do not reply—I merely glance at my coat-sleeve where are a few washed-out, reddish blood stains. It is Weil's blood. Weil shot down by Heel's order. So far we have come. There is war again ; but no comradeship——

4

Tjaden is celebrating his marriage to the horse-butchery. The business has developed into a perfect gold mine and Tjaden's interest in Mariechen has increased proportionately.

In the morning the bridal pair drive to the church in a black lacquered coach, bedecked in white silk—four-in-hand, of course, as is only proper for a union that owes its origin to horses. Willy and Kosole have been chosen as witnesses. For such a festive occasion Willy has bought himself a pair of white gloves, made of pure cotton.—That cost us a great deal of trouble. Karl had first to get us half a dozen orders to purchase, and then for two whole days the search continued—nowhere did they stock Willy's size. But it was worth all the trouble. The chalk-white sacks that he finally settled on, go so stunningly with his newly dyed swallow-tail. Tjaden has on a frock-coat, and Mariechen is in a wedding dress, all complete with veil and orange blossom.

Shortly before their departure for the registry office there is a slight mishap. Kosole arrives, sees Tjaden in his frock-coat, and has an attack of hysteria. No sooner has he more or less recovered himself, than he will glance again in the direction where Tjaden's fly-away ears are gleaming over his stand-up collar, and the trouble starts all over again. There is no help for it—he would be sure to break down again in the middle of the church and endanger the whole ceremony—so at the last moment I am obliged to take his place as best man.

The entire butchery has been decked out with garlands. At the entrance are flowers and young birch trees, and even the slaughter-house has a garland of fir branches, to which Willy, amid general acclamation, adds a placard with the word " *Welcome!* "

Of course there is not a skerrick of horse-flesh on the table ; nothing but the best quality pork is steaming in the dishes and before us stands an enormous joint of roast veal ready carved.

After the veal Tjaden removes his frock-coat and takes off his collar. This enables Kosole to go to work in more comfort, for until now he has not dared let his gaze wander without running the risk of bringing on a choking fit.—We all follow Tjaden's example and things begin to be comfortable.

During the afternoon his father-in-law reads a document making Tjaden a partner in the butchering business. We all congratulate him, and then Willy in his white gloves solemnly bears in our wedding present—a brass tray with a set of twelve cut-crystal schnapps glasses. Also three bottles of cognac from Karl's stock. The father-in-law is so touched by it that he offers Willy a position as manager of a chop-house he is proposing to open during the next few weeks somewhere or other. Willy agrees to think over the matter.

Ludwig also looks in for a moment during the course of the evening. At Tjaden's special request he comes in uniform, for Tjaden is anxious to show his people that he had a real Lieutenant for his friend at the Front. He soon goes again, but the rest of us stay until nothing is left on the table but bare bones and empty bottles.

It is midnight when we turn out at last into the street. Albert makes the suggestion that we now go to the Café Gräger.

" That's all shut down long since," says Willy.

" We can get in round the back," persists Albert. " Karl knows how."

We none of us have any real desire to go now, but Albert insists so long, that at last we give in. It surprises me rather, because usually Albert is the first to want to go home.

Although the front of the Café Gräger is all quiet and in darkness, when we cross the courtyard at the back we find everything still in full swing.—Gräger's is the profiteers' haunt, and every day business goes on there into the small hours of the morning.

One part of the room is made up of little cubicles with red velvet curtains. That is the wine department. Most of the curtains are drawn. Squeals and laughter issue from behind them. Willy grins from ear to ear : " Gräger's Private Moll-Shop, eh ? "

We find seats for ourselves well to the front. The café is chock full. To the right are the tables for whores. Where business prospers gaiety flourishes, so twelve women are none too many here. But even they have competition, so it seems. Karl points out Mrs. Nickel to us, a voluptuous, dark-eyed hussy. Her husband is a profiteer in just a small way of business, who, but for her, might well have starved long ago. She helps him out by treating alone with his business confrères at her flat, usually for one hour.

At every table there is an excited back and forth of mumblings, whispers, asides and confused din. Fellows wearing English-made suits and new hats are led aside into corners by others in swallow-tails and no collars ; with an air of secrecy packets and samples are brought out of side-pockets, examined, handed back, proffered again ; notebooks appear, pencils are in motion ; every now and then somebody will get up and go off to the telephone, or outside ; and the air is humming with talk of truck-loads, of tons, of butter, herrings, bacon, flasks, dollars, gulden, stocks and shares, and figures.

Close beside us a particularly hot dispute is raging over a truck-load of coal. But Karl dismisses it with a scornful gesture. " That's just hot-air business ! Somebody has heard tell of something or other, a second passes it on, a third interests a fourth; they run up and down and make a great deal of fuss, but there's seldom anything in it really. They're just the hangers-on, who will be happy if they can pick up a little commission by the way. The real profiteer-captains deal only with one or at most two middlemen, whom they know at first hand. That fat chap over there, for instance, bought two truck-loads of eggs in Poland yesterday. At the moment, they're ostensibly on their way to Holland, so I'm told; they'll be labelled afresh en route, and then come back again to be sold as Dutch new-laid eggs at three times the price. Those fellows ahead there are cocaine dealers; they make immense profits, of course. That's Diederichs sitting over there on the left—he deals only in bacon. Also very good."

" And it's for these swine we have to go round with a bellyache ! " growls Willy.

" You'd have to do that anyway," replies Karl. " Why, only last week there were ten kegs of butter sold off by the State, because they'd been let go rotten through long standing. And it's the same thing with corn. Bartscher has just bought a couple of truck-loads for a few pence, because it had been allowed to get soaked with rain in some tumbledown State storehouse and was all mildewed."

" Who did you say ? " asks Albert.

" Bartscher. Julius Bartscher."

" Is he here often ? "

" Oh, yes, I think so," says Karl. " Want to make a deal with him ? "

Albert shakes his head : " Has he got much money ? "

" Like hay," replies Karl, with a certain tone of respect.

" I say ! just look ! there comes Arthur ! " cries Willy, laughing.

The canary-yellow mackintosh enters by the back door. A couple of people stand up and make toward him. He brushes them aside, nods to this one and that one patronisingly, and walks on down the tables like a general. I notice with surprise what a hard, unpleasant air his face has taken on, a look that is there even when he smiles.

He salutes us rather loftily. " Sit down, Arthur," smirks Willy. Ledderhose hesitates, but he cannot resist the opportunity of showing us, in his own domain here, what a big noise he has become.

" Only for a moment, then," says he, taking Albert's chair, who is now ranging through the room as if in search of somebody.—I am about to go after him but refrain, supposing that he has merely to go into the yard a moment. Ledderhose calls for schnapps, and is already chaffering about five thousand pairs of army boots and twenty truck-loads of old stores with a fellow whose fingers are fairly flashing with diamonds. With an occasional glance Arthur re-assures himself every now and then that we are also listening.

But Albert is going along the cubicles. Someone has said something to him that he cannot believe, but which, for all that, has stuck in his brain all the day like a thorn. When he peers through a chink into the last cubicle but one, it is as if an immense axe were suddenly descending upon him. He reels a moment, then he rips the curtain aside.

On the table are champagne glasses, and beside them a bouquet of roses. The table-cloth is awry and hanging half on the floor. Beyond the table a fair-haired person is curled in a settle. Her clothing is in disarray, her hair dishevelled, and her breasts are still bared. The girl's back is toward Albert, and she hums a tune as she combs her hair before a little mirror.

" Lucie," says Albert hoarsely.

She swings round and stares at him as if he were a ghost. She tries desperately to smile, but as she sees Albert's gaze fixed on her naked breasts, the twitching dies in her face. It is no use lying now. Frightened she pushes in behind the settle. " Albert —it wasn't my fault—" she stammers—" he, it was he—" then all at once she gabbles quickly : " He made me drunk, Albert—and I wouldn't—and he kept on giving me more, and then I didn't know what I was doing any more ; Albert, I swear——"

Albert does not answer.

" What's the meaning of this ? " demands someone behind him.

Bartscher has come back from the yard and now stands there swaying slightly to and fro. He blows the smoke of his cigar into Albert's face. " Pimping, eh ? Be off with you ! Clear out ! "

For a moment Albert stands there dumbly before him. Then suddenly, with awful vividness the protruding belly, the brown check suit, the gold watch-chain and the wide, red face of the other man stamps itself into his brain.

At that moment Willy looks up casually from our table. He leaps up, knocks over a couple of people and tears down the café. But too late. Before he can arrive Albert has drawn his field revolver and fired. We dash across.

Bartscher tried to shield himself with a chair ; but he had only time to raise it to the level of his eyes. Albert has planted his shot one inch above it, square in the forehead. He hardly even took aim—he was always the best shot in the company and with his service revolver he had no equal. Bartscher falls crashing to the floor. His feet twitch. The shot was fatal. The girl screams. " Out ! " bawls Willy, holding back the onrushing guests. We run Albert, who is standing motionless staring at the girl, out through the courtyard, across the street, round the first corner to a dark square, where there are two furniture vans standing. Willy follows us. " You must clear out at once ! to-night ! right now ! " he says panting.

Albert looks at him as if he had only just waked up. Then he shakes himself free. " No, Willy, let me alone," he answers dully, " I know what I have to do."

" Are you mad ? " snorts Kosole.

Albert sways a little. We hold him. Again he wards us off. " No, Ferdinand," he says quietly, as if he were very tired, " who does the one thing must do the other also."

He goes slowly back to the street.

Willy runs after him and argues with him. But Albert only shakes his head and turns the corner into Mill Street. Willy follows him.

" We'll have to take him by force ! " cries Kosole. " He'll give himself up to the police ! "

" I don't think it's any good, Ferdinand," says Karl hopelessly, " I know Albert."

" Giving himself up won't bring the man back to life ! " cries Kosole. " What good will that do ? Albert must get away ! "

We sit round in silence waiting for Willy.

" But whatever can have made him do it ? " Kosole asks after a while.

" He banked so much on the girl," I answer.

Willy comes back alone. Kosole jumps up. " Is he away ? "

Willy shakes his head. " Gone to the police ! I couldn't do anything with him. He almost fired on me too, when I tried to drag him off."

" Oh, Christ ! " Kosole rests his head on the shaft of the cart. Willy sinks down on the grass. Karl and I lean against the side of the furniture van.

Kosole, Ferdinand Kosole, is sobbing like a little child.

5

A shot has been fired, a stone has been loosed, a dark hand has reached in among us. We fled before a shadow ; but we have run in a circle and the shadow has overtaken us.

We have clamoured and searched ; we steeled ourselves and yet have surrendered ; we tried to elude it, yet it has sprung upon us ; we lost our way, yet we still ran on farther—but ever we felt the shadow at our heels and tried to escape it.—We thought it was pursuing us.—We did not know we were dragging it with us ; that there where we were, it was also, silently standing—not behind us, but within us—in us ourselves.

We have thought to build us houses, we desired gardens with terraces, for we wanted to look out upon the sea and to feel the wind—but we did not think that a house needs foundations. We are like those abandoned fields full of shell-holes in France, no less peaceful than the other ploughed lands about them, but in them are lying still the buried explosives —and until these shall have been dug out and cleared away, to plough must be a danger both to plougher and ploughed.

We are soldiers still without having been aware of it.—Had Albert's youth been peaceful and without interruption, then he would have had many things familiar and dear to him, that would have grown up with him, and that now would have sustained and kept him. But all that was broken in pieces, and when he returned he had nothing—his repressed youth, his gagged desires, his hunger for home and affection then cast him blindly upon this one human being whom he supposed that he loved. And when that was all shattered, he knew of nothing but to shoot—he had been taught nothing else. Had he never been a soldier he would have known many another way. As it was, his hand did not falter— for years he has been accustomed to shoot and not to miss.

In Albert, the dream-ridden adolescent, in Albert, the shy lover, there still sat Albert, the soldier.

The wrinkled old woman cannot understand it.— " But how could he have done it ? He was always such a quiet child ! " The ribbons of her old-lady's cap are trembling, the handkerchief is trembling, the black mantilla is trembling—the whole woman is one quivering piece of anguish. " Perhaps it is because he has had no father. He was only four when his father died.—But then, he was always such a quiet, good child——"

" And so he is still, Frau Trosske," I say. She grasps at the straw and begins to talk of Albert's childhood. She must talk, she says, she can't bear it any more—the neighbours have been in, and acquaintances, two teachers, too—none of them could understand it——

" What they should do is to hold their tongues," I say. " They're to blame for it, partly."

She looks at me uncomprehendingly. But then she runs on again and tells me how Albert first learned to walk, how he never cried like other children, indeed, how he was almost too quiet for a young boy—and now, to have done a thing like this ! But how could he have done it ?

I look at her in wonder. She doesn't know anything about Albert ! It would probably be the same with my mother.—Mothers know only to love, that is their one understanding.

" But, Frau Trosske," I say warily, " Albert has been at the war, you must remember."

" Yes, yes," she replies. But she does not see the connection.—" This Bartscher, was he a bad man ? " she then asks quietly.

" He was a blackguard," I affirm roundly, for I don't mind betting he was.

She nods in her tears. " I couldn't understand it otherwise. He never hurt a fly in his life. Hans now, he did pull their wings off. But Albert never. —What do you think they will do to him now ? "

" They can't do much," I say to comfort her ; " he was very excited, you see, and that is almost the same as doing it in self-defence."

" Thank God," she sighs. " The tailor upstairs said he would be hanged for it."

" Then the tailor's mad," I retort.

" Yes, and he said, Albert was a murderer, too ! And he isn't ! never, never, never ! " she bursts out.

" You leave that tailor to me, I'll fix him," I say savagely.

" I hardly dare to go outside the door, now," she sobs. " He is always standing there."

" I'll come along with you, Frau Trosske," I say.

We reach the outer door of the house. " There he is again," whispers the old woman fearfully, and points to the door. I brace myself.—If he says one word I will pound him to pulp, though it should cost me ten years in the clink.—But he gives us a wide berth, as do the two women also who are loafing there with him.

Once inside the flat Albert's mother shows me a picture of Hans and Albert as boys, and then begins to weep anew. But she stops again almost at once, as if she were ashamed.—Old women are like children in that—tears come to them quickly ; but they dry up quickly also.—In the passage, as I am about to go, she asks me : " Do you think he gets enough to eat ? "

" Yes, I'm sure he does," I reply. " Karl Bröger will see to that ; he can get plenty."

" I have still a few pancakes left ; he likes them so much. Do you think they would let me take him some ? "

" There's no harm in trying," I answer ; " And if they do let you, you just say this to him : I know you're not guilty, Albert.—Only that."

She nods. " Perhaps I did not think of him enough. But Hans, you see Hans hasn't got any feet——"

I reassure her. "The poor boy ! " she says, "and now he is sitting there all alone——"

I give her my hand. " Now I'll just have a word with that tailor.—He won't trouble you next time, I promise."

The tailor is still standing at the door. A commonplace, stupid, little bourgeoise face. He leers at me maliciously, his mouth ready to start blabbing as soon as I am gone. I take hold of him by the coat lapels. " You bloody snip ! if ever you say another word to the old lady up there, I'll knock bloody hell out of you, hear me ? you pack-thread athlete, you washerwoman ! " I shake him like a sackful of old rags and bump his backside against the knob of the door. " You lousy, stinking skunk ! if I have to come again I'll break every bone in your body, you miserable, bloody scissor-grinder ! " Then I land him one on each cheek.

I am already a long way off when he shrieks after me : " I'll take you to court ! It will cost you a hundred marks, at the least." I turn round and walk back. He disappears.

Dirty and travel-worn Georg Rahe is sitting in Ludwig's room. He read the report about Albert in the newspaper and has come back at once.—" We must get him out," says he.

Ludwig looks up.

" With half a dozen bright fellows and a motor car," Rahe continues, " it couldn't possibly miss. The best time would be when he is being taken across to the court-house. All we do is to jump in among them, make a bit of a shindy while two run with Albert to the car."

Ludwig listens a moment, then he shakes his head. " It's no good, Georg. We would only make things worse for Albert, if it miscarried. As it is, he does at least stand a chance of getting off fairly lightly.—Not that that's any argument—I'd be with you at once—But Albert—we wouldn't get Albert to come. He doesn't want to."

"In that case we'll just have to make him," explains Rahe after a while—"He's got to get out—and if I once start——"

Ludwig says nothing.

"I don't think it's any use either, Georg," I say—"even if we did get him away, he would only come straight back again. He almost shot Willy, when he tried to lug him off."

Rahe puts his head in his hands. Ludwig looks grey and wasted. "It's my idea we are all lost," says he hopelessly.

No one answers. Silence and trouble weigh like death in the room.

I continue to sit alone with Ludwig a long time. He props his head in his hands. "It is all in vain, Ernst. We are finished, but the world goes on as if the war had never been. It won't be long now before our successors on the school benches will be listening, eager-eyed, to stories of the war, and wishing they had been there too, rid of all the tedium of school.—Even now they are trooping to join the Free Corps—at seventeen years guilty of political murder !—I'm so tired, Ernst——"

"Ludwig——" I sit down beside him and put my arm about his slight shoulders.

He smiles cheerlessly. Then he says quietly : "I had a schoolboy love affair once, Ernst, before the war. I met the girl again a few weeks ago. She seemed to me to have grown even more beautiful ; it felt as if those days had come to life again in one human being. We used to see one another fairly often afterwards.—And then all at once I realised—" He rests his head on the table. When he looks up again his eyes are dead from anguish—" such things are not for me, Ernst—I am terribly sick."

He gets up and opens the window. Outside the night is warm, and many stars. I continue to stare before me gloomily. For a long time Ludwig stands there looking out. Then he turns to me : " Do you remember how as youngsters we used to go off at night with a volume of Eichendorff into the woods ? "

" Yes, Ludwig," I answer quickly, glad that he is now thinking of something else, " it was in late summer. One time we caught a hedgehog ! "

His faces relaxes. " And we imagined it might turn into a real adventure, with stage-coaches, and winding-horns and stars—remember that ?—how we wanted to go off to Italy ? "

" Yes, but the coach that was to take us never came ! And we hadn't money for the train ! "

Ludwig's face brightens, ever clearer and clearer, it looks almost unearthly, so serene is it. " And then we started to read *Werther*——" he says.

" And to drink wine," I prompt him.

He smiles : " And *Green Heinrich* ! Remember how we used to whisper together about Judith ? "

I nod. " But afterwards you preferred Hölderlin to all the others."

A strange peace seems to have come over Ludwig. He is talking easily and quietly. " What schemes we had ! and how noble and good we were to be ! A nice mess we have made of it, Ernst—poor ninnies——"

" Yes," I say meditatively. " What has come of it all——"

Side by side we lean out over the window-sill. The wind is asleep in the cherry trees. They whisper softly. A shooting star falls. The clock strikes twelve.

" We must be going to sleep." Ludwig gives me his hand.

" Good night, Ernst."

" Sleep well, Ludwig."

Late in the night someone thunders on my door. With a sudden start I sit upright. " Who's there ? "

" It's me ! Karl ! Open the door ! "

I spring out of bed.

He bursts in. " Ludwig——"

I grab hold of him. " What's wrong with Ludwig ? "

" Dead——"

The room spins round. I fall back on the bed. " Get a doctor ! "

Karl smashes a chair on to the floor so that it splinters. " Dead, Ernst—artery cut——"

I do not know how I put on my clothes. I do not know how I came here. But suddenly a room is there, piercing light, blood, an intolerable glitter and sparkle of quartzes and stones, and in a settle before it, an unutterably weary, thin, collapsed figure, a shockingly pale, sharp face with half-shut, extinguished eyes——

I do not know what is happening. The landlady is there, Karl is there, noise is there—one of them is speaking to me : to stay here—I understand : they want to fetch someone—I nod ; I crouch into the

281

sofa, doors rattle, I cannot move, cannot speak. Suddenly I am alone with Ludwig and look at him——

Karl was the last to be with him. He found him calm and almost gay. After he had gone, Ludwig put his few things in order and wrote for some time. Then he drew a chair to the window and set a basin with warm water on the table beside him. He locked the door, sat himself in the settle, and with his arm in the water he cut the artery. The pain was slight. He saw the blood flowing, a scene he had often thought on—to let this hateful, poisoned blood pour out of his body.

His room became very clear. He saw every book, every nail, every glint of the quartzes, the iridescence, the colours ; he absorbed it : his room. It gathered about him, it passed in with his breath and was one with his life. Then it receded. Uncertain. His youth began, in pictures. Eichendorff, the woods, homesickness. Reconciled, without pain. Beyond the woods rose up barbed-wire entanglements, little white shrapnel clouds, the burst of heavier shells. But they alarmed him no longer. They were muffled, almost like bells. The bells became louder, but the woods were still there. The bells pealed in his head so loudly that he felt it must burst. Then it grew darker. The pealing sounded fainter, and the evening came in at the window, clouds floated up under his feet. He had wished once in his life to see flamingoes ; now he knew—these were flamingoes, with broad, pinkish-grey wings, lots of them, a phalanx—did wild ducks not once fly so toward the very red moon, red as poppies in Flanders ?—The landscape receded farther and farther, the woods sank deeper, rivers rose up, gleaming, silver, and islands ; the pinkish-grey wings flew ever higher and higher, and the horizon became ever brighter—the sea—— Now, suddenly, a dark cry swelled in his throat, hot, insistent, a last thought spilled over out of the brain into the failing consciousness : Fear, rescue, bind it up !—he tried to rise, staggering, to lift his hand—the body jerked, but already it was too weak. All spun round and spun round, then it vanished ; and the giant bird with dark pinions came very gently with slow sweeps and the wings closed noiselessly over him.

A hand pushes me away. People are there again, they are taking up Ludwig, I pull the first one away, no one shall touch him ! But then all at once his face is before me, bright and cold, changed, harsh, strange—— I know him no more and stagger back, out.

I do not know how I come to be in my room. My mind is vacant, my arms lie limp along the rests of the chair.

I have done, Ludwig. I, too, have done. Why should I stay ? We none of us belong here. Uprooted, burned, ashes—— Why did you go alone ?

I stand up. My hands are hot, my eyes burning. I feel feverish. My thoughts are whirling. I do not know what I am doing. " Take me," I whisper, " take me too ! "

My teeth chatter with cold. My hands are wet. I stumble forward. Big black circles vibrate before my eyes.

I stiffen suddenly.—Was that a door? a window rattling? A shudder runs through me. I stagger up. In the moonlight through the open door of my room I see my old tunic hanging on the wall beside the violin. I move toward it stealthily, on tip-toe, so that it shall not observe me; I sneak on this grey tunic that has destroyed so much in us, our youth and our life—I pull it down and think to fling it away, but then I smooth it lightly with my hand, I put it on, I feel it taking possession of me through the skin, I shiver, my heart thuds heavily in my throat—— A note twangs out in the silence! I start and turn round, I take fright, press back against the wall——

In the pale light of the open door stands a shadow. It sways and hovers, it comes nearer and beckons, a figure, a face with dark eye-sockets, between them a great cleft gaping, a mouth speaking without sound. Is that——? " Walter——" I whisper. Walter Willenbrock, killed in August '17, at Passchendaele. Am I mad then? am I dreaming? am I ill?—But behind him another is already pushing his way in, pale, crippled, bowed down—Friedrich Tomberge, whose back was broken by a shell-splinter at Soissons, while he was sitting on the stairs of a dugout. And now they press in, with dead eyes, grey and ghastly, a swarm of shadows, they have come back again and are filling the room.—Franz Kemmerich, with his eighteen summers, who had his leg amputated and died three days after.—Stanislaus Katczinsky, with dragging feet and drooping head, whence trickles a thin, dark, stream.—Gerhard Feldkamp, blown to pieces by a trench mortar bomb at Ypres. Paul Bäumer, killed in October '18, Heinrich Wessling,

Anton Heinzmann, Haie Westhus, Otto Matthes, Franz Wagner, shadows, shadows. A long procession, an unending line, they press in, they perch on the books, they clamber up to the window, they fill the room.

But suddenly the horror, the astonishment breaks in me—for slowly a stronger, a darker shadow has arisen. Propped on its arms it creeps in through the door, it takes on life, bones grow within it, a body drags itself in, teeth gleam chalky-white out of the black face, eyes too now flash in the deep sockets—— Rearing like a seal he crawls in, toward me—the English captain ! and trailing behind him, rustling, the puttees. With a slight lurch he flings himself upwards, reaches toward me with clutching hands— " Ludwig ! Ludwig ! " I cry, " Ludwig, help me ! "

I catch up piles of books and fling them at the hands.—" Bombs, Ludwig ! " I groan ; I wrench the aquarium from its stand and heave it toward the door, it crashes and shatters in pieces ; I hurl the butterfly-case after it, the violin ; I seize a chair and strike at that grin : " Ludwig ! " I shout, " Ludwig ! " I rush at him, I burst through the door, the chair crashes. I rush out—cries behind me, frightened cries—but louder, nearer the gasping, panting—he is chasing me ! I fly down the stairs, he stumps after me, I gain the street, he is there, I run, the houses rock.—" Help ! Help ! " Squares, trees, a clutch at my shoulder, he has caught me ! I roar, howl, stumble ; uniforms, fists, raging, flashes and the full thunder of the gleaming axe that strikes me to the ground——

PART VII

I

Has it been years? Or was it only weeks? Like a mist, like a distant thunderstorm the past hangs on the horizon. I have been ill a long time, and whenever the fever lessened the troubled face of my mother was always there. But then came an immense weariness that took away all obdurateness, a waking sleep in which all thoughts were resolved, a feeble surrender to the gentle singing of the blood and the warmth of the sun.

The meadows are glowing with the splendour of late summer. Just to lie in the grasses!—the spears are higher than one's face. They bend over, they are the world, nothing is here but gentle swaying to the rhythm of the wind. In places where grass alone grows the wind has a soft humming note like the sound of a distant scythe—there where sorrel is, its note is deeper, more sombre. One must be still a long time and listen intently to hear it.

Then the stillness comes to life. Tiny flies with black, red-spotted wings sit close side by side on the spike of sorrel and rock to and fro with the swaying of the stem. Bumble bees hum like little aeroplanes above the clover, and a lady-bird, solitary and persistent, climbs to the topmost limit of a spray of shepherd's purse.

An ant reaches my wrist and disappears into the

tunnel of my coat sleeve. He is dragging after him a piece of dry grass, much longer than himself. I feel the light scratching on my skin and am unable to decide whether it is the ant or the little piece of grass that traces this exquisitely delicate wake of life down my arm, dissolving every moment in little shudders. But now the wind blows into my sleeve, and I think that the lightest caress of love must be uncouth beside this breath on the skin.

Butterflies come eddying along, given up utterly to the wind, as though they swam upon it, the white and golden skiffs of the air. They alight upon flowers, and suddenly, when next I lift my eyes, I see two sitting still on my chest, one like a yellow leaf with red spots, the other outspread with violet peacock's eyes on deep velvet brown. Ribbons, decorations of summer. I breathe very lightly and slowly, even so my breath moves their wings—but they stay with me. The bright sky hangs above the grasses and a dragonfly with whirring wings is poised over my shoe.

White Mary's threads, cobwebs, shimmering gossamers float in the air. They hang from the stalks and the leaves, the wind bears them along, they catch on my hands, on my clothes, they spread themselves over my face, my eyes, they cover me up. My body, now even my body is passing into the meadow. Its boundaries are becoming uncertain, it is no longer apart, the light breaks down its contours and at the edges it is beginning to be unsure.

Above the leather of my shoes rises the breath of the grasses, into the woollen pores of my clothing presses the odour of the earth, through my hair blows the moving sky, which is wind—and the blood knocks against the skin, it rises to meet the incoming thing, the nerve-ends are erect and quivering, already I feel the butterfly's feet on my breast, and the tread of the ant echoes in the concave chambers of my veins—then the wave gathers strength, stronger, the last resistance has carried away and now I am a hill without a name, grass and earth.

The noiseless streams of the earth ebb and flow, and my blood flows with them ; it is borne along with them and has part in them all. Through the warm dark of the earth it is flowing with the meaning of crystals and quartzes, it is in the secret sound of the weight with which drops sink down among the roots and assemble to thin runnels in search of the springs. With them it breaks out again from under the ground ; it is in brooks and in rivers, in the glistening banks, in the breadth of the sea and in the moist silver vapour the sun draws up again to the clouds—it circles and circles, it takes ever more and more of me with it and empties it into the earth and underground streams ; the chest sinks and collapses, the arms fall away, slowly and without pain the body disappears ; it is gone ; now only the fabric, only the husks remain. The body has become the trickling of underground springs, the talk of the grasses, moving wind, rustling leaf, and silent, resounding sky. The meadow comes nearer, flowers grow through it, blossoms sway over it ; I have sunk down, forgotten, poured away under poppies and yellow marsh mari-golds, over which butterflies and dragon-flies hover.

Lightest of movements—gentlest of tremors.—Is this the last vibration before the end ? Is it only the rocking of the poppy flowers, and the grasses ? Is it only the trickling among the roots of the trees ?

But the movement increases. It becomes regular, passes over into breathing, pulsating; wave returns upon wave and pours back—back from rivers, trees, leaf and earth. The cycle begins anew, but now it does not impoverish, it brings ever more in, and it stays; it becomes vision, perception, feeling, hands, body—the husks are no longer empty—the earth again laps about my body, released, light and winged —I open my eyes——

Where am I? Where was I? Have I been sleeping? The mysterious sense of union is still there, I listen, not daring to move. But it stays, and ever stronger and stronger grows the joy and the lightness, the skimming, radiating. I lie on the grass; the butterflies have gone, and more remote the sorrel rocks to and fro, the ladybird has reached its goal, the gossamers cling to my clothes; the undulation, pulsation remains, it mounts into my chest, to my eyes. I move my hands, what pleasure! I bend my knees, I sit up, my face is wet; and only then do I discover that I am weeping, incontinently weeping, as if all that were now over, gone for ever——

I still rest a while. Then I get up and walk off toward the cemetery. I have not been there before. To-day is the first time since Ludwig's death I have ventured out alone.

An old woman goes with me to point out Ludwig's grave. It lies behind a beech hedge and is planted with periwinkle. The earth is still loose, and forms a hill against which are leaning a few withered wreaths. The gilt lettering of the inscription has faded already, it is no longer legible.

I have been rather afraid to come here. But this

stillness is without alarms. The wind blows lightly over the graves, the September sky stands golden beyond the crosses, and in the plane trees a blackbird is singing.

Ah, Ludwig, to-day for the first time I have felt something of home and peace, and you are not here! Even now I hardly dare to believe it, I still suspect it is but weakness and weariness. But perhaps it will yield to us some day; we have only to wait, perhaps, and be silent, and it will come to us of itself; perhaps just these, our bodies and the earth, perhaps these only have not abandoned us, and perhaps we need do nothing but just listen and follow them.

Ah, Ludwig! and there we were searching and searching; we lost our way and fell down; we were looking for a purpose, and we tripped over ourselves; we did not find it—and you have gone under! And now, is it to be just a breath of wind over the grasses, a blackbird singing at evening, that rallies us and leads us back home? Can a cloud on the horizon, a tree in summer, have more power then, than so much will?

I do not know, Ludwig. I cannot believe it, for I had given up hope. But it is true that we do not yet know what surrender is, we have not felt its strength. We know only power.

But if it should prove a way, Ludwig—what is that to me?—without you——

Night is rising up slowly beyond the trees, bringing with it again unrest and melancholy. I stare down at the grave.

Footsteps crunch on the gravel. I look up. Georg Rahe! He observes me with concern and urges me to go home.

" It's a long while since I saw you, Georg," I say.
" Where have you been ? "

He makes a vague gesture. " I've been trying
my hand at a lot of things."

" Aren't you a soldier, then ? " I ask.

" No," he answers harshly.

Two women in mourning are coming down the
path between the plane trees. They have little green
watering-cans in their hands, and begin to water the
flowers on an old grave. The perfume of mignonette
and wallflowers floats across.

Rahe looks up. " I thought to find some remnant
of comradeship there, Ernst. But it was mere barbar-
ised gang spirit, a thin, ghostly caricature of the war.
People who imagined that by stowing away a few
dozen rifles they would be able to deliver the
Fatherland !—hard-up, out-of-work officers who knew
nothing better to do with themselves than to be on the
spot wherever there was any prospect of trouble—hoboes,
permanent tramps who had lost touch with everything,
and went merely in fear of having to get back into
civil life again—the last, toughest clinkers of war. And
among them a few idealists and a mob of curious young
lads out for adventure—hunted, embittered, desperate
and mistrusting each other. Yes, and then——"

He is silent a while and remains staring before him.
With sidelong glances I study his face. He is nervous
and haggard, there are dark shadows round his eyes.
Then he straightens himself up. " Why shouldn't I
tell you, Ernst—I've chewed on it long enough, God
knows ! We had a bit of a fight one day. Against
Communists, so they said. But then when I saw the
dead, workers, some of them still in their old army
tunics and military boots, former comrades, something

inside me tore. I cleaned up half a company of Englishmen once with my aeroplane—that didn't worry me at all, war was war. But these dead comrades here in Germany—shot down by their own former comrades—no, not for me, Ernst!"

I think of Weil and Heel, and nod.

A chaffinch starts to sing just above us. The sun is descending, more golden. Rahe spits out a shred of tobacco. "Yes, and then—then a bit later two of our fellows were suddenly missing. They had some scheme for betraying the whereabouts of one of our plants of rifles, so it was said. And without any investigation at all their own comrades beat them to death with clubs one night in the forest. *Feme*, they call it, but lynching is what it is. One of the dead men had been a corporal under me at the Front. A real gem of a fellow! So then I chucked it." He looks at me. "And that's what it has turned into, Ernst. Yes, and to think of those other days! to think with what a will, what a sally we set out in those other days!" He flings his cigarette away. "Where the hell is it now?" Then after a pause he says quietly, "And how could this other thing ever have come out of that?—that's what I'd like to know——"

We get up and go off down the avenue of plane trees to the exit. The sunlight plays in the leaves and flickers over our faces. It is all so unreal—the things we have been talking of, and this soft, warm wind of late summer, the blackbirds and the cold breath of memory.

"And what are you doing now, Georg?" I ask.

He tops the heads of the thistles with his stick as we walk. "I've had a look at most things, Ernst—professions, ideals, politics—but I don't fit into this show. What does it amount to?—everywhere profiteering, suspicion, indifference, utter selfishness——"

I feel rather exhausted with walking, so we sit on a seat on the Klosterberg.

The spires of the town below shimmer green, the roofs steam, and smoke rises silver from the chimneys. Georg points down there : " Like spiders they lurk there in their offices, their shops, their professions, each one of them ready to suck the other man dry. And then the rest hanging over each of them—families, societies, authorities, laws, the State ! One spider's web over another ! True, one may call that life, if one likes, and a man may even pride himself on crawling about under it his forty years and more ; but I learned at the Front that time is not the measure of life. Why should I climb down forty years ? I have been putting all my money for years on one card and the stake has always been life. I can't play now for halfpence, and small advances."

" You weren't in the trenches the last year, Georg," I say. " Things may have been different with the Air Force, but sometimes for months together we would never see a single man of the enemy—we were just so much cannon fodder. There was no play, I assure you, no bidding, and nothing to put into the pool—there was merely waiting, till a man stopped his packet at last."

" I'm not talking of the war at all, Ernst—I am talking of the youth and the comradeship——"

" Yes, that's all finished," I say.

" We have lived as it were in a hot-house," says Georg meditatively, " and now we are old men. But it's as well to be clear about it. I am not complaining : I'm merely balancing accounts. For me all roads are shut. There is nothing left but to vegetate. And I don't mean to do that. I mean to be free."

" Ach, Georg," I reply, " what you say only means

an end of things. But somewhere, somehow, there must be a beginning for us too. I believe I had a first glimpse of it, to-day. Ludwig knew it, but he was too sick——"

Georg puts an arm round my shoulder. "Yes, yes, I know—you mean just be useful, Ernst——"

I lean against him. "When you say it, it sounds unctuous and hateful; but there must be a comradeship in it somewhere, Georg, though we don't understand it as yet."

I should like to tell him something of what I experienced there in the meadow. But I cannot hold it in words.

We sit in silence side by side. "Well, what are you going to do now, Georg?" I ask after a while.

He smiles thoughtfully. "I, Ernst?—It was damned bad luck I wasn't killed.—As things are now I am merely rather ridiculous."

I push his hand away and look at him. "I think I'll go off again for a bit first——" he reassures me.

He toys with his walking-stick and looks idly ahead. "Do you remember what Giesecke said once? In the asylum up there? He wanted to go to Fleury—back, you see. He thought that might help him——"

I nod. "He's still up there. Karl went to see him the other day——"

A light breeze has risen. We look out over the town to the long row of poplars, where as boys we used to build tents and play at Red Indians. Georg was always the Chief; and I loved him as only boys, who know nothing about it, can love.

Our eyes meet. "Old Shatterhand!" says Georg solemnly, and then he smiles.

"Winnetou!" I reply just as quietly.

The nearer the day comes for the trial, the more often I think of Albert. And suddenly, one day, clear and vivid before me I see a wall of mud, a loophole, a rifle with a telescopic sight, and behind it a cold, watching, tense face : Bruno Mückenhaupt, the best sniper in the battalion, who never missed.

I jump up—I must go and see what he is doing—what he makes of it all now.

A high house with many flats. The stairs are running wet. It is Saturday, and everywhere there are buckets, scrubbing-brushes and women with their dresses tucked up.

A shrill bell, far too noisy for the door. Hesitatingly someone opens. I ask for Bruno. The woman admits me. Mückenhaupt is in his shirt sleeves on the floor playing with his daughter, a little girl of five or thereabouts, with straw-coloured hair and a big blue bow. With silver paper he has laid down a river over the carpet and set little paper boats on it. Some have tiny tufts of wadding fixed on them—these are the steamers, with little celluloid dolls for passengers. Bruno is contentedly smoking a long, curly pipe. On the porcelain bowl is a picture of a soldier kneeling and taking aim, with the legend : *Use Eye and Hand for the Fatherland!*

" Hullo, Ernst," says Bruno, giving the little girl a pat and leaving her to go on with her play. We go to the sitting-room—a sofa and chairs of red plush, crochetted antimacassars spread over the backs, the floor so polished that I slip on it. Everything is neatly in its place ; big conch shells, knick-knacks and photographs on the sideboard, and among them, in the middle, on red velvet under a glass dome, Bruno's medals.

We talk about the old times.—" Have you still got your marksman's card ? " I ask.

" But what do you think, man ! " protests Bruno reproachfully. " That has an honoured place ! "

He brings it out from the drawer and turns over the pages with evident enjoyment. " Of course, summer was always my best time—you could see then till so late into the evening. Here—no, wait a minute—yes—June 18th, four head shots ; 19th, three ; 20th, one ; 21st, two ; 22nd, one ; 23rd, none—wash out ! —The sons of bitches got wise to it and were more careful—but here, look you, the 26th—a new lot came up who hadn't heard tell of Bruno—nine heads ! what do you say to that now ? "

He beams at me. " And all in two hours ! It was comical—I don't know how it was, perhaps I was catching them under the chin and blowing them out, but anyway they shot up one after the other breast high above the trench like so many billy-goats.— But see here now—29th June, 10.2 p.m., head shot— no joking mind you, Ernst—I had witnesses—see there it is : *Confirmed. Company Sergeant-Major Schlie !* Ten o'clock at night ! almost in the dark ! that's shooting for you, what ? Man, but those were the times ! "

" Yes, Bruno," I say, " the shooting was marvellous, no doubt about it,—all the same—what I mean to say is, don't you feel a bit sorry for the poor blighters sometimes ? "

" What ? " he says in amazement.

I repeat what I have said. " Of course, Bruno, one was right in the thick of it then—but to-day, it all looks rather different somehow."

He pushes back his chair. " Man ! Why, you're a Bolshevik, I declare !—It was our duty ! Orders ! What——" Thoroughly offended he wraps up his scoring book in its tissue paper again and puts it back in the drawer.

I pacify him with a good cigar. He takes a few puffs and is reconciled. Then he begins to tell me about his rifle club that meets every Saturday. " We had a ball there just a while back. Classy, I tell you ! And next time it's to be skittles, with prizes. You must come along sometimes, Ernst ; you can get a beer at the bar, the like as I've rarely tasted, so smooth.— And a penny a pint cheaper, too, than elsewhere. Mounts up, that does—every night, you know.—It's smart and yet it's cosy like, if you understand me. Here "—— he points to a gilt collar-chain—" *Champion shot*. Bruno 1st. Pretty good, what ? "

The child comes in. One of the boats has come unfolded. Bruno carefully sets it right again and strokes the little girl's hair. The blue ribbon crackles.

Then he takes me to a sideboard laden with every conceivable sort of object.—He won them in the shooting-gallery at the annual fair. Three shots a penny, and whoever shot a certain number of rings could select his own prize. Bruno was not to be dragged from the gallery the whole day. He shot down whole heaps of teddy bears, cutglass dishes, cups, beer mugs, coffee pots, ash trays, balls, and even two wicker armchairs.

" At the finish they wouldn't let me in anywhere," he laughs happily. " I'd have bankrupted the whole works before I'd done. Once bitten twice shy, eh ? "

I go down the dark street. Light, and swilling water is flooding from the doorways.—Bruno will be playing again with his little girl. His wife will be bringing in the evening meal. And afterwards he will go for his beer. On Sunday he will take the family for an outing. He is an affectionate husband, a good father, a respected citizen. There is nothing to be said against him. Nothing to be said against him.

And Albert ? And us ?

Already an hour before the beginning of Albert's trial we are standing in the corridor of the courthouse. At last the witnesses are called. With thudding heart we go in. Albert, very pale, is leaning back in his chair, gazing at the floor in front of him. We try to speak to him with our eyes : Courage, Albert ! We won't leave you in the lurch.—But he does not look up.

After our names have been read over we have to leave the court-room again. As we go out we discover Tjaden and Valentin sitting in the front row of the audience. They wink at us.

One after another the witnesses are called. With Willy it lasts a particularly long time. Then comes my turn. A quick glance at Valentin—an imperceptible shake of the head. So—Albert has refused to make any statement. I expected as much. He sits there vacantly beside his counsel. But Willy is red about the gills. Watchful as a wolfhound, he is eyeing the Prosecutor. The two have had a dust-up apparently.

I am sworn in. Then the President of the Court starts to interrogate. He wants to know whether Albert had not previously spoken of his intention of getting square with Bartscher. When I say No, he states that several witnesses were struck by the fact that Albert had been so cool and deliberate.

" He always is," I reply.

" Deliberate ? " interjects the Prosecutor.

" Cool," I retort.

The President leans forward. " Even in such circumstances ? "

" Of course," I say. " He was cool in far worse situations than that."

" In what worse situations ? " asks the Prosecutor pointing a quick finger.

" In a bombardment."

He withdraws the finger. Willy grunts contentedly. The Prosecutor gives him an angry look.

" So he was cool then ? " asks the President once again.

" As cool as now," I answer sourly. " Can't you see how coolly he sits there, though everything within him is boiling and raging !—He was a soldier ! He learned there not to go hopping about and flinging up his arms to heaven in despair, merely because a situation was critical. Else he wouldn't have any now !"

The Counsel for the Defence makes some notes. The President looks at me a moment. " If that is so why did he shoot ? " he asks. " Surely it was not so grievous a matter that the girl should go to the café with another man for once."

" It was more grievous to him than a bullet in the guts," I reply.

" How so ? "

" Because the girl was the only thing he had in the world."

" He had his mother," interjects the Prosecutor.

" He could not marry his mother," I retort.

" And why was it so important he should marry ? " asks the President. " Is he not much too young still ? "

" He was not too young to be a soldier," I oppose. " And he wanted to marry because after the war he was lost, because he went always in fear of himself and of his memories and looked for something whereby to steady himself. And this girl was that to him."

The President turns to Albert : " Prisoner at the bar, are you now willing to answer ? Is it true, what this witness has said ? "

Albert delays a while. Willy and I fix him with our eyes. " Yes," he then answers reluctantly.

" And would you now tell us, why you had a revolver with you ? "

Albert is silent.

" He always had it with him," I interpose.

" Always ? " asks the President.

" Of course," I reply, " just the same as his hand-kerchief and his watch."

The President looks at me in astonishment. " But a revolver is a rather different thing from a pocket handkerchief ! "

" True," I say, " he found the handkerchief less necessary. He was often without one."

" And the revolver——"

" It saved his life more than once. He has carried it for three years, and he brought the habit back with him."

" But he does not need it now ! You see, it is peace time."

I shrug my shoulders. " We have not yet found it so."

The President turns to Albert. " Prisoner at the bar, do you not wish to unburden your conscience ? Do you not repent what you have done ? "

" No," says Albert apathetically.

All is hushed. The jury listens. The Prosecutor leans forward, Willy looks as if he would throw himself on Albert. I stare at him desperately.

" But you have killed a man," says the President impressively.

" I have killed many men," answers Albert indifferently.

The Prosecutor jumps up. The juryman by the door stops biting his nails. " What have you done ? " asks the President breathlessly.

" In the war," I interrupt hastily.

" That is quite another matter," declares the Prosecutor, disappointed.

Then Albert lifts his head. " How is that a different matter ? "

The Prosecutor rises. " Do you mean to compare what you did here with fighting in defence of the Fatherland ? "

" No," retorts Albert. " The people I shot then had done me no injury——"

" Monstrous ! " says the Prosecutor in disgust and turns to the President. " I must implore——"

But the President is calmer. " Where should we be, if every soldier thought as you do ? " says he.

" True enough," I say. " But that is not our responsibility. Had this man "—I point to Albert— " had this man not been trained to shoot men, he would not have shot one now."

The Prosecutor is as red as a turkey. " It is unheard of that witnesses, unasked, should——"

The President overrides him.—" I think we may venture to depart for once from the usual procedure."

In the meantime I am set aside and the girl is called. Albert huddles together and presses his lips tight. The girl is wearing a black silk dress and has had her hair newly waved. She advances self-consciously. It is apparent that she feels herself an important personage.

The judge inquires into her relationships with Albert and with Bartscher. She describes Albert as quarrelsome, Bartscher on the other hand was an amiable man. She had never contemplated marriage with Albert; on the contrary, she was as good as engaged to Bartscher. "Herr Trosske is much too young," she explains and swings on her hips.

The sweat pours down Albert's forehead, but he does not stir. Willy is kneading his hands. We can hardly contain ourselves.

The President asks what was her relation with Albert.

"Quite harmless," she says, "we were merely acquainted."

"Was the accused excited at the time?"

"Of course," she replies enthusiastically. That appears to flatter her.

"How do you account for that?"

"Well, you see"—she smiles and turns coyly aside—"he was very much in love with me."

Willy groans aloud, hollowly. The Prosecutor fixes him through his spectacles.

"Dirty bitch!" resounds suddenly through the court-room.

A tremendous hubbub. "Who spoke there?" asks the President.

Tjaden rises proudly.

He is awarded a fine of fifty marks for contempt of court.

"Cheap," says he, taking out his pocket-book. "Do I have to pay now?"

He gets a further fine of fifty marks and is ordered from the court.

The girl has become distinctly less brazen.

" And what passed between you and Bartscher that evening ? " the President interrogates further.

" Nothing," she protests uncomfortably. " We were just sitting together."

The judge turns to Albert. " Have you anything to say ? "

I bore him with my glance. " No," he says quietly.

" The statements are correct, then ? "

Albert smiles bitterly, his face is grey. The girl looks fixedly at the Christ hanging on the wall above the President. " It is possible they are correct," says Albert. " I hear them to-day for the first time. In that case I was mistaken."

The girl breathes again. But too soon. For now Willy jumps up. " Liar ! " he shouts. " She lies like a dog ! She had been having a grind with the fellow —she was still half naked when she came out."

Tumult. The Counsel for the Prosecution protests. The President reprimands Willy, but he is now beyond control. Albert looks at him despairingly. " Though you went down on your knees to me, I must say it ! " he calls to him. " She was whoring, and when the prisoner confronted her, she told him Bartscher had made her drunk ; then he went mad and fired. He told me so himself, when he went to give himself up."

The Counsel for the Defence pounces on it. " So he did—so he did ! " the girl shrieks in confusion. The Prosecutor is gesticulating wildly : " The dignity of the Court——"

Willy turns on him like a bull. " Don't you get on your high horse, you pedantic, old snake ! Do you think we care for your wigs and your trappings ? Try and turn us out if you can ! What do you know about us anyway ? The boy there was gentle and quiet, ask his mother if he was not. But to-day he shoots, as once he might have thrown pebbles. Remorse? Remorse? How should he feel remorse now for killing a fellow who has smashed in pieces everything he had in the world, when for four years he has had to shoot down innocent men?—The only mistake he made was that he shot the wrong person. It was the woman he should have done in!—Do you think then that four years killing can be wiped off the brain with the flabby word ' Peace' as with a wet sponge?— We know well enough we cannot shoot up our private enemies at will, but once let anger take us, and we are confused and overpowered, think then where it must land us!"

There is wild confusion in the court. The President tries in vain to restore order.

We stand side by side, Willy looks terrific, Kosole's fists are clenched; they can do nothing against us for the moment, we are too dangerous. The one policeman is taking no risks. I jump forward and face the bench where the jury is seated. "We are pleading for a comrade!" I cry. "Do not condemn him! He had no desire to become so indifferent to life and death —none of us did! But we had to abandon all such values out there, and since we came back no man has lifted a hand to help us! Patriotism, Duty, Home— we said all these things to ourselves again and again, merely to endure it, to justify it. But they were only abstractions—there was too much blood there, it swept them away."

Suddenly Willy is standing beside me.

" It is not a year yet since this man "—he points to Albert, " was lying out alone with his two mates in a machine-gun post—the only one in the sector—and an attack came. But the three were quite calm; they set their aim and waited, they didn't fire too soon, they merely sighted exactly at belly level. Then when the columns before them, supposing everything clear, began to advance, not till then did they open fire; and so it went on again and again—it was a long time before they could get reinforcements. But the attack was repulsed in the end. And afterwards we brought in those who had been shot down by the machine-gun; there were twenty-seven beautiful belly hits, every one as true as the next, almost all of them fatal—and that is not counting the rest, the thigh-wounds, the wounds in the balls, in the guts, in the chest, in the head.— This man alone "—he points to Albert again—" with his two mates had taken care of enough to fill a whole hospital—though, of course most of the stomach-wounds never got that far. And for that he was awarded the Iron Cross, First Class, and congratulated by the Colonel. Do you understand now why this man is not subject to your points of law and your civil code?—It is not for you to judge him! He is a soldier, he belongs to us, and we pronounce him Not Guilty!"

The Prosecutor has the floor at last. "Such monstrous disorder——" he gasps, and shouts to the policeman to put Willy under arrest.

Renewed uproar. But Willy keeps them all at bay and I start in again. "Disorder is it? Then whose fault is that? Yours, I say! You, everyone of you, should stand before our tribunal! It is you with your war, who have made us what we are! Lock us away too, with him, that's the safest thing to do. What did you ever do for us when we came back? Nothing, I tell you! Nothing! You wrangled about 'Victory ' ! You unveiled war memorials ! You spouted about heroism ! and you denied your responsibility !

" You should have come to our help !—But no, you left us alone in that worst time of all, when we had to find a road back again. You should have proclaimed it from every pulpit ; you should have told us so when we were demobilised; again and again you should have said to us : ' We have all grievously erred ! We have all to find the road back again ! Have courage ! It will be hardest for you, you left nothing behind you that can lead you back again ! Have patience ! ' You should have shown us again what life is ! You should have taught us to live again ! But no, you left us to stew in our juice ! You left us to go to the dogs ! You should have taught us to believe again in kindliness, in order, in culture, in love ! But instead you started again to falsify, to lie, to stir up more hatred and to enforce your damned laws. One of us has gone under already ! And there stands the second."

We are quite beside ourselves. All the anger, the bitterness, the disillusionment in us has seethed up and boiled over. There is wild disorder in the room. It continues a long time, but at last comparative quiet is restored. We all get one day's imprisonment for contempt of court and have to leave the place at once. Even now we might easily break away from the policeman and escape ; but that is not what we want. We want to go into prison with Albert. We pass close by him to show him that we are all with him.

Later we learn that he was condemned to three years' imprisonment and that he received sentence without a word.

3

One idea had become rooted in Georg Rahe's mind. He would see his past once again, eye to eye.—He contrived to come by a foreigner's passport and so to cross over the frontier. He travelled on through towns and villages, he waited about on big and little railway stations, and by nightfall is at last there where he wishes to be.

Without delay he sets off down the street, through the town, and beyond it toward the heights.

Children are playing in the pools of light under the gas lamps. Workmen returning home come toward him. A couple of motor-cars whir past. Then it is quiet.

The twilight is still enough to enable him to see. And anyway, Rahe's eyes are used to the dark. He leaves the road and goes off across country. After a while he trips up ; rusty barbed-wire has caught in his trousers and ripped a hole. He stoops to release it. It is the barbed-wire entanglement along an old battered trench. Rahe straightens himself up. Ahead stretch away the barren fields of battle.

In the uncertain twilight they appear a tormented, frozen sea, a petrified storm; Rahe detects the sickly odour of blood, of powder and earth, the wild smell of death, who is still in this landscape and here has authority. Involuntarily he draws in his head, his shoulders hunch, his arms hang loosely forward, hands ready for a fall—no more the gait of the cities—but the crouching, stealthy slinking of the beast, the wary alertness of the soldier again——

He stops and studies the field. An hour ago it was still strange to him, but now he knows it again, every fold in the ground, every valley. He has never been away from it. In the rekindling of memory the months shrivel up like paper, they are consumed and vanish away like smoke. Once more Lieutenant Georg Rahe is crawling along through the night on patrol—and there has been nothing between. About him, only the silence of the evening and the faint wind in the grasses—but in his ears, the battle roars again. He sees the explosions heaving; parachute rockets hang in the sky above the desolation like gigantic arc lamps; the heaven coughs glowing-black and the earth, thundering from horizon to horizon, is churned into fountains and sulphurous craters.

Rahe clenches his teeth.—He is no dreamer, but he cannot withstand it—memory overwhelms him like a whirlwind.—Here is not peace, not the make-believe peace of the rest of the world; here is still struggle and war; here destruction is still mysteriously raging and its eddies lose themselves in the sky.

The earth clutches for him, it reaches out after him, as with hands; the yellow, thick clay, sticks to his shoes and makes his steps heavy, as though the dead would drag him, the survivor, down to themselves.

He is running over the black field of craters. The wind is growing stronger, the clouds are driving fast and occasionally the moon pours its pale light over the landscape. And each time the light comes then Rahe stops dead, his heart stands still; he flings himself down and lies motionless, glued to the earth. He knows it is nothing—but again the next time, startled, he springs into a shell-hole. With open eyes and well aware, he yet submits to the law of this ground over which no man can walk upright.

The moon is a gigantic parachute rocket. The

tree-stumps in the coppice stand out black in the moonlight. Beyond the ruins of the farm there slopes the gully through which no attack ever came. Rahe squats in a trench. Bits of a belt are lying there, a couple of mess-tins, a spoon, hand-grenades covered in mud, ammunition pouches, and beside them grey-green wet cloths, threadbare, already half turned to clay, the remains of a soldier.

He lies long on the ground, his face to the earth—and the silence is beginning to speak. In the earth is an immense hollow rumbling gasping breath, roaring, and again rumbling, clapping and clinking. He clutches his fingers into the earth and presses his head down against it, he thinks he hears voices and cries; he would like to ask, to speak, to cry out; he listens and waits for an answer, an answer to his life——

But only the wind rises, the clouds drive more swiftly and lower, and shadow chases shadow over the field. Rahe picks himself up and walks on without direction a long time, till at last he is standing before the black crosses, erect, one behind another in long rows, like a company, a battalion, a brigade, an army.

And suddenly he understands all.—Before these crosses the whole fabric of grand abstractions and fine phrases comes crashing down. Here alone the war still exists, no longer as in the minds and distorted memories of those who have come away from it. Here stand the lost years that have not been fulfilled, like a will o' the wisp over the graves; here the unlived life that finds no rest, cries out in roaring silence to the sky; here the strength and the will of a generation of youth that died before it could begin to live, is poured out in one vast lament upon the night.

Shudders creep over him. At one shrill burst he

recognises the empty jaws where the truth, the valour and the life of a generation disappeared. The thought chokes him, it destroys him.

" Comrades ! " he shouts to the wind and the night : " Comrades ! We have been betrayed. We must march again ! Against it ! Against it ! Comrades!"

He stands in front of the crosses. The moon breaks through, and he sees them gleaming, they rise out of the earth with widespread arms, already their tread comes on menacing ; he stands before them, marks time. He stretches his hand onward : " Comrades— march ! "

And his hand goes to his pocket and again the arm is lifted—a tired, lonely shot that is caught up by the wind and swept away—he staggers, he is down on his knees, he props on his arms and with a last effort turns again to the crosses—he sees them marching. They stamp and are in motion, they are marching, slowly, and their way is far ; it will take long, but it leads forward ; they shall come there and fight their last battle, the battle for life. They are marching in silence, a dark army, the longest way, the way into the heart. It will take many years—but what is time to them ? They have broken camp, they are marching, they come——

His head sinks down. It grows dark about him, he falls forward : he is marching with the column. As one late finding his way home he lies there on the ground, his arms outspread, his eyes dull already and his knees drawn up. The body twitches once more, then all has become sleep ; and now only the wind is still there on the desolate, dark waste, it blows and blows ; above are the clouds and the sky, the fields and the endless wide plains with the trenches and shell-holes and crosses.

EPILOGUE

I

THE earth is smelling of March and violets. Snow-drops are showing above the damp mould. The furrows of the field are shimmering purple.

We walk down a path through the woods—Willy and Kosole in front, Valentin and I behind them. It is the first time for months that we have all been together. We do not often see one another.

Karl has lent us his new car for the day. He could not come himself, he has not the time. He has been making a mint of money these last few months, for the mark is falling and that favours his business. So his chauffeur has driven us out.

" What are you doing exactly, Valentin ? " I ask.

" Going the round of the fairs," he replies. " With the swingboats."

I look at him in surprise. " Since when ? "

" Oh, a long time. My partner—you remember her ? she soon chucked me. She dances in a restaurant now. Fox-trots and tangoes. There's more demand for that these days. And, well you see, an old army hobo's not smart enough for that sort of thing."

" Do swingboats bring in much, then ? " I ask.

He shakes his head. " Don't talk about it ! Not enough to live on, yet too much to die on, if you follow me. And this everlasting traipsing about ! We're on the road again to-morrow. To Krefeld this time.

Properly up the pole, as you might say, Ernst.—What's become of Jupp, do you know ? "

I shrug my shoulders. " Left town I think. Same as Adolf. One never sees anything of them."

" And Arthur ? "

" He's well on his way to being a millionaire," I reply.

" He knows a thing or two ! " nods Valentin sadly.

Kosole halts and stretches his arms. " Well, boys, it's grand walking, no mistake—if only a man hadn't to be out of work in order to do it ! "

" Don't you think you'll get something again soon ? " asks Willy.

Ferdinand shakes his head. " It's not so easy. I'm on the black list, you see. Not docile enough. Still a man's healthy, that's something. I sting Tjaden for a bit every now and then just to keep me going. He's well dug in among the suet."

We call a halt at a clearing in the wood. Willy hands round a box of cigarettes that Karl has given him. Valentin's face brightens. We sit down and smoke.

The tops of the trees creak softly. A few tits are twittering, and the sun is already strong and warm. Willy yawns largely and then stretches out on his overcoat. Kosole makes himself a sort of pillow of moss and lies down likewise. Valentin is sitting pensively on the trunk of a beech tree, watching a green ground beetle.

I look at the old familiar faces and in a moment everything seems changed—here we are, all squatting together again, as so often before—only we are fewer now—but are we really together still ?

Kosole pricks up his ears. Out of the distance

comes a sound of voices. Young voices. It will be the Wandervögel, the birds of passage, making a first ramble with their guitars and their ribbons this silver misted day. We used to do the same before the war—Ludwig Breyer and Georg Rahe and I——— I lean back and think of those times—the evening round the camp fire, the folk-songs, the guitars and the lovely nights full of stars over the tent. That was our youth. In the Wandervögel of those days was all the fresh romance and enthusiasm of youth, that afterwards still lingered on in the trenches a short while, only to collapse at last in 1917 under the awful horrors of the battle of machines.

The voices are coming nearer.

I prop myself on my arms and raise my head to see the procession go by. It is strange—only a few years back we still belonged to all that, and now it seems as if they were an entirely new generation, a generation to follow ours, that can take up again the things we had to let fall———

Shouts resound. A full chime, almost a choir. Now but a single voice again, indistinct, not yet to be understood. Twigs break and the ground trembles to many footsteps. Again a shout. Again the footsteps; they stop; silence. Then, sharp and clear, a command: " Cavalry approaching on the right !—By squads, right wheel !—double march ! "

Kosole jumps up. I also. We stare at one another.—Are we bewitched ?—What can that mean ?

Already they are breaking cover from the undergrowth in front of us ; they run to the edge of the wood and throw themselves on the ground. " Range four hundred ! " snaps the same voice as before. " Covering fire—Fire ! "

A rattling clatter. A long line of sixteen- and eighteen-year-old boys lying side by side along the edge of the wood. They all wear waterproof jackets with leather girdles buckled about them like soldiers' belts. All are dressed alike, grey jackets, puttees, caps with badges—uniformity has been deliberately emphasised. Each has a walking-stick with a steel point, with which he is battering on the tree-trunks in imitation of machine-gun fire.

But from under the warlike caps there look out young, red-cheeked children's faces. Watchful and excited they peer away to the right in search of approaching cavalry. They do not see the tender miracle of the violet among the brown leaves—nor the purple bloom of the coming spring that lies over the ploughed fields—nor the downy, soft fur of the leveret that is hopping there along the furrows.—Ah, yes, they do see the leveret !—but they are aiming their sticks at it and the clatter on the tree-trunks swells mightily. Behind them stands a powerful fellow with a bit of a paunch, also in waterproof jacket and puttees. He beefs out his commands : " Slow fire ! Two hundred yards ! " He has a pair of spy-glasses and is observing the enemy.

" Holy Jesus ! " I exclaim in horror.

Kosole has recovered from his astonishment. " What sort of bloody nonsense do you call this ? " he growls.

But he gets himself in hot waters. The leader, who is now joined by two confrères, glares and thunders. The soft spring air is loud with bold words. " Shut your mugs, you damned shirkers ! You enemies to the Fatherland ! You dirty push of traitors ! "

The boys now join in eagerly. One shakes his slight

fist. "We'll have to give you a good hiding!" he pipes up in his high-pitched voice. "Cowards!" chimes in another. "Pacifists!" cries a third. "These Bolsheviks must all be rooted out, or Germany will never be free!" shouts a fourth glibly and pat.

"That's right!" The leader pats him on the shoulder and makes toward us. "Run them off, lads!"

At that moment Willy wakes up. He has been asleep until now. He is still a good soldier in that: if he lies down for long he at once goes to sleep.

He stands up. The leader pulls up short at once. Willy looks about him in surprise and explodes into laughter. "What's this? A fancy dress ball?" he asks. Then he grasps the situation. "Well, well— so there you are!" he growls at the leader, "we've been wondering what had become of you for a hell of a time now! Yes, yes, I know, the Fatherland—it's all yours, by deed of settlement, what? And everyone else is a traitor, what? Funny thing then, that three quarters of the German Army were traitors. Just you hop off now, you jackanapes! Why can't you let the kids enjoy the few years that are left to them, while they need still know nothing about it?"

The leader draws off his army.—But the wood is spoiled for us. We go back into the village. Behind us, rhythmical and syncopated, echoes the cry: "Frontheil! Frontheil! Frontheil!"

"Frontheil——" Willy clutches his hair. "If any-one had said that to the lads up the line!"

"Yes," says Kosole sourly, "so it begins all over again——"

Just outside the village we find a little beer garden

where already there are a few tables standing out in the open. Though Valentin is due back at his swingboats in an hour, we still sit ourselves down for a quick one, to make the best of our time—for who knows when we shall be together again——

A pale sunset is colouring the sky. I cannot help thinking of that scene back in the wood. " My God, Willy," I say, " here we are alive still and only just out of it—how in God's name is it possible there should already be such people to do that sort of thing——"

" There will always be such people," answers Willy unusually earnest and thoughtful, " but don't forget us, we are here, too. And there's a lot of people think as we do. Most of them, probably. Ever since then —you know, since Ludwig and Albert—all sorts of things have been going round in my head, and I've come to the conclusion that everybody can do something in his own way, even though he may have nothing but a turnip for a head. My holidays are over next week, and I'll have to go back to the village as a school-teacher again. And, you know, I'm positively glad of it. I mean to teach my youngsters what their Fatherland really is. Their homeland, that is, not a political party. Their homeland is trees, fields, earth, none of your fulsome catchwords. I've considered it all off and on a long time, and I've decided that we're old enough now to do some sort of a job. And that's mine. It's not big, I admit. But sufficient for me— and I'm no Goethe, of course."

I nod and look at him a long while. Then we set off.

The chauffeur is waiting for us. The car glides softly through the slowly gathering twilight. We are already approaching the town and the first lights have shown up when there mingles with the crunching and grinding of the tyres a long-drawn, hoarser, throaty sound—in an easterly direction across the evening sky there moves a wedge-shaped flight—a flock of wild geese——

We look at it—— Kosole is about to say something, but then is silent. We are all thinking the same thing. Then comes the town with streets and noise. Valentin climbs out. Then Willy. Then Kosole——

2

I was in the wood the whole day. Weary now, I have turned in at a little country inn and taken a room for the night. The bed is already open, but I do not want to sleep yet. I sit down in the window and listen to the stirrings of the spring night.

Shadows flit about among the trees and up from the woods come cries, as though wounded were lying there. I look quietly and composedly out into the darkness, for I am afraid of the past no longer. I look into its quenched eyes without flinching. I even go out to meet it, I send my thoughts back into the dugouts, and shell-holes—but when they return they bring back neither fear nor horror with them, but only strength and will.

I have awaited a storm that should deliver me, pluck me away—and now it has come softly, even without my knowledge. But it is here. While I was despairing thinking everything lost, it was already quietly growing. I had thought that division was always an end. Now I know that growth also is division.

And growth means relinquishing. And growth has no end——

One part of my life was given over to the service of destruction; it belonged to hate, to enmity, to killing. But life remained in me. And that in itself is enough, of itself almost a purpose and a way. I will work in myself and be ready; I will bestir my hands and my thoughts. I will not take myself very seriously, nor push on when sometimes I should like to be still. There are many things to be built and almost everything to repair; it is enough that I work to dig out again what was buried during the years of shells and machine-guns. Not everyone need be a pioneer—there is employment for feebler hands, lesser powers. It is there I mean to look for my place. Then the dead will be silenced and the past not pursue me any more—it will assist me instead.

How simple it is—but how long it has taken to arrive there! And I might still be wandering in the wilderness, have fallen victim to the wire snares and the detonators, had Ludwig's death not gone up before us like a rocket, lighting to us the way. We despaired when we saw how that great stream of feeling common to us all—that will to a new life shorn of follies, a life recaptured on the confines of death—did not sweep away before it all surviving half-truth and self-interest, so to make a new course for itself, but instead of that merely trickled away in the marshes of forgetfulness, was lost among the bogs of fine phrases, and dribbled away along the ditches of social activities, of cares and occupations. But to-day I know that all life is perhaps only a getting ready, a ferment in the individual, in many cells, in many channels, each for himself—and if the cells and channels of a tree but take up and carry farther the onward urging sap, there will emerge at the last rustling and sunlit branches, crowns of leaves, and freedom. I will begin.

It will not be that consummation of which we dreamed in our youth and that we expected after the years out there. It will be a road like other roads, with stones and good stretches, with places torn up, with villages and fields—a road of toil. And I shall be alone. Perhaps sometimes I shall find someone to go with me a stage of the journey—but for all of it, probably no one.

And I may often have to hump my pack still, when my shoulders are already weary; often hesitate at the crossways and boundaries, often have to leave something behind me, often stumble and fall—but I will get up again and not just lie there, I will go on and not look back. Perhaps I shall never be really happy again, perhaps the war has destroyed that, and no doubt I shall always be a little inattentive and nowhere quite at home—but I shall probably never be wholly unhappy either—for something will always be there to sustain me, be it merely my own hands, or a tree, or the breathing earth.

The sap mounts in the stems, the buds burst with faint noises, and the darkness is full of the sound of growth. There is night in the room, and the moon. There is life in the room. It creaks in the furniture, the table cracks and the wardrobe also. Many years ago someone felled these and split them, planed them and worked them into things of utility, into chairs and beds—but each springtime, in the darkness of the sap, it stirs and reverberates in them again, they waken, they stretch themselves, mere objects of use no longer, no longer chairs for a purpose ; once again they have part in the streaming and flowing outside. The boards under my feet creak and move of themselves, the wood of the window-sill cracks under my hands, and in front of the door even the splintered, decaying trunk of a lime tree by the road-side is thrusting out fat, brown buds. In a few weeks it too will have little silken green leaves, as surely as the wide spreading branches of the plane-tree overshadowing it.

PRINTED IN GREAT BRITAIN BY
WYMAN AND SONS, LIMITED, LONDON, FAKENHAM AND READING.